THE GOLDEN AGE OF SOVIET THEATRE

Vladimir Mayakovsky (1893–1930) was one of the great revolutionary figures of twentieth-century poetry. An active revolutionary in his teens, he later supported the October Revolution and the young Soviet state. He dreamt of creating a new art that would correspond to a new order of society. His influence among poets has been incalculably great and Stalin remarked that 'Mayakovsky was, and remains, the greatest Soviet poet'. *The Bedbug*, one of his great satirical dramas, was begun two years before his suicide in 1930.

Isaac Babel (1894–?1941) published his first stories in 1916. During the First World War he fought with the Tsarist army and in 1917 went over to the Bolsheviks. He served with the *Cheka* and when in 1920 war broke out between Poland and the Soviet Russia, he was sent to Poland as a war correspondent. He disappeared in Stalin's purges in the 1930s. The official date of his death was 17 March 1941. *Marya* (1933–5) deals with the fate of individuals and groups confronted by the dissolution of a whole order of society.

Yevgeny Schwartz (1897–1958) began his career as a professional writer of children's stories and plays in 1925. For sheer charm, his dramatized fairy-tales for adults, whether written for the stage, the puppet-theatre or the cinema, are among the loveliest works of their kind produced in Europe since those of Hans Andersen. However, Schwartz's talent was not confined to simple tales and his work was ultimately recognized as controversial and important. *The Dragon*, written in 1943, is his most outspoken and most hilarious debunking of political tyranny.

THE GOLDEN AGE OF SOVIET THEATRE

EDITED BY MICHAEL GLENNY

THE BEDBUG

Vladimir Mayakovsky

Translated by Max Hayward

MARYA

Isaac Babel

Translated by Michael Glenny and Harold Shukman

THE DRAGON

Yevgeny Schwartz

Translated by Max Hayward and Harold Shukman

PENGUIN BOOKS

PENGUIN BOOKS

Published by the Penguin Group
27 Wrights Lane, London W8 5TZ, England
Viking Penguin Inc., 40 West 23rd Street, New York, New York 10010, USA
Penguin Books Australia Ltd, Ringwood, Victoria, Australia
Penguin Books Canada Ltd, 2801 John Street, Markham, Ontario, Canada L3R 1B4
Penguin Books (NZ) Ltd, 182–190 Wairau Road, Auckland 10, New Zealand

Penguin Books Ltd, Registered Offices: Harmondsworth, Middlesex, England

This collection published in Penguin Books 1966 under the title 'Three Soviet Plays'
Reprinted under the present title 1981
3 5 7 9 10 8 6 4

The Bedbug
First published 1929
This translation first published by Meridian Books 1960

Marya
First published Moscow 1935
This translation first published by Penguin Books 1966

The Dragon
First published 1960
This translation first published by Penguin Books 1966

Made and printed in Great Britain by
Richard Clay Ltd, Bungay, Suffolk
Set in Monotype Bembo

CONTENTS

INTRODUCTION

THE twenty years after the Russian revolution were the golden age of the Soviet theatre, in which it led the world in vitality, innovation and popularity with its audiences. People at such opposite poles of the world of drama as Granville Barker and Cecil B. de Mille endorsed the supremacy of the inter-war Soviet theatre. In physical capacity alone its growth after 1917 was astonishing. In that year Moscow had sixteen theatres; in 1934 it had sixty. Today the number has dropped to twenty-nine, of which only eighteen belong to the 'legitimate stage' as opposed to opera, ballet, puppets, and the circus, although during the same period the population of Moscow has doubled. At the end of tsarist rule, Russia could count a total of 250 theatres; twenty years later the Soviet Union had 560 permanent theatres, to say nothing of countless amateur and semi-professional theatres run by the armed forces, trade unions, collective farms, etc.

This explosion of activity began with the revolution, itself an intensely dramatic not to say theatrical series of events played out virtually on one stage – Petrograd – in the blinding limelight of the world's attention. Theatres played a peculiarly important role in those days before radio broadcasting, as being virtually the only media for addressing and influencing large numbers of people simultaneously. The theatre also moved out of doors to deliver the revolutionary message to vast crowds who had never before seen any kind of dramatic performance. The methods used were inevitably crude, oversimplified and exaggeratedly rhetorical, but they were highly effective both as political propaganda, and as a means of democratizing the theatre and of awakening a taste for drama and spectacle among the masses. A classic example of this 'mass theatre' was Mayakovsky's wild extravaganza *Mystery-Bouffe*, performed on the first anniversary of the revolution in Petrograd and then in a circus in Moscow for the Congress of the Soviets; another was the extraordinary mixture of morality play and pageant staged on 7 November 1920 for the third anniversary of the revolution, *The Storming of the Winter Palace*. The director, Yevreinov, used eight thousand actors and staged it on the very spot in the vast square in front of the Winter Palace on which the actual event had occurred three years before. The cruiser *Aurora* was used for 'noises off', repeating the firing of her historic salvo; rockets flared and the audience of one hundred thousand sang the *Internationale* as a colossal red flag was hoisted.

These colourful manifestations did not survive for long, largely because they were fantastically expensive to produce and, when the period of dazed exaltation known as War Communism was ended by Lenin's decree of 9 August 1921 establishing the New Economic Policy, the Soviet state was obliged to husband its meagre resources and these politico-dramatic extravaganzas were stopped.

As Soviet society gradually settled down, people looked back on these heroic open-air beginnings of the revolutionary theatre with slightly embarrassed amusement, but there is no doubt that they greatly helped in creating a huge and enthusiastic new audience. It is difficult nowadays to grasp the scale of enthusiasm for the theatre that began to be aroused in the early twenties. To begin with, there was a blessed return to peace and relative calm; it was a new beginning, an era of work, reconstruction, optimism and boundless new hopes. Life was often hard and drab, but there was always the theatre, now available to all. The old regime's ban on public assembly was removed and the tyranny of the box office was abolished; under Lunacharsky, first Commissar for Public Education and himself a playwright, generous subsidies were handed out to theatres and to the 'shock brigades' of mixed professionals and amateurs which set out all over the country to carry the theatre to the people. The Bolshevik government fully realized the power of the theatre as a propaganda force; religion was in discredit and the new theatre with its spectacle and dynamism could become the secular replacement for the only body which had once supplied the masses with a place of assembly and an aesthetic experience: the church. Every evening as their doors opened the theatres were literally stormed by their eager, impressionable new fans. It was a producer's dream.

The Russian theatre, both before and after the revolution, nurtured many great producers. They, the actors and dancers they trained and the designers they encouraged are perhaps the greatest of all Russia's contributions to the arts in this century. Among the many brilliant theatre directors of this period there stand out two giants who – after due credit is given to their colleagues and rivals – literally created the modern Russian theatre and directed it throughout the age of its predominance: Konstantin Alexeyev – known as Stanislavsky – and Vsevolod Meyerhold.

Both men had already made their mark well before the revolution. By 1917, in fact, their theories and those of other pioneering directors such as Yevreinov, Taïrov, and Vakhtangov had already been developed and tried in practice. The theatrical revolution began a good twenty years before the political overthrow of the old regime. Stanislavsky was rich and began his acting career as an amateur in a private company. The creation of the modern Russian theatre dates from his historic conversation in 1897 with his playwright friend Nemirovich-Danchenko which lasted twenty hours and whose direct result was the foundation of the Moscow Art Theatre. It opened on 14 October 1898 with a play by Alexei Tolstoy (a distant cousin of Leo Tolstoy), *Tsar Fyodor Ivanovich*, a colourful if undistinguished historical romance; but the true brilliance and depth of perception of Stanislavsky's technique was only revealed in his epoch-making productions of Chekhov's plays:

The Seagull in 1898; *Uncle Vanya* in 1899; and the most impressive of all, his two Chekhov premières – *The Three Sisters* in 1901 and *The Cherry Orchard* in 1904. Stanislavsky was the founder and unsurpassed master of psychological realism: his theatre was based on an intensive 'dialogue' between actors and author, in which the actors immersed themselves not only in the text and in the author's mind but in the invisible and unwritten psychological background of every character, however small the part. The actors were mercilessly trained to emotional receptivity and to physical control of expression by yoga-like exercises, discussions, criticism and a grinding programme of rehearsal. To have fifty dress rehearsals of a new production was normal practice.

It was a perfectionist theatre, fortunately made possible before 1917 by Stanislavsky's personal wealth and after the revolution by massive state subsidies. In stage design and costume, Stanislavsky's counterpart to psychological realism was the most subtle and painstaking naturalism; such was the scholarship lavished on a new production that productions of, for instance, *Othello* and *Julius Caesar* meant expeditions by members of the company to Cyprus and Rome. In speech, the M.A.T. actors were schooled to the utmost extension of their resources and absolute physiological mastery of vocal technique; whilst giving an impression of effortless naturalism their speech was as carefully planned as the rest of Stanislavsky's technique and based on musical rhythms. A visitor to almost any Soviet theatre today will find Stanislavsky's methods still faithfully observed, although it is now perilously close to becoming the very sort of ossified academic style against which Stanislavsky himself reacted so violently in his time.

One of the Master's first actor-disciples at the M.A.T. and in his way as great a theatrical genius as Stanislavsky was Vsevolod Meyerhold. Stanislavsky appointed him early in his career to be the first director of the Studio Theatre attached to the M.A.T. Here he was allowed to stage experimental productions, but not for long. His ideas on design and stagecraft were at complete variance with Stanislavsky's naturalism and the two were simply unable to work together. Meyerhold left Moscow and went as producer to Komissarzhevskaya's theatre in St Petersburg, where he rapidly developed the techniques of stylization which were to lead to the boldest and most extreme forms of theatrical Expressionism. Meyerhold was a natural 'leftist' by temperament (he later joined the Communist Party, as Stanislavsky never did) and a restless, dynamic innovator throughout his career. Long before 1914 Meyerhold had declared war on naturalism and was producing Maeterlinck's *Death of Tintagiles* with totally non-realistic designs made to look like bas-reliefs. After the revolution he was in the thick of the boiling upsurge of extremist left-wing art movements; he had an instinctive affinity with Mayakovsky and produced his *Mystery-Bouffe* in 1918 and THE BEDBUG, the first play in this volume, in 1928.

Although themselves originally influenced by German Expressionism, Meyerhold and his fellow Constructivists, Taïrov and Vakhtangov, had such scope for development in Russia that they in turn exercised an even more profound effect on Piscator and Brecht in Germany and are thus the real progenitors of the Brechtian theatre of today. The concept of alienation – the assertion of unreality as the very essence of the stage – had been fully worked out and put into practice by the 'left wing' of the Russian theatre well before Brecht's first play *Drums in the Night* was produced by Reinhardt in 1922. Of the three giants of the non-realistic Russian theatre, Vakhtangov is the only one whose memory is still officially honoured in the Soviet Union with a theatre named after him (even the M.A.T. has been renamed in honour of Gorky). In fact, owing to his untimely death in 1923, the extent of his contribution to the Soviet theatre was notably less than that of Meyerhold and Taïrov, but his methods have proved to have lasting qualities. At least one of his productions is still in the repertory outside

Russia – *The Dybbuk*, performed by the Jewish Habima Theatre (an Israeli company founded as a Hebrew-language theatre in Moscow and at one time under Vakhtangov's direction). Like Meyerhold, Vakhtangov also began his career under the aegis of Stanislavsky, for whom he started work as a director in the First Studio of the M.A.T. in 1913. In 1920 he was appointed director of the Third Studio of the M.A.T., where he stayed until his death three years later; this theatre is still in existence in Moscow under the name of the Vakhtangov Theatre. Although he rejected Stanislavsky's almost photographic naturalism, Vakhtangov was equally out of sympathy with Meyerhold's often extreme stylistic formalism. While he fully exploited the 'theatricality' of the stage, he achieved his effects with a minimum of staging and scenery. He relied on an extraordinary degree of intuitive understanding with his actors to achieve a kind of controlled spontaneity which broke down the barrier between illusion and reality, between performers and audience.

Alexander Taïrov was another leading Soviet director whose aesthetic ideas had largely matured before 1917. He was appointed director of the Chamber ('Kamerny') Theatre in 1914 and achieved the feat, extraordinary under Soviet conditions, of remaining at the same post until shortly before his death in 1950. In his early days Taïrov was strongly influenced by Yevreinov's idea of 'synthetic theatre', in which the divisions between traditional genres – farce, tragedy, pantomime, comedy, and opera – were swept away to make a total spectacle of all these elements. To put this into practice Taïrov made his actors into masters of all trades, able to be singers, acrobats and dancers as well as versatile 'straight' actors. It was Taïrov also who brought Constructivist décor into the Russian theatre, although its use was eventually carried much further by Meyerhold. Constructivism, a form of abstract art whose most celebrated exponent and theoretician was Vladimir Tatlin, was an attempt to extend the Cubist technique of collage into three dimensions. It used a variety of materials – wire, glass, sheet metal, wood, etc. – as much for their ability to outline space, to define and emphasize spatial relationships, as for their intrinsic textural and rhythmic values. Constructivism was essentially architectonic; Taïrov used it not for its scenic application but for the very opposite reason – because it was a spatial medium which allowed the actor to become the mobile centre of the stage, freed from the distraction and limitation of conventional scenery. Taïrov's theatre however was never dominated by one style; he was a brilliant eclectic whose personal sensitivity and sense of theatrical fitness were the only fixed criteria of his Chamber Theatre. He brought many productions from the Western theatre into the Russian repertoire, including the works of Shaw, O'Neill, Shakespeare, and Racine, and produced a sparkling version of the Brecht–Weill *Threepenny Opera* in 1930, only two years after its première in Berlin. After 1930, as the Party began to exercise an ever closer control over the repertoire, he was obliged to concentrate more on Soviet authors. Of these productions one of his best was Vsevolod Vishnevsky's *Optimistic Tragedy*, which had its première at Taïrov's theatre in 1933.

In a country such as the Soviet Union where the Communist Party claims exclusive political competence, many things that in a capitalist society are private undertakings subject only to the dictates of economics, taste and public opinion become matters of state concern. So it was with the Russian theatre in the twenties and thirties. While for much of that time the theatre retained considerable independence in matters of staging, method and style, Party control over the producer's choice of plays was increased by degrees. General political developments cast their shadows on the theatre. During the N.E.P. period (1921–8), for the first half of which Lenin was still alive, relative freedom reigned. Then, as Stalin manoeuvred with increasing success for supreme power, a parallel strengthening of Party control over literature and the theatrical repertoire took place. In 1927, the year that Stalin succeeded in having Trotsky expelled from the Party, the Agitprop Department of the Central Committee of the Party met to reinforce their hold over the theatre, their declared aim being to wipe out what they called the 'spiritual N.E.P.' – in plain language 'freedom of thought' – which had developed during the twenties. Three methods were to be used: Communists were to be appointed as theatre directors; 'artistic councils' within theatres were to be set up to criticize and select plays; and the role of 'activists' was to be emphasized, i.e. Party-inspired pressure-groups drawn from the Komsomol, trade unions, etc., would badger theatre managements in the press, in meetings and in the auditorium to make them put on Party-line plays. Although this programme was a sign of the way things were to go, it was not particularly effective.

By 1928 Stalin felt sufficiently sure of himself to show his hand. In January Trotsky was exiled to central Asia. An official end was declared to the N.E.P., which meant the complete extinction of all significant forms of private finance and trading; the enforced collection of grain marked the overture to farm collectivization, and in October the first Five Year Plan, Stalin's crash programme of industrialization, was launched. In 1929 Stalin put into action his ruthless policy of rural expropriation by terror and the forcible establishment of collective farming.

For theatre directors and playwrights 1929 was the year in which direct state control began to be effectively exercised over the repertoire. The Narkompros (one of those rather sinister-sounding Soviet abbreviations, the full version of which is literally translated 'People's Commissariat of Enlightenment' or more plainly Ministry of Education) spawned another body known as the Chief Repertoire Committee, or Glavrepertkom for short, with the task of censoring and 'filtering' plays, filtering meaning handing them back to authors for alteration into line with official doctrine. Glavrepertkom pursued its watchdog role with increasing vigour until by 1936 it was turning down half the new plays presented by the main theatres for the 1936–7 season. As an example of this activity, Glavrepertkom intervened in 1934 to prevent the production of Babel's MARYA (the second play in this volume) when it was already in rehearsal under the distinguished director Salomon Mikhoels at two theatres simultaneously, the Vakhtangov and the State Jewish Theatre. The piece was therefore never publicly performed in the Soviet Union, but since Glavrepertkom's writ ran only in the theatre, *Marya* was passed by the literary censorship, Glavlit. It was allowed publication in March 1935 in the magazine *Teatr i Dramaturgiya*, and with minor alterations in book form in June of the same year, although in what was for Soviet conditions an extremely small edition of three thousand copies. Because of Glavrepertkom's interdiction on it for the theatre, the published version ends with a specific editorial admonition that this edition is 'for reading'.

The censorship was only the ultimate, fine-mesh filter through which any literary work had to pass before reaching the Soviet public in any authorized form; beginning also in 1929, Stalin began a successful campaign of controlling literature at source by dragooning all writers into a single Party-dominated organization, outside which they had little hope of having original works published. This process, known generally by its German name of *Gleichschaltung* as a result of Hitler's efforts in the same direction, was carried out by Stalin's officials with a thoroughness and efficiency never achieved by the Nazis. In 1929 there existed, aside from various splinter-groups, two main literary organizations: the Vserossiisky Soyuz Pisatelei ('All-Russian Union of Writers') and the Rossiiskaya Assotsiatsiya Proletarskikh Pisatelei ('Russian Association of Proletarian Writers', universally referred to by its Russian initials as R.A.P.P.). The former was non-political, rather similar in character to P.E.N., and contained mostly fellow-travellers rather than Party members. It had no ideological or aesthetic programme and was concerned primarily with writers' welfare; its members included most of the famous names of Russian literature of the day, such as the novelist and dramatist Leonid Leonov. R.A.P.P., by contrast, was an avowedly militant organization of writers, blessed by the Party though not specifically affiliated to it and dedicated to the bold if vague principle of the 'supremacy of the proletariat' in literature. It tended to be a young man's organization, many of its members being sincere idealists with a mission to create a new, revolutionary culture, although it also had its inevitable quota of opportunists who merely wanted to be on the most promising bandwagon. The Party egged them on to bully the non-R.A.P.P. writers into line, and in 1929 they began the campaign by attacking two stalwarts of the All-Russian Union, the novelist Boris Pilnyak and the novelist and playwright Yevgeny Zamyatin. These two and all other leaders of the All-Russian Union were ousted from their posts; under R.A.P.P. pressure the union was renamed the All-Russian Union of *Soviet* Writers and ceased from then on to perform any significant function.

For two years R.A.P.P. was allowed almost complete control, until suddenly in 1932 it was disbanded without warning. In its place a sole organization, the Union of Soviet Writers, was created, to which in effect every writer was forced to belong in order to practise professionally. The leaders of R.A.P.P., all keen Marxists, had served their purpose of whipping-in the herd and were now removed. To circumscribe the writers' freedom even further, Zhdanov defined the official doctrine of 'Socialist Realism' at the first Congress of Soviet Writers in August 1934. For the playwrights this meant a drastic cramping of their style. From now on they were required to write nothing but stereotyped pieces on a few officially approved themes, all of them little more than aspects of the Party's urge to condition the population into the required patterns of behaviour. In their predictability, conformity to pattern and in intellectual content Socialist Realist plays were about on a level with Aldwych farces or second-feature westerns, but lacking even their redeeming traces of humour and crude entertainment value. Authors of undoubted talent, such as Katayev and Afinogenov, were made to distort their vision so that a play which began with an honest and originally conceived conflict in the first two acts ended by being resolved with dreary predictability according to the canon of the inevitable victory of 'socialist' forces.

Yet the theatre still flourished as the most vital sector of the arts in Soviet Russia, still managed to be original and stimulating for a few more years thanks to its tremendous heritage of vigour and experimentation. An American eyewitness of the period, Philip E. Moseley, while noting that literary life was dangerous but lively, described the theatrical scene of the early thirties as follows:

> Only the Moscow theatre seemed relatively unconcerned in its both old and new vitality. New plays and new interpretations of older ones were awaited eagerly and discussed with vigour. The theatre was a bond among the intelligentsia, even more than the novel. At its worst it could never be insignificant....
>
> In the difficult conditions of overwork, overcrowding and undernourishment it seemed at times as if the intelligentsia was being given 'theatre and potatoes' instead of 'bread and circuses'.

Moseley then goes on to draw a very perceptive distinction between two types of writer:

> In its own way intelligentsia opinion resisted the pressure of the new conformity as long as it could. It divided educated people, according to its own standard, into *intelligenty* ('intellectuals') and *inzheniery* ('engineers'). *Intelligenty* were people who had opinions of their own, who asserted some intellectual independence and personal sincerity. 'Engineers', regardless of their various professions, were those who mouthed the slogans of the regime and renounced all judgement of their own.

At the risk of over-simplification, the Soviet playwrights of the inter-war period can be divided with reasonable justice into Moseley's two categories. Not that the *inzheniery* were exclusively talentless hacks, though many were. There were genuinely gifted men among them who could go through the motions, who had an ear for dialogue and the technical skill to construct a play, but having once shown that they were willing to be used by the official dogmatists they were exploited to put across the Party line until they became little more than sounding brass, dead instruments which only responded to manipulation. Typical of such Establishment playwrights was Nikolai Pogodin, who beginning in 1929 wrote at least thirteen plays until his last work in 1958 and who could be relied upon every two or three years to turn out an efficient if generally lifeless piece on the approved topic of the day. Another talented writer, Trenyov, who in 1926 had written a classic piece on the Civil War called *Lyubov Yarovaya* in which husband and wife find each other on opposite sides of the battle-lines, continued to write during the thirties, but compared with the vigour of his earlier work his plays grew increasingly hollow and flaccid. Throughout this period it was as if a cloud of paralysing gas had been sprayed over the world of literature, leaving those who survived alive but capable of little but robot-like behaviour.

As Zamyatin accurately said soon after his deposition from the All-Russian Union of Writers, 'The Russian theatre leads the world'; but, he went on, 'incomprehensible though this may seem . . . the repertoire is its weak point . . . you can count on your fingers the contemporary Russian plays which have stood the test of time'. He mentioned his own play *The Flea*, Vsevolod Ivanov's *Armoured Train 14–69*, Katayev's *Squaring the Circle*, Bulgakov's *The White Guard* (also known as *The Day of the Turbins*), Afinogenov's *The Eccentric*, Trenyov's *Lyubov Yarovaya*, and Kirshon's *The Rails are Humming*. All the plays he mentions were written during the twenties, and apart from some patriotic pieces written during and just aftei the Second World War the Soviet theatre had to wait twenty-five years until the post-Stalin thaw before any works appeared which even remotely approached the quality of the plays written in the first post-revolutionary decade. Zamyatin dismissed without distinction all the 'boy-meets-tractor' plays of the R.A.P.P. and Socialist Realist periods as

> abortions – conceived in haste and immature. Like all abortions their heads are disproportionately large, stuffed with first-class ideology, whilst their puny and rachitic bodies proved incapable of supporting the weight of so much ideology. Like all abortions they need artificial nourishment and soon perished, despite the efforts of the critics to bottle-feed them. All these pieces were cut to the same invariable pattern: the scene showed the inevitable factory (or kolkhoz), a saboteurs' plot and finally the punishment of vice or the triumph of virtue.

There were some authors who managed to continue writing for the theatre whilst skirting the depths of the abyss. They achieved this either by the sheer talent which enabled them to write decently entertaining plays even while sticking to official themes by choosing such tolerated non-Party themes as young love, or by sticking firmly to historical subjects dealing with those tsars and tsarinas lucky enough to bear the seal of approval of the Soviet ideologues. Among the permitted monarchs for stage treatment were Ivan the Terrible, Peter the Great, and Catherine the Great. (Interestingly enough Alexander II, who liberated the Russian serfs three years before Lincoln freed the American slaves, has never been accepted into the canon of Soviet-approved tsars.) The most notable author of historical plays on these lines was Alexei Tolstoy; in the early days after the revolution he had written some extremely good adaptations of foreign plays which were original enough in treatment to be more than mere translations, including Büchner's *Danton's Death* and Čapek's *R.U.R.*, retitled *The Revolt of the Machines*. The latter was very typical of the slightly naïve Futurism of the early post-revolutionary period, but Tolstoy found a more durable genre in historical chronicle plays. The other reasonably safe playwright's refuge – love stories – were in Soviet language 'lyrical drama'. Two authors who maintained a reasonably constant output of adequate plays during the barren thirties by concentrating on this subject were Arbuzov and Afinogenov. Arbuzov's *Tanya*, written in the late thirties, about a couple who marry too young, divorce, and meet again years later to find that they are still incompatible, would easily stand repetition today. Afinogenov is probably best known in Britain for his *Distant Point*; written in 1935 it is still in the Russian repertoire and had a modest success in war-time London. Apart from *The Eccentric* his best play is probably *Fear*, dealing with the agony of an intellectual in coming to terms with the new Soviet society. It received a very impressive M.A.T. production in 1930 which largely concealed the weakness of its puerile R.A.P.P.-imposed ending.

If the 'engineers' – the hacks, the conformists and the compromisers – among the Soviet playwrights of the twenties and thirties are winnowed away like so much lightweight chaff, what good grain is left? One could catalogue a fair number of interesting plays written in the comparatively libertarian atmosphere of the twenties. After the first flush of ultra-left experiments had blown themselves away by their own extravagance, Lunacharsky exhorted Soviet dramatists to go 'back to Ostrovsky', i.e. to return to the inescapable fundamentals of well-made plays and to remember their social responsibility of educating a huge new, unsophisticated public to appreciate the theatre. The discipline of writing accessible plays was generally beneficial, and a new school of purely Soviet drama began to take shape. Most of those who had the will and talent to write had been through the tempering fires of revolution, civil war and famine and this experience naturally occupied their minds to the exclusion of practically all else. Inevitably the dramatic subject-matter of the twenties tended to be concentrated on the Russian revolution, historic revolutions of the past, the struggle of the working class abroad and above all the civil war at home.

Typical of such playwrights was Bill-Belotserkovsky, a working-class Jew by origin who had been a sailor, had emigrated to America and experienced the black underside of life in a capitalist society, earning his keep for twelve years as a navvy and stevedore in the U.S.A. A number of his plays, including his first two rather brash efforts, *Echo* and *Hard A'port*, were slices of life taken directly from his days as a docker and seaman in America. Others who celebrated the glories and miseries of the civil war and the Polish campaign in straightforward, vigorous, epic style were Vishnevsky in *First Cavalry Army*, Vsevolod Ivanov, with a famous piece commissioned for the tenth anniversary of the revolution, *Armoured Train 14–69*, and Leonid Leonov in *The Badgers*, a dramatization of his own novel of the same name. Although these plays were written by authors of undeniable talent, they do not wear well when removed from their context of time and place. Obsessed with a particular interpretation of the violent events of the recent past, they tend to be heavily over-simplified and declamatory in style. The public of today, even in the Soviet Union, is out of sympathy with their red-flagwagging heroics.

The choice of plays for inclusion in this volume has of necessity been narrowed down to those rare Soviet writers whose writing possesses the qualities of imaginative power, originality and unconcern with the deadening ephemera of ideology. There were other candidates than the three represented in the necessarily limited compass of this book; their common denominator besides literary talent was a degree of artistic integrity which brought them into conflict with Stalin's regime, generally with tragic results. Yesenin, who wrote a remarkable but unfinished verse play called *Rogues' Country*, committed suicide, as did the temperamentally not dissimilar Mayakovsky.

Babel was forced into becoming what he ironically called a master of 'the genre of silence' and was arrested on a false denunciation in 1939; during his years of silence he wrote a lot, including a play which he regarded as 'greatly superior' to *Marya*. In writing it he claimed to have discovered his true gift as a playwright, but all his unpublished manuscripts, including that play, were impounded at his arrest and probably destroyed by the N.K.V.D.

Mikhail Bulgakov managed to avoid arrest, although for most of his life as a writer he was permanently at odds with Stalin's cultural bureaucrats. He spent the first years after the revolution as an *émigré*, but returned to Russia. His finest and best-known play *The Day of the Turbins* (adapted from his own novel *The White Guard* and known in its first English translation under that title) is a profound study, equally sympathetic to both sides, of the Reds and the Whites during the civil war. Between 1926 and 1928 he wrote three plays in quick succession; two of them, *Zoë's Apartment* and *The Purple Island*, were sharp satires on contemporary manners and morals and were harshly treated by the Party critics. The best of these plays, *Flight*, a satirical, even grotesque study of a group of *émigrés*, had to wait until 1957 before it was performed, seventeen years after Bulgakov's death. Of the five known plays written by Zamyatin, at least three, *The Fires of San Domingo*, *Attila*, and *The African Guest*, merit translation and revival. It is to be hoped that this may one day be undertaken, as Zamyatin is a writer of great imagination, irony and humour and is too little known. Nor is it generally known that Zoshchenko, famous for his humorous short stories, also wrote at least three plays. One of the great might-have-beens of Soviet literature was Yuri Olesha, who wrote only four plays and then dried up as a writer, an advanced case of paralysis induced by Stalin's all-pervasive nerve gas. One of his best works, *A List of Assets*, has been translated. Another Olesha play, *The Conspiracy of Feelings*, would make a good play in translation if only it were possible to find a full and correct text. The fact that Yevgeny Schwartz, the author of the third play in this collection, THE DRAGON, managed to live longer than most of his fellow non-conforming writers is a tribute to his good fortune and skill in sticking to a politically safe occupation as an editor of children's books and magazines under Samuel Marshak. He wrote a great number of stories, plays and playlets for children which are gay, charming and totally free of sentimentality. His second play for the adult stage was a satirical comedy of manners called *The Shadow*. It was produced by the famous Leningrad director, N. P. Akimov, in 1940 at the Comedy Theatre. His first and third plays, *The Naked King* (1934) and *The Dragon* (1943), had to wait until Stalin's death before they could be put on a Soviet stage, with the exception of a single performance of *The Dragon* in 1943; again the director was Akimov, who achieved a triumph with his productions of *The Shadow*, *The Naked King*, and *The Dragon* in the 1960–1 season of the Leningrad Comedy Theatre. Despite their brilliantly organized fairy-tale form, the latter plays are two of the most penetrating and certainly the funniest studies ever made of tyranny and the moral corruption of both tyrant and subjects. *The Shadow* is available in an American translation.

The handful of great plays which are the most that can be plucked from the barren soil of the Soviet Union of Lenin and Stalin are more than anything else evidence of the loss sustained by Russia and the world from the repression of original and brilliant writers. It seems to us ridiculous that Stalin could really have imagined that his power was in serious danger from a scattering of playwrights and directors. From our viewpoint it is clear how easily the magnificent apparatus of the Russian theatre could have been brought to even greater triumphs by giving a measure of freedom to its dramatists. It can only be hoped that the small advances towards a more liberal attitude since 1954 will be held and pressed forward.

MICHAEL GLENNY

WORKS CONSULTED

Theater in a Changing Europe, ed. T. H. Dickinson: Part II A, 'The Theater of Soviet Russia', by Joseph Gregor, and Part II B, 'The Development of Soviet Drama', by Henry Wadsworth Dana, Putnam, New York, 1938.

Le Théâtre russe contemporain, Yevgeny Zamyatin, Cahiers du monde russe et soviétique, ed. Pierre Forgues, Paris, 1964.

Men, Years, Life, Ilya Ehrenburg, translated Anna Bostock and Yvonne Kapp, MacGibbon & Kee, 1962–4.

Das russische Theater, René Fülöp-Miller, Berlin, 1928; English version, *The Russian Theatre*, Harrap, 1930.

My Life in Art, Konstantin Sergeyevich Stanislavsky, translated J. J. Robbins (first English edition), Geoffrey Bles, 1924.

Isaac Babel: The Lonely Years, 1925–1939, ed. Natalie Babel, Farrar, Straus, New York, 1964.

Literature and Revolution in Soviet Russia, ed. M. Hayward and L. Labedz, Oxford University Press, 1963.

The Bedbug and Selected Poetry, Vladimir Mayakovsky, translated M. Hayward and G. Reavey, ed. Patricia Blake, Meridian Books, New York, 1960.

Entertainment in Russia, Faubion Bowers, Thomas Nelson, New York, 1959.

Deutsches Theater des Expressionismus, ed. Joachim Schöndorff, Langen-Müller, Munich, 1962.

Tvorchesky Teatr, P. M. Kerzhentsev, Gosizdat, Moscow-Petrograd, 1923.

Literaturnaya Entsiklopediya, vol. 8, Moscow, 1934.

Kratkaya Literaturnaya Entsiklopediya, vols. 1–2, Moscow, 1962– 4.

From Gorky to Pasternak, Helen Muchnic, Methuen, 1963.

Marya, I. E. Babel. Goslitizdat, Moscow, 1935.

A. Afinogenov – Dnevniki i Zapisniye Knizhki, Sov. Pisatel, Moscow, 1962.

Teatr i Zhizn, N. Pogodin, Iskusstvo, Moscow, 1953.

K. A. Trenyov – Ocherki Tvorchestva, R. Feinberg, Goslitizdat, Moscow, 1962.

Survey, No. 55, ed. Walter Z. Laqueur, London, April 1965.

Russian Theatre, Marc Slonim, Methuen, 1962.

Yevgeny Schwartz, S. Tsimbal, Sov. Pisatel, Leningrad, 1961.

THE BEDBUG

Vladimir Mayakovsky

An extravaganza in nine scenes translated
by Max Hayward with an introduction
by Patricia Blake

INTRODUCTION TO *THE BEDBUG*

In 1928, Mayakovsky was passing into the most tragic period of his life. During the two years before his suicide he came closest to an awareness of the nature of the society he had once acclaimed. He saw the conflict between the individual and the collective, between the artist and the bureaucrat. And, although this knowledge ultimately proved intolerable, it is to Mayakovsky's honour that, at the last, he chose to confront it in his art.

He began writing *The Bedbug* [*Klop*] in the autumn of 1928, during his travels to Germany and France, and completed it in Moscow at the end of December 1928. He had been in a great hurry to finish the play and rush back to Paris to meet Tatyana Yakovleva, with whom he had fallen in love. On 28 December he wrote in a letter to Tatyana:

> We – your Waterman and I – have written a play. We read it to Meyerhold. We wrote it twenty hours a day without food and drink. My head got swollen from this kind of work – even my cap won't fit any more. . . . I work like a bull – my mug with its red eyes lowered over the desk. . . . I still have mountains and tundras of work and I'm finishing it off and I'll rush to see you.

Mayakovsky had another, incidental reason for rushing *The Bedbug*; he was longing to make enough money to buy a Renault car in Paris and bring it back to Moscow. Although Mayakovsky succeeded in buying the Renault, the play was to be a disappointment in every other respect.

The Bedbug is one of the most devastating satires of Communist society in contemporary literature. In the first half of the play, Mayakovsky sees the Russia of 1928 in terms of the Soviet bourgeoisie: the profiteers, the Party fat cats, the proletarian philistines. His villain is Prisypkin, the bedbug-infested, guitar-strumming, vodka-soaked vulgarian who is the proud possessor of a Party card and a proletarian pedigree. In the second half, Mayakovsky foresees the Communist millennium. Now, in 1978, the excesses of a Prisypkin are unthinkable. Sex, vodka, tobacco, dancing and romance are merely items in the lexicon of archaisms. The hero? None other than Prisypkin, who has been resurrected as a zoological curiosity and who begins to look nearly human in this dehumanized world. He is lost, frightened, utterly deprived of love: in short, he is a caricature of his author. To sharpen the resemblance on stage, Mayakovsky took pains to teach the actor who played Prisypkin his own mannerisms.

Prisypkin's last lines are an ominous invitation. Momentarily released from his cage, he walks to the footlights and addresses the audience: 'Citizens! Brothers! My own people! Darlings! How did you get here? So many of you! ... Why am I alone in the cage? Darlings, friends, come and join me! Why am I suffering? Citizens!'

But Mayakovsky's first audiences were not ready to recognize his warning. Then, *The Bedbug* appeared to be dealing with periods in time which did not exist for the literal-minded. In the first part of the play, Mayakovsky had chosen to identify his repulsive characters with N.E.P. (New Economic Policy) which had already been supplanted by the first Five-Year Plan. As for the second part, the nature of the Stalinist utopia was as yet beyond the imagination of all but prophets, madmen and poets.

The Bedbug opened at the Meyerhold Theatre in Moscow on 13 February 1929, and remained in the repertoire until 16 May 1930. It was directed by Vsevolod Meyerhold in his most controversial style, with Mayakovsky as assistant director. Meyerhold thought highly of the author.

Mayakovsky knew what theatre is ... [he wrote], he was not only a brilliant playwright but also a brilliant director. I have been staging plays for many years but I never allowed myself the luxury of letting a dramatist work with me directing a play. But not only did I permit

Mayakovsky to work with me, but I found I could not work without him.

The incidental music for the original production of *The Bedbug* was composed by Dmitry Shostakovich. The composer recalls that Mayakovsky asked him to write a score that would be suitable for a 'local firemen's band'. Although this was not exactly in Shostakovich's line, he did his best. On hearing the music for the first time, Mayakovsky merely remarked: 'Well in general, it will do.' The score has since been lost.

Mayakovsky tried unsuccessfully to sell the play to a German publisher and to the German producer Erwin Piscator. Having failed in Moscow, it failed in Leningrad as well, where it was performed at the Great Drama Theatre in 1929. After 1929 it was produced only a few times and for very brief runs, and usually in abridged form.

Nowadays, the Russian audience that has endured the Stalin era is more appreciative of *The Bedbug*. When the authorities permitted a full-scale repertory production in Moscow in 1955 (staged by Sergei Yutkevich and Valentin Pluchek at the Satire Theatre), it became a smash hit. Since then it has been staged, with great success, in cities all over the country. Significantly, some of these productions have heightened the immediacy of Prisypkin's plight quite beyond Mayakovsky's intention. In the original production, his cage was a fantasy of glass and string; today it has iron bars and is provided with some familiar furnishings of contemporary Soviet life: the fringed orange lampshade, the fake tapestry hanging and the frilled boudoir pillow. The puritans of 1978 who express their repugnance for romance and vodka now do so against a backdrop showing the new University of Moscow building, completed in 1953. In at least one production, Prisypkin has become a tragic hero. When the resurrected Prisypkin has been abandoned in horror by the doctors of the brave new world, the lights in the laboratory dim; a single spotlight illuminates him as he kneels beating his head on the stage. His cry,

'Alone!' howled into the darkness, is surely one of the most hair-raising effects in modern theatre.

Bold as such productions appear in Moscow today, the Meyerhold–Mayakovsky version was a far riskier enterprise as Russia entered the Stalin era. There can hardly be anyone among those who now throng to see *The Bedbug* who does not know the fate of its creators. In 1937 Meyerhold was accused in *Pravda* of consistently producing anti-Soviet plays. He was arrested in 1939 and perished in a concentration camp during the war. Mayakovsky would unquestionably have joined Meyerhold if he had not taken his execution into his own hands.

The cultural bureaucrats tolerated Mayakovsky's satire of the communist millennium in *The Bedbug*, but they were determined not to let him get away with assailing the regime of the day, as he did in his next play *The Bathhouse*. After a first reading in February 1930, Glavrepertkom, the theatre censorship committee, declared that the play was not acceptable in its present form. After some alterations it was produced the following month and failed as badly as *The Bedbug*. A few reviews had a sinister ring. Vladimir Ermilov, for example, insinuated in *Pravda* that Mayakovksy was playing the game of the Trotskyist opposition.

Always hypersensitive to criticism and stricken by failure, Mayakovsky believed he was now the victim of persecution. His presentiment of tragedy was, as always, uncanny; the purges of the intelligentsia were at hand. Mayakovsky evidently sensed that he would be among the first to be condemned. On April 1930 an acquaintance ran into him in the lobby of the Meyerhold Theatre:

> He was very gloomy. I started talking to him about . . . an article in *Pravda* giving an objective assessment of *The Bathhouse*. Mayakovsky replied: 'Never mind. It's too late now.'

Four days later Mayakovsky was dead.

PATRICIA BLAKE

CHARACTERS

IVAN PRISYPKIN (otherwise known as PIERRE SKRIPKIN), a former Party member, former worker, and now the fiancé of

ELZEVIR DAVIDOVNA RENAISSANCE, manicurist and cashier of a beauty parlour

ROSALIE PAVLOVNA RENAISSANCE, her mother

DAVID OSIPOVICH RENAISSANCE, her father

ZOYA BERYOZKINA, a working girl

OLEG BARD, an eccentric house-owner

MILITIAMAN

PROFESSOR

DIRECTOR OF ZOO

FIRE CHIEF

FIREMEN

USHER AT WEDDING

REPORTER

WORKERS

CHAIRMAN OF CITY SOVIET

ORATOR

HIGH-SCHOOL STUDENTS

MASTER OF CEREMONIES

MEMBERS OF PRESIDIUM OF CITY SOVIET, HUNTERS, CHILDREN, OLD PEOPLE

SCENE ONE

1929. Tambov, U.S.S.R. Centre: Huge revolving door of State Department Store. Sides: Display windows full of goods. People entering empty-handed and coming out with bundles. Private pedlars[1]* *walking through the aisles.*

MAN SELLING BUTTONS: Why get married on account of a button? Why get divorced on account of a button? Just press your thumb against your index finger and you won't lose your trousers, citizens! Dutch press-studs! They sew themselves on! Twenty kopecks for half a dozen!
Here you are, gentlemen!

MAN SELLING DOLLS: Dancing dolls!
Straight from the ballet studios!
The best toy for indoors and outdoors!
Dances to the order of the People's Commissar!

WOMAN SELLING APPLES: We ain't got no pineapples!
We ain't got no bananas!
Top-grade apples at fifteen kopecks for four!
Like some, lady?

MAN SELLING WHETSTONES: Unbreakable German whetstones!
Any one you choose for thirty kopecks!
Hones where you like and how you like!
Sharpens razors, knives – and tongues for political discussions!

MAN SELLING LAMPSHADES: Lampshades! Lampshades!
All sizes and colours!
Blue for comfort and red for passion!
Get yourselves a lampshade, comrades!

* Notes are at the end of the play.

MAN SELLING BALLOONS: Sausage balloons!
Fly like a bird!
Nobile[2] could have used one at the North Pole!
Step right up, citizens!

MAN SELLING SALTED HERRINGS: Best herrings! Best herrings!
Indispensable with pancakes and vodka!

WOMAN SELLING UNDERWEAR: Brassières! Brassières!
Lovely fur-lined brassières!

MAN SELLING GLUE: Why throw out your broken crockery?
Famous Excelsior glue!
Fixes anything from Venus de Milo to a chamber-pot!
Like to try it, lady?

WOMAN SELLING PERFUME: Coty perfume by the ounce!
Coty perfume by the ounce!

MAN SELLING BOOKS: What the wife does when the husband's away!
A hundred and five funny stories by the ex-Count Leo Nikolayevich Tolstoy!
Fifteen kopecks instead of a rouble twenty!

WOMAN SELLING UNDERWEAR: Lovely brassières!
Fur-lined brassières!

[*Enter* PRISYPKIN, ROSALIE PAVLOVNA, *and* OLEG BARD.]

PRISYPKIN [*excitedly*]: Look at those aristocratic bonnets!

ROSALIE: They're not bonnets, they're . . .

PRISYPKIN: Think I'm blind? Suppose we have twins? There'll be one for Dorothy and one for Lillian when they go out walking together. . . . That's what I'm going to call them: Dorothy and Lillian – aristocratic – like the Gish sisters. Now you buy those bonnets, Rosalie . . . my house must be like a horn of plenty.

OLEG BARD [*giggling*]: Buy 'em, buy 'em, Rosalie Pavlovna! He doesn't mean to be vulgar – that's how the up-and-coming working class sees things. Here he is, bringing an immaculate proletarian origin and a union card into your family and you count your kopecks! His house must be like a horn of plenty.

[ROSALIE *buys with a sigh.*]

OLEG BARD: Let me carry them – they're quite light. Don't worry – it won't cost you any more . . .

MAN SELLING TOYS: Dancing dolls from the ballet studios . . .

PRISYPKIN: My future children must be brought up refined. There, buy one, Rosalie Pavlovna!

ROSALIE PAVLOVNA: Comrade Prisypkin . . .

PRISYPKIN: Don't call me comrade! You're not a proletarian yet – not till after the marriage!

ROSALIE PAVLOVNA: Well, *Mister* Prisypkin, for this money fifteen men could have a shave – beards, whiskers, and all. What about an extra dozen beers for the wedding instead?

PRISYPKIN [*sternly*]: Rosalie Pavlovna, my house must be filled like a horn . . .

OLEG BARD: His house must be like a horn of plenty. Beer must flow like a river, and dancing dolls, too – like out of a cornucopia.

[ROSALIE PAVLOVNA *buys.*]

OLEG BARD [*seizing the parcels*]: Don't worry – it won't cost you any more.

MAN SELLING BUTTONS: Why get married on account of a button?

Why get divorced on account of a button?

PRISYPKIN: In our Red family there must be no petty bourgeois squabbles over fly buttons. There we are! Buy them, Rosalie Pavlovna!

OLEG BARD: Rosalie Pavlovna, don't provoke him until you get that union card. He is the victorious class and he sweeps away everything in his path, like lava, and Comrade Prisypkin's trousers must be like a horn of plenty . . .

[ROSALIE PAVLOVNA *buys with a sigh.*]

OLEG BARD: Allow me . . . I'll take them and it won't cost you . . .

MAN SELLING SALTED HERRINGS: Finest republican herrings!
Indispensable with every kind of vodka!

ROSALIE PAVLOVNA [*brightening, pushing everybody aside, loudly*]: Yes! salted herrings! Now that's something for the wedding, I'll sure take some of them. Let me through, sir! How much is this sardine?

MAN SELLING SALTED HERRINGS: This salmon costs two-sixty the kilo.

ROSALIE PAVLOVNA: Two-sixty for that overgrown minnow?

MAN SELLING SALTED HERRINGS: Really, madam! Only two-sixty for this budding sturgeon!

ROSALIE PAVLOVNA: Two-sixty for these marinated corset stays! Did you hear that, Comrade Skripkin? Oh, how right you were to kill the Tsar and drive out Mr Ryabushinsky![3] Oh, the bandits! I shall claim my civic rights and buy my herrings in the Soviet State Co-op!

OLEG BARD: Wait a moment, Comrade Skripkin. Why get mixed up with petty bourgeois elements and haggle over herrings like this? Give me fifteen roubles and a bottle of vodka and I'll fix you up with a wedding in a million.

PRISYPKIN: Comrade Bard, I'm against all this petty bourgeois stuff – lace curtains and canaries. . . . I'm a man with higher needs. What I'm interested in is a wardrobe with a mirror . . . .

[ZOYA BERYOZKINA *nearly runs into them as they stand talking. Steps back in astonishment and listens.*]

OLEG BARD: When your cortège . . .

PRISYPKIN: What's that? Some kind of card-game?

OLEG BARD: Cortège, I say. That's what they call processions of all kinds, particularly wedding processions, in these lovely foreign languages.

PRISYPKIN: Well, what do you know!

OLEG BARD: As I was saying, when the cortège advances I'll sing you the epithalamium of Hymen.

PRISYPKIN: Huh? What's that about the Himalayas?

OLEG BARD: Not the Himalayas ... an epithalamium about the god Hymen. That was a god these Greeks had. I mean the ancient republican Greeks, not these mad-dog guttersnipe opportunists like Venizelos.

PRISYPKIN: What I want for my money is a real Red wedding and no gods! Get it?

OLEG BARD: Why, of course, Comrade Skripkin! Not only do I understand, but by virtue of that power of imagination which, according to Plekhanov,[4] is granted to Marxists, I can already see as through a prism, so to speak, the triumph of your class as symbolized by your sublime, ravishing, elegant, and class-conscious wedding! The bride steps out of her carriage and she's all red – that is, she's all steamed up. And leading her by the arm is her red escort, Yerikalov, the book-keeper – he's fat, red, and apoplectic ... and you are brought in by the red ushers, the table is covered with red hams, and the bottles all have red seals.

PRISYPKIN [*approvingly*]: That's it! That's it!

OLEG BARD: The red guests shout 'Kiss, kiss!'[5] and your red spouse puts her red lips to yours ...

ZOYA BERYOZKINA [*seizes both of them by the arms; they remove her hands and dust off their sleeves*]: Vanya! What's he talking about, this catfish in a cravat? What wedding? Who's getting married?

OLEG BARD: The Red nuptials of Elzevir Davidovna Renaissance and ...

PRISYPKIN: I love another, Zoya,
She's smarter and cuter
With a bosom held tighter
By a beautiful sweater.

ZOYA BERYOZKINA: But what about me, Vanya? Who

do you think you are? A sailor with a girl in every port?

PRISYPKIN [*wards her off with outstretched hand*]: 'We part like ships in the sea . . .'

ROSALIE PAVLOVNA [*rushing from the shop, holding a herring above her head*]: Whales! Dolphins! [*To the herring pedlar*] Now then, show me that snail! [*She compares. The street-vendor's herrings are larger. Wrings her hands.*] Longer by a tail's length! What did we fight for, Comrade Skripkin, eh? Why, oh, why did we kill the Tsar? Why did we throw out Mr Ryabushinsky? This Soviet regime of yours will drive me to my grave. . . . A whole tail's length longer!

OLEG BARD: My dear Rosalie Pavlovna, try comparing them at the other end. They're only bigger by a head and what do you want the heads for? You can't eat them and you'll cut them off and throw them out anyway.

ROSALIE PAVLOVNA: Did you hear that? If I cut off your head, Comrade Bard, it will be no loss to anyone, but if I cut off these herrings' heads I lose ten kopecks to the kilo. Well, let's go home. . . . I sure want a union card in the family, but my daughter's in a good business, and that's nothing to sniff at!

ZOYA BERYOZKINA: We were going to live and work together . . . so it's all over . . .

PRISYPKIN: Our love is liquidated. I'll call the militia if you interfere with my freedom of love as a citizen.

ROSALIE PAVLOVNA: What does she want, this slut? Why have you got your hooks on my son-in-law?

ZOYA BERYOZKINA: He's mine!

ROSALIE PAVLOVNA: Ah! She's pregnant! I'll pay her off, but I'll smash her face in first!

MILITIAMAN: Citizens! Stop this disgusting behaviour!

SCENE TWO

Hostel for young workers. INVENTOR *huffs and puffs over a blue-print.* YOUTH *lolls around.* GIRL *sits on the edge of the bed.* YOUTH IN SPECTACLES *with nose buried in a book. Whenever the door opens, a long corridor with doors off and light-bulbs is seen.*

BAREFOOT YOUTH [*howling at the top of his voice*]: Where are my boots? Someone's swiped my boots again! Am I supposed to check them every night in the baggage room at the Kursk Station? Is that what I've got to do? Is that it?

CLEANER: Prisypkin took them to go see his lady-love, his she-camel. He cursed while he put them on. 'This is the last time,' he said. 'In the evening,' he said, 'I shall present myself in a get-up more appropriate to my new social status.'

YOUTH: The bastard!

YOUNG WORKER [*tidying up the room*]: The trash he leaves behind him is kind of more refined nowadays. It used to be empty beer-bottles and fish-tails and now it's cologne bottles and ties all the colours of the rainbow.

GIRL: Shut your trap! The kid buys a new tie and you curse him like he was Ramsay MacDonald.

YOUTH: That's just what he is – Ramsay MacDonald! The new tie don't matter. Trouble is that he's tied to the tie – not the tie to him. He don't even use his head any more, so his tie shouldn't get twisted.

CLEANER: If there's a hole in his sock and he's in a hurry, he paints it over with indelible ink.

YOUTH: His feet are black anyway.

INVENTOR: But maybe not black in the places where the holes are. He ought to just switch his socks from one foot to the other.

CLEANER: There's the inventor for you! Why don't you take out a patent before somebody steals the idea?

[*Whisks a duster over the table, upsets a box from which visiting-cards drop out fanwise. Bends down to pick them up, holds them to the light, laughs so hard he can barely manage to motion his comrades towards him.*]

ALL [*reading and repeating after each other*]: Pierre Skripkin![1] Pierre Skripkin!

INVENTOR: That's the name he's invented for himself. Prisypkin. Who is Prisypkin? What good's Prisypkin? What's the point of Prisypkin? But Pierre Skripkin – that's not a name, it's a romance!

GIRL [*dreamily*]: But it's true! Pierre Skripkin is very fine and elegant. You roar your heads off but how do you know he's not carrying out a cultural revolution in his own home?

YOUTH: Yeah, Pushkin's got nothing on him with those sideburns of his. They hang down like a pair of dog's tails and he doesn't even wash them to keep them neat.

GIRL: There's that movie star with sideburns ...

INVENTOR: Prisypkin got the idea from him.

YOUTH: And what does his hero's hair grow on, I'd like to know? He's got no head at all, but a whole halo of fuzz. Wonder what makes it grow? Must be the dampness.

YOUTH WITH BOOK: Anyway, he's no movie star. ... He's a writer. I don't know what he's written, but I know he's famous! They've written about him three times in *Evening Moscow*: they say that he sold Apukhtin's[2] poetry as his own, and Apukhtin got so mad he wrote a denial. And so what's-his-name came back and said: 'You're all crazy, it's not true, I copied it from Nadson.'[3] I don't know which of them is lying. It's true they don't print him any more, but he's very famous. He gives lessons to young people – how to write verse, how to dance, and, well, you know ... how to borrow money.

YOUTH WITH BROOM: Painting over holes with ink – that's no way for a worker to behave!

[MECHANIC, *grease-covered, comes in half-way through this sentence. Washes his hands and turns around.*]

MECHANIC: He's no worker. He quit his job today. He's marrying a young lady – a hairdresser's daughter. She's the cashier and the manicurist too. Mademoiselle Elzevir Renaissance'll clip his claws for him now....

INVENTOR: Elzevir – that's the name of a type face.

MECHANIC: I don't know about her type face, but she's certainly got a figure! He showed her picture to our pay clerk today...

What a honey, what a peach –
Both her breasts weigh eighty pounds each!

BAREFOOT YOUTH: He's sure fixed himself up!

GIRL: Jealous, eh?

BAREFOOT YOUTH: So what? When I get to be foreman and earn enough to buy myself a pair of boots, I'll start looking around for a cosy little apartment.

MECHANIC: Here's my advice to you: get yourself some curtains. You can either open them and look out at the street or close them and take your bribes in private. It's better to work with other people, but it's much more fun to eat your chicken by yourself. Right? We had men who tried to run away from the trenches, too, and we just swatted them down like flies. Well, why don't you just get out?

BAREFOOT YOUTH: Okay. Okay. Who do you think you are? Karl Liebknecht?[4] If a dame gives you the glad eye out of a window, I bet you fall for it, too, hero!

MECHANIC: I'm no deserter. You think I like wearing these lousy rags? Like hell I do! There are lots of us, you know, and there just aren't enough Nepmen's[5] daughters to go around. ... We'll build houses for everybody! But we won't creep out of this foxhole with a white flag.

BAREFOOT YOUTH: You and your trenches! This isn't 1919. People want to live their own lives now.

MECHANIC: Well, isn't it like the trenches in here?

BAREFOOT YOUTH: Nuts!

MECHANIC: Look at the lice!

BAREFOOT YOUTH: Nuts!

MECHANIC: Our enemies attack silently now – that's the only difference. And people shoot with noiseless powder!

BAREFOOT YOUTH: Nuts!

MECHANIC: Look at Prisypkin – he's been shot by a two-eyed, double-barrelled gun!

[*Enter* PRISYPKIN *in patent-leather shoes. In one hand he holds a pair of worn-out shoes by the laces and tosses them over to* BAREFOOT YOUTH. OLEG BARD *carries his purchases. He stands between* PRISYPKIN *and the* MECHANIC, *who is dancing a jig.*]

OLEG BARD: Don't pay any attention to this vulgar dance, Comrade Skripkin, it will only spoil the refined taste that is awakening in you.

[*The youths in the hostel turn their backs.*]

MECHANIC: Quit bowing and scraping. You'll crack your skull.

OLEG BARD: I understand, Comrade Skripkin! You are too sensitive for this vulgar crew. But don't lose your patience for just one more lesson. The first foxtrot after the nuptial ceremonies is a crucial step – it should leave a deathless impression. Well now, take a few steps with an imaginary lady.... Why are you stamping your feet like at a May Day parade?

PRISYPKIN: Comrade Bard, let me take my shoes off: they pinch and besides they'll wear out.

OLEG BARD: That's the way! That's right! Tread softly like you were coming back from a saloon on a moonlit night, full of sadness and dreams. That's the way! But don't wriggle your hind parts! You're supposed to be leading your partner, not driving a pushcart. . . . That's the way! . . . Where's your hand? Your hand's too low!

PRISYPKIN [*passes his hand over an imaginary shoulder*]: It won't stay up!

OLEG BARD: And now, Comrade Skripkin, you discreetly locate the lady's brassière, hook your thumb into it, and rest your hand – it's pleasant for the lady and makes it easier for you. Then you can think about your other hand. . . . Why are you rolling your shoulders? That's not a foxtrot. You're giving a demonstration of the shimmy.

PRISYPKIN: No, I was just scratching myself.

OLEG BARD: That's not the way to do it, Comrade Skripkin! If any such emergency occurs while you're carried away by the dance, roll your eyes, as if you were jealous of the lady, step back to the wall in the Spanish manner, and rub yourself rapidly against some statue or other. In the smart society where you'll be moving there's always a hell of a lot of statues and vases. So rub yourself, screw up your face, flash your eyes, and say: 'I understand, tr-r-reacherous one, you are playing a game with me. . . .' Then you start dancing again and pretend you're gradually calming down and cooling off.

PRISYPKIN: Like this?

OLEG BARD: Bravo! Well done! How clever you are, Comrade Skripkin! A man of such talents just doesn't have elbowroom in Russia, what with capitalist encirclement and the building of socialism in one country. I ask you – is Lower Goat Street a worthy scene for your activities? You need a world revolution, you must break through into Europe. Once you've smashed the Chamberlains, the Poincarés, you will delight the Moulin Rouge and the Pantheon with the beauty of your bodily movements. Just remember that! Now hold it! Hold it! Magnificent! But I must be off. I have to keep an eye on the ushers. I'll give them one glass in advance before the wedding and not a drop more. When they've done their job, they can drink straight out of the bottle, if they like. *Au revoir!* [*Shouts from the doorway as he leaves*] And don't put on two ties at once – particularly if they're different colours. And remember, you can't wear a starched shirt outside your trousers!

[PRISYPKIN *tries on his new clothes.*]

YOUTH: Vanya, why don't you cut it out?

PRISYPKIN: Mind your own goddamn business, respected comrade! What did I fight for? I fought for the good life, and now I've got it right here in my hands – a wife, a home, and real etiquette. I'll do my duty, if need be, but it's only we who held the bridgehead who have a right to rest by the river! So there! Mebbe I can raise the standards of the whole proletariat by looking after my own comforts. So there!

MECHANIC: There's a warrior for you! A real Suvorov![6] Bravo!

For a while I worked my best
Building a bridge to Socialism
But before I was through I wanted a rest
By the bridge to Socialism.
Now it's grown with grass that's grazed by sheep
And all I do is lie and sleep
By the bridge to Socialism.

So that's it, eh?

PRISYPKIN: Leave me alone with your cheap propaganda ditties . . . [*Sits down on bed and sings to guitar.*]

On Lunacharsky Street
There's an old house I know
With stairs broad and neat
And a most elegant window.

[*A shot.* ALL *rush to the door.*]

YOUTH [*from the doorway*]: Zoya Beryozkina's shot herself! They'll give her hell for this at the Party meeting!

VOICES: Help!
First aid!

Help!
First aid!

A VOICE [*on the phone*]: First aid! Help! What? She's shot herself! Right through the breast! This is Lower Goat Street, number sixteen.

[PRISYPKIN *alone. Hurriedly collects his belongings.*]

MECHANIC: And a woman like that shoots herself on account of you, you hairy skunk! [*Grabs* PRISYPKIN *by the jacket and throws him out of the room, hurling his belongings after him.*]

CLEANER [*running in with doctor; jerks* PRISYPKIN *to his feet and gives him his hat, which has fallen off*]: You're walking out on your class with a hell of a bang!

PRISYPKIN [*turns away and yells*]: Cab! Seventeen Lunacharsky Street – and my luggage!

SCENE THREE

Huge beauty parlour. Mirrors decorated with paper flowers. Liquor bottles on small shaving-tables. On the left a grand piano. On the right a coal stove whose pipes climb all around the walls. In the middle of the room a banquet table at which sit PIERRE SKRIPKIN, ELZEVIR RENAISSANCE, *the* BEST MAN (*an accountant*), *and the* MATRON OF HONOUR (*accountant's wife*). OLEG BARD *is master of ceremonies and sits in the centre of the table.*

ELZEVIR: Shall we begin, Skrippy my pet?

PRISYPKIN: Just a minute.

ELZEVIR: Skrippy darling, shall we start?

PRISYPKIN: Wait. I said I wished to get wed in an organized fashion – in the presence of the guests of honour, and particularly in the presence of the secretary of our factory committee, respected Comrade Lassalchenko. . . . Here we are!

GUEST [*running in*]: My dear bride and bridegroom, please forgive me for being late and allow me to convey to you the congratulations of our respected leader, Comrade Lassalchenko. 'Tomorrow,' he says, 'I would even go to the church, if need be, but today,' he says, 'I can't make it. Today,' he says, 'is a Party meeting, and like it or not, I have to go to the Party cell. . . .' So let us proceed to current business, as the saying goes.

PRISYPKIN: I hereby declare the wedding open.

ROSALIE PAVLOVNA: Comrades and *Messieurs*! Please eat! Where would you find pigs like these nowadays? I bought this ham three years ago in case of a war with Greece or Poland. . . . But there's still no war and the ham is getting mouldy. . . . Eat, gentlemen!

ALL [*raising their glasses*]: Kiss! Kiss![1]

[ELZEVIR *and* PIERRE *kiss.*]

Kiss! Kiiii-ss-ss!

[ELZEVIR *throws herself around* PIERRE*'s neck and he kisses her staidly, conscious of his working-class dignity.*]

BEST MAN: Let's have some Beethoven! Shakespeare! Give us a show! What do they think we celebrate their anniversaries for?

[*The piano is dragged to centre of stage.*]

VOICES: By the side! Grab it by the side! Look at its teeth – makes you want to smash them in!

PRISYPKIN: Don't trample on the legs of my piano!

OLEG BARD [*stands up, staggers, and spills his glass*]: I am happy, I am happy to see, as we are gathered here today, that the road of Comrade Skripkin's fighting career has come to such a splendid conclusion. It's true that along that road he lost his Party card, but, on the other hand, he did acquire many state lottery tickets. We have succeeded in reconciling, in coordinating the couple's class and other contradictions. We who are armed with the Marxist vision cannot fail to see, as in a drop of water, so to speak, the future happiness of humanity – or as it is called in popular parlance: socialism.

ALL: Kiss! Kiss!

[ELZEVIR *and* PRISYPKIN *kiss.*]

OLEG BARD: What gigantic steps we are making on the road to the rebuilding of family life! When we all lay dying at the battle of Perekop,[2] and when many of us, indeed, did die, could we have foreseen that such fragrant roses would blossom forth in this day and age? Could we have imagined, when we groaned under the yoke of autocracy, could even our great teachers Marx and Engels have imagined in their dreams, or dreamed in their imaginations that the bonds of Hymen would one day join together Labour – obscure but grandiose – and Capital – dethroned but ever enchanting?

ALL: Kiss! Kiss!

OLEG BARD: Respected comrades! Beauty is the motive force of progress! What would I have been as a simple worker? Botchkin[3] – just plain Botchkin! What could Botchkin do except bray like an ass? But as Oleg the Bard I can do anything you like! For instance:

I'm Oleg the bard
A happy drunkard.

And so now I'm Oleg Bard and enjoy all the blessings of culture as an equal member of society. And I swear – well, no swearing here – but at least I can talk like an ancient Greek:

Prithee, give me, Elzevir
A herring and a glass of beer!

And the whole country responds, just like they were troubadours:

Here's to you, Oleg dear,
A herring's tail and a glass of beer,
To whet your whistle
In style and good cheer!

ALL: Bravo! Hurray! Kiss!

OLEG BARD: Beauty is pregnant with ...

USHER [*jumps up, menacingly*]: Pregnant? Who said 'pregnant'? I'll ask you to watch your language in the presence of the newly-weds!

[USHER *is dragged off.*]

ALL: Give us Beethoven! Give us the Kamarinsky![4]

[OLEG BARD *is dragged to the piano.*]

OLEG BARD:

The tramcars drew up to the Registry Office
Bringing the guests to a Red marriage service. . . .

ALL [*singing in chorus*]:

Dressed in his working clothes was the spouse
And a union card stuck out of his blouse!

ACCOUNTANT: I get the idea! I get the whole thing!

Hail to thee, Oleg Bardkin
Curly-headed like a lambkin. . . .

HAIRDRESSER [*poking his fork at the* MATRON OF HONOUR]: No, madam, no! Nobody has curly hair now, after the Revolution! Do you know how we make a *chignon gaufré*? You take the curling-iron [*he twists his fork*], heat it on a low flame – *à l'étoile* [*thrusts his fork into the blazing stove*], and then you whip up a kind of *soufflé* of hair on the crown of the head . . . like this.

MATRON OF HONOUR: You insult my honour as a mother and a virgin. . . . Leave me alone, son of a bitch!!!

USHER: Who said 'son of a bitch'? I'll ask you to watch your language in the presence of the newly-weds!

[*The* ACCOUNTANT *separates them and continues his song, turning the handle of the cash register as though it were a barrel-organ.*]

ELZEVIR [*to* OLEG BARD]: Ah, play us the waltz 'Makarov's Lament for Vera Kholodnaya'. . . .[5] Ah, it's so *charmant*; it's simply a *petite histoire*. . . .

USHER [*armed with a guitar*]: Who said '*pissoir*'? I'll ask you to watch . . .

[OLEG BARD *separates them and pounces on the piano keys.*]

USHER [*looks over his shoulder, threateningly*]: Why do you play only on the black keys? I suppose you think black is good enough for the proletariat. You play on all the keys only for the bourgeoisie, is that it?

OLEG BARD: Please, citizen, please! I'm concentrating on the white ones!

USHER: So you think white is best? Play on both!

OLEG BARD: I *am* playing on both!

USHER: So you compromise with the Whites,[6] opportunist!

OLEG BARD: But, comrade ... the keyboard is ...

USHER: Who said 'bawdy'? And in the presence of the newlyweds! Take that! [*Hits him on the back of the neck with guitar. The* HAIRDRESSER *sticks his fork into the* MATRON OF HONOUR'*s hair.* PRISYPKIN *pushes the* ACCOUNTANT *away from his wife.*]

PRISYPKIN: What do you mean by sticking a fish into my wife's breast? This is a bosom, not a flower-bed, and that's a fish, not a chrysanthemum!

ACCOUNTANT: And who gave us salmon to eat? You did, huh? So what are you screaming about, huh?

[*In the tussle the bride is pushed on to the stove. The stove overturns. Her wedding veil catches fire. Flames. Smoke.*]

VOICES: We're on fire! ... Who said 'on fire'? ... Salmon! ... 'The tramcars drew up to the Registry Office. ...'

SCENE FOUR

A fireman's helmet gleams in the darkness, reflecting the light of a near-by fire. FIREMEN *rush on stage, report to their* CHIEF *and exit.*

FIRST FIREMAN: We can't control it, Comrade Chief! We weren't called for two hours ... the drunken swine! It's burning like a powder magazine. [*Exit.*]

CHIEF: No wonder it burns – cobwebs and liquor.

SECOND FIREMAN: It's dying down . . . the water's turning to icicles. The cellar looks like a skating rink. [*Exit.*]

CHIEF: Found any bodies?

THIRD FIREMAN: One with a smashed skull – must have been hit by a falling beam. Sent it straight to the morgue. [*Exit.*]

FOURTH FIREMAN: One charred corpse of undetermined sex with a fork in its hand.

FIRST FIREMAN: An ex-woman found under the stove with a wire crown on her head.

THIRD FIREMAN: One person unknown of pre-war build with a cash register in his hands. Must have been a bandit.

SECOND FIREMAN: No survivors . . . one person unaccounted for – since the corpse has not been found, I assume it must have burned up entirely.

FIRST FIREMAN: Look at the fireworks! Just like a theatre, except that all the actors have been burned up!

THIRD FIREMAN:

They were driven from the marriage
In a Red Cross carriage. . . .

[*A bugler summons the* FIREMEN. *They form ranks and march through the aisles of the theatre reciting.*]

FIREMEN:

Comrades and citizens!
vodka is toxic!
Drunks can easily
burn up the Republic!
A primus stove or an open fire
can turn your home into a funeral pyre!
You can start a fire
if you chance to doze off
So no bedside reading
of Nadson and Zharov![1]

SCENE FIVE

Fifty years later. An immense amphitheatre for conferences. Instead of human voters, radio loudspeakers equipped with arms like direction indicators on a car. Above each loudspeaker, coloured electric lights. Just below the ceiling there are movie screens. In the centre of the hall a dais with a microphone, flanked by control panels and switches for sound and light. Two technicians – an OLD MAN *and a* YOUTH *– are tinkering around in the darkened hall.*

OLD MAN [*flicking dust from loudspeakers with a bedraggled feather duster*]: It's an important vote today. Check up on the voting apparatus of the agricultural zones and give it a spot of oil. There was a hitch last time....

YOUTH: The agricultural zones? Okay! I'll oil the central zones and polish up the throat of the Smolensk apparatus – they were a bit hoarse again last week. I must tighten up the arms on the metropolitan auxiliary personnel – they're deviating a bit – the right arm tangles with the left one.

OLD MAN: The Ural factories are ready. We'll switch in the Kursk metalworks – they've just installed a new apparatus of sixty-two thousand votes for the second group of Zaporozhe power stations. It's pretty good and doesn't give any trouble.

YOUTH: And you remember how it was in the old days? Must have been queer, wasn't it?

OLD MAN: My mother once carried me to a meeting in her arms. There weren't many people – only about a thousand. They were just sitting there, the parasites, and listening. It was some important motion and it was passed by a majority of one. My mother was against it but she couldn't vote because she was holding me in her arms.

YOUTH: Yes.... That was amateur stuff, of course!

OLD MAN: Apparatus like this wouldn't even have been any good in the old days. A fellow used to have to raise his hand to draw attention to himself – he'd thrust it right in the chairman's face, put both his hands right under his nose. He could have used twelve hands like the ancient god Isis. And lots of people avoided voting. They tell a story about one fellow who sat out some important discussion in the men's room – he was too frightened to vote. He just sat and thought, trying to save his skin.

YOUTH: And did he?

OLD MAN: I'll say he did! But they appointed him to another job. Seeing how much he liked the men's room they put him there permanently in charge of the soap and towels.... Everything ready?

YOUTH: Everything!

[*They run down to the control panels. A man with glasses and beard flings open the door and walks straight to the rostrum. Standing with his back to the auditorium, he raises both hands.*]

ORATOR: Plug in all the zones of the Federation!

OLD MAN *and* YOUTH: Okay!

[*All the red, green, and blue bulbs light up simultaneously.*]

ORATOR: Hello, hello! This is the President of the Institute for Human Resurrection. The motion has been circulated by telegram and has been discussed. The question is clear and simple. At the corner of 62nd Street and 17th Avenue in the former town of Tambov a building brigade, while excavating at a depth of seven metres, has discovered a caved-in, ice-filled cellar. A frozen human figure is visible through the ice. In the opinion of the Institute this individual, who froze to death fifty years ago, could be resurrected. Let us regulate the difference of opinions!

The Institute considers that the life of every worker must be utilized until the very last second.

An X-ray examination has shown that the hands of the individual are calloused. Half a century ago callouses were the distinguishing mark of a worker. And let me remind you that after the wars that swept over the world, after the civil wars that led to the creation of our World Federation, human life was declared inviolable by the decree of November 7th, 1965. I have to bring to your attention the objections of the Epidemiological Office, which fears a spread of the bacteria known to have infected the former inhabitants of what was once Russia.

In putting the question to the vote, I am fully aware of my responsibility. Comrades, remember, remember, and once again remember:

We are voting
for a human life!

[*The lights are dimmed, a high-pitched bell rings. The text of the motion is flashed on to a screen and read out by the* ORATOR.]

For the sake of research into the labour habits of the proletariat, for the sake of comparative studies in human life and manners, we demand resurrection!

[VOICES *from half the loudspeakers: 'Quite right! Adopted!' Some other* VOICES: *'Rejected!' The* VOICES *trail off and the screen darkens. A second bell. A new motion is flashed on to the screen and the* ORATOR *reads it out.*]

Moved by the sanitary-inspection stations of the metallurgical and chemical enterprises of the Don Basin: In view of the danger of the spread of the bacteria of arrogance and sycophancy, which were epidemic in 1929, we demand that the exhibit remain in its refrigerated state.

[VOICES *from the loudspeakers: 'Rejected!' A few shouts of 'Adopted!'*]

ORATOR: Any further motions or amendments?

[*Another screen lights up and the* ORATOR *reads from it.*]

The agricultural zones of Siberia request that the resurrection be postponed until the autumn – until the termination of work in the fields – in order to make possible the presence of the broad masses of the people.

[*Overwhelming majority of loudspeakers: 'Rejected!' The bulbs light up.*]

I put it to a vote. All in favour of the first motion please raise their hands!

[*Overwhelming majority of the steel hands are raised.*]

Who is in favour of the amendment from Siberia?

[*Two lone hands are raised.*]

The Assembly of the Federation accepts the motion in favour of RE-SUR-RECTION!

[*Roar from all the loudspeakers: 'Hurrah!' The* VOICES *die away.*]

The session is closed!

[REPORTERS *rush in through swinging doors. The* ORATOR *cannot restrain himself and shouts joyfully.*]

Resurrection it is! Resurrection! Resurrection!

[*The* REPORTERS *pull microphones from their pockets.*]

FIRST REPORTER: Hello! 472·5 kilocycles calling. . . . *Eskimo Izvestiya.* . . . Resurrection!

SECOND REPORTER: Hello! Hello! 376 kilocycles. . . . *Vitebsk Evening Pravda.* . . . Resurrection!

THIRD REPORTER: Hello! Hello! Hello! 211 kilocycles. . . . *Warsaw Komsomol Pravda.* . . . Resurrection!

FOURTH REPORTER: *Armavir Literary Weekly.* . . . Hello! Hello!

FIFTH REPORTER: Hello! Hello! Hello! . . . 44 kilocycles. . . . *Izvestiya of Chicago Soviet.* . . . Resurrection!

SIXTH REPORTER: Hello! Hello! Hello! . . . 115 kilocycles. . . . *Red Gazetet of Rome.* . . . Resurrection!

SEVENTH REPORTER: Hello! Hello! Hello! . . . 78 kilocycles. . . . *Shanghai Pauper*. . . . Resurrection!

EIGHTH REPORTER: Hello! Hello! Hello! . . . 220 kilocycles. . . . *Madrid Dairy-Maid*. . . . Resurrection!

NINTH REPORTER: Hello! Hello! . . . 11 kilocycles. . . . *Kabul Pioneer*. . . . Resurrection!

[*Newsboys burst in with news-sheets fresh from the press.*]

FIRST NEWSBOY:

Read how the man froze
Features in verse and prose!

SECOND NEWSBOY:

World-wide poll on number one question!
Can obsequiousness spread by infection?

THIRD NEWSBOY:

Feature on ancient guitars and romances
And other means of drugging the masses!

FOURTH NEWSBOY:

Interview! Interview! Read all about it!

FIFTH NEWSBOY:

Complete list of so-called 'dirty words'.
Don't be scared, keep your nerve!

SIXTH NEWSBOY:

Science Gazette! Science Gazette!
Theoretical discussion of ancient problem –
Can an elephant die from a cigarette?

SEVENTH NEWSBOY:

It'll make you cry
and give you colic –
Explanation of
the word 'alcoholic'!

SCENE SIX

Sliding door of frosted glass behind which gleam metal parts of surgical apparatus. In front of it are an old PROFESSOR *and his elderly assistant, who is recognizable as* ZOYA BERYOZKINA. *Both are in white hospital gowns.*

ZOYA BERYOZKINA: Comrade! Comrade professor! Don't do this experiment, I beg you! Comrade professor, that awful business will start all over again. . . .

PROFESSOR: Comrade Beryozkina, you have begun to live in the past and you talk an incomprehensible language. Just like a dictionary of obsolete words. What's 'business'? [*Looks it up in the dictionary*] Business . . . business . . . bootlegger . . . Bulgakov . . . bureaucracy . . . ah, here we are: 'business: a kind of activity that prevented every other kind of activity'. . . .

ZOYA BERYOZKINA: Well, this 'activity' nearly cost me my life fifty years ago. . . . I even went so far as to attempt suicide. . . .

PROFESSOR: Suicide? What's 'suicide'? [*Looks in dictionary*] . . . supertax . . . surrealism . . . here we are: 'suicide'. [*Surprised*] You shot yourself? By a court order? A revolutionary tribunal?

ZOYA BERYOZKINA: No . . . by myself. . . .

PROFESSOR: By yourself? Carelessness?

ZOYA BERYOZKINA: No . . . love. . . .

PROFESSOR: Nonsense! Love should make you build bridges and bear children. . . . But you . . . my-my-my!

ZOYA BERYOZKINA: Let me go; I simply can't face it!

PROFESSOR: That really is . . . what was the word? . . . 'a business'. My-my-my! A business! Society needs you. You must bring all your feelings into play so as to enable this being, whom we are about to unfreeze, to recover from his fifty anazooic years with the maximum of ease. Yes, upon my word! Your presence is very, very important! . . . He and she – that's you I mean! Tell me, were his eyelashes brittle? They might break during the process of rapid defrigeration.

ZOYA BERYOZKINA: Comrade professor, how can I remember eyelashes of fifty years ago!

PROFESSOR: Fifty years ago . . . that was yesterday! And how do you think I manage to remember the colour of the hairs on the tail of a mastodon that died half a million years ago? My-my-my! Well, do you remember whether he dilated his nostrils very much while breathing in a state of excitement?

ZOYA BERYOZKINA: Comrade professor, how can I remember? It's thirty years since people dilated their nostrils under such conditions.

PROFESSOR: Well, well, well! And do you have information about the size of his stomach and liver? In case there is any quantity of alcohol that might ignite at the high voltage we require. . . .

ZOYA BERYOZKINA: How can I remember all that, Comrade professor? I know he had a stomach. . . .

PROFESSOR: Ah, you don't remember anything, Comrade Beryozkina! But you can at least tell me, was he impulsive?

ZOYA BERYOZKINA: I don't know . . . perhaps . . . but not with me.

PROFESSOR: Well, well, well! I fear that while we're unfreezing him, you are freezing up! My-my-my! Well, let's proceed.

[*The* PROFESSOR *presses a button. The glass door slides back silently. In the middle a shining, zinc-covered, man-sized box on an operating table. Around it are taps with pails under them. Wires lead into the crate. Oxygen cylinders. Six calm, white-clad* DOCTORS *stand around the crate. Six washbasins in the foreground. Six towels hang, as though suspended in mid-air, on an invisible wire.*]

PROFESSOR [*to first doctor*]: Switch on the current only at my signal. [*To second doctor*] Bring the temperature up to 98·6 at intervals of fifteen seconds. [*To third doctor*] Have the oxygen cylinder ready. [*To fourth doctor*] Drain off the water gradually as you replace the ice with air pressure. [*To fifth doctor*] Raise the lid at once. [*To sixth doctor*] Follow the stages of his revival in the mirror.

[*The* DOCTORS *nod their heads to show they have understood. They watch the temperature. Water drips. The* SIXTH DOCTOR *stares at a mirror in the right side of the crate.*]

SIXTH DOCTOR: His natural colour is returning! [*Pause.*] He's free from ice! [*Pause.*] His chest is heaving! [*Pause.*] Professor, look at these unnatural spasms!

PROFESSOR [*comes up and looks closely; in a calm voice*]: That's a normal movement – he's scratching himself. Evidently the parasites inseparable from these specimens are reviving.

SIXTH DOCTOR: Professor, what do you make of this? That movement of his left hand from the body. . . .

PROFESSOR [*looking closely*]: He's what used to be called a 'sentimental soul', a music lover. In antiquity there was Stradivarius and there was Utkin. Stradivarius made violins and Utkin played on this thing – 'guitar' they called it. [*He inspects thermometer and apparatus registering blood pressure.*]

FIRST DOCTOR: 98·6.

SECOND DOCTOR: Pulse 68.

SIXTH DOCTOR: Breathing regular.

PROFESSOR: To your places!

[*The* DOCTORS *walk away from the crate. The lid flies open and out comes* PRISYPKIN. *He is dishevelled and surprised. He looks around, clutching his guitar.*]

PRISYPKIN: Well, I've slept it off! Forgive me, comrades, I was sozzled, of course! What militia station is this?

PROFESSOR: This isn't the militia. This is the defrigeration station. We have unfrozen you.

PRISYPKIN: What's that? Unfrozen me? We'll soon see who was drunk! I know you doctors – always sniffing at alcohol! I can prove my identity; I've got my documents on me [*jumps down from crate and turns out his pockets*] . . . seventeen roubles, sixty kopecks in cash . . . paid up all my dues . . . Revolutionary Defence Fund . . . Anti-illiteracy campaign. . . . Here you are, look! . . . What's this? A marriage certificate. [*Whistles.*] . . . Where are you, my love? Who is kissing your finger tips? There'll be hell to pay at home! Here's the best man's receipt. Here's my union card. [*Happens to see the calendar; rubs his eyes, looks around in horror.*] May 12th, 1979! All my unpaid union dues! For fifty years! The forms I'll have to fill out! For the District Committee! For the Central Committee! My God! My wife! Let me out of here! [*Shakes the hands of the* DOCTORS *and makes for the door.*]

[*Alarmed,* ZOYA BERYOZKINA *goes after him. The* DOCTORS *crowd around the* PROFESSOR *and speak in chorus.*]

DOCTORS: What's that he was doing – squeezing our hands like that?

PROFESSOR: An antihygienic habit they had in the old days.

[*The six* DOCTORS *and the* PROFESSOR *thoughtfully wash their hands.*]

PRISYPKIN [*bumping into* ZOYA BERYOZKINA]: For heaven's sake, who are you? Who am I? Where am I? You wouldn't be Zoya Beryozkina's mother? [*Turns his head at the screech of a siren.*] Where the hell am I? Where've they put me? What is this? Moscow, Paris, New York??? Cab! [*Blaring of automobile horns.*] Not a soul in sight! Not a single horse! Just cars, cars, cars! [*Presses against door, scratches his back, gropes with his hand, turns around, and sees a bedbug crawling from his collar on to the white wall.*] A bedbug! My sweet little bedbug, my darling little bedbug, my own little bedbug! [*Plays a chord on guitar and sings*] 'Leave me not, abide with me awhile ...' [*Tries to catch bedbug with his hand, but it crawls away.*] 'We part like ships in the sea ...' He's gone! ... I'm all alone! 'No one replies, alone I am again, alone ...' Cab! Cars! ... Seventeen Lunacharsky Street, no luggage ... [*Clutches his head, swoons into the arms of* ZOYA BERYOZKINA, *who has run out after him.*]

SCENE SEVEN

A triangular plaza. Three artificial trees. First tree has green square leaves on which stand enormous plates with tangerines. Second tree has paper plates with apples. Third tree has open perfume bottles shaped like pine cones. Sides: glass-fronted buildings. Long benches running along the sides of the triangle. Enter REPORTER *and four other people, men and women.*

REPORTER: Over here, comrades! In the shade! I'll tell you about these grim and astonishing events. In the first place ... Pass me some tangerines. How right the municipality was to make the trees tangerine today. Yesterday it was pears – so dry, insipid, unnutritious!

[GIRL *takes a plate of tangerines from the tree. The people sitting on the bench peel them, eat them, and turn expectantly to the* REPORTER.]

FIRST MAN: Well, come on, comrade, let's have all the details.

REPORTER: Well, the ... how juicy they are! Want some? Well, okay, here's the story. ... How impatient you are! ... Naturally, as dean of the correspondents I know everything. ... Look, look! See that?

[*A* MAN *with a box full of thermometers walks quickly through.*]

He's a vet. The epidemic's spreading. As soon as it was left alone this resurrected mammal made contact with the domestic animals in the skyscraper, and now all the dogs have gone mad. It taught them to stand on their hind legs. They don't bark or frisk around any more – all they do is 'beg'. They pester everybody at meal-times, whining and fawning. The doctors say that humans bitten by these animals will get all the primary symptoms of epidemic sycophancy.

ALL: O-h!

REPORTER: Look, look!

[*A* MAN *staggers past. He is loaded with hampers containing bottles of beer.*]

PASSER-BY [*singing*]:

Back in the nineteenth cent-ury
A fella could live in lux-ury
Drinking beer and drinking gin
His nose was blue and hung down to his chin!

REPORTER: See? That man's sick – finished! He's one of the one hundred and seventy-five workers of the Second Medical Laboratory. To make its transitional existence easier the doctors ordered the resurrected mammal to be fed with a mixture that is toxic in large doses and repulsive in small ones – 'beer' it's called. The poisonous fumes made them dizzy and some of them took a swig of it by mistake, as a refresher. Since then they've had to change the working personnel three times. Five hundred and twenty workers are in the hospital, but the terrible epidemic continues to rage, mowing everybody down on its foaming path.

ALL: A-h!

MAN [*dreamily and longingly*]: I don't mind sacrificing myself in the cause of science. Let them inoculate me with a dose of this mysterious illness!

REPORTER: He's done for, too. . . . Quiet! Don't startle this sleepwalker! . . .

[GIRL *comes by. She stumbles through the steps of a foxtrot and the Charleston and mutters verses from a booklet held between two fingers of one outstretched hand. She holds an imaginary rose between two fingers of the other hand. Presses it to her nose and inhales imaginary fragrance.*]

Poor girl. She lives next door to this crazed mammal and at night, when the town is asleep, she hears the throb of his guitar through the wall – and then there are long heart-rending sighs and sobs. What was it they called this sort of thing? 'Crooning', wasn't it? . . . It was too much for the poor girl and she began to go out of her mind. Her parents were heartbroken and called in the doctors. The professors say it's an acute attack of an ancient disease they called 'love'. This was a state in which a person's sexual energy, instead of being rationally distributed over the whole of his life, was compressed into a single week and concentrated in one hectic process. This made him commit the most absurd and impossible acts.

GIRL [*covers her face with her hands*]: I'd better not look. I can feel these 'love' microbes infecting the air!

REPORTER: She's finished, too. The epidemic is taking on oceanic proportions.

[*Thirty* CHORUS GIRLS *dance on to the stage.*]

Look at this thirty-headed centipede! Just think, this raising of the legs is what they [*he turns to the audience*] called art!

[*A foxtrotting couple comes on.*]

The epidemic has reached it . . . its – what's the word? – [*looks in dictionary*] its 'apo-gee'. . . . Well, this is nothing less than a hermaphrodite quadruped.

[DIRECTOR *of zoo runs in. He is carrying a small glass case. After him comes a crowd of people armed with telescopes, cameras, and fire ladders.*]

DIRECTOR [*to all*]: Seen it? Seen it? Where is it? Oh, you've seen nothing! A search party reported they saw it here about a quarter of an hour ago. It was making its way up to the fourth floor. Its average speed is one and a half metres an hour, so it can't have got very far. Comrades, search the walls immediately!

[*The searchers extend their telescopes. The people sitting on the benches jump up and, shading their eyes with their hands, peer into the distance. The* DIRECTOR *gives instructions.*]

VOICES: This the way to find it? We should put a naked man on a mattress in every window. It goes for humans. . . .

Don't shout! You'll frighten it away!

I won't give it to anybody if I find it!

Don't you dare; it's public property! . . .

EXCITED VOICE: Found it! Here it is, crawling . . .!

[*Binoculars and telescopes are all focused on one spot. The silence is interrupted only by the clicking and whirring of cameras.*]

DIRECTOR: Yes . . . that's it! Put guards around it! Firemen, over here!

[*People with nets surround the place. The firemen put up their ladder and people clamber up in Indian file.*]

DIRECTOR [*lowering telescope. In tearful voice*]: It's got away! . . . Crawled to the next wall. . . . SOS! It'll fall and kill itself! Volunteers! Heroes! This way!

[*The ladder is run up a second wall. People climb up. Others watch with bated breath.*]

EXCITED VOICE [*from above*]: Got it! Hurrah!

DIRECTOR: Quick! Careful! Don't let it go! Don't crush the insect's legs! [*The insect is passed down the ladder and handed to the* DIRECTOR. *He puts it in the glass case and flourishes it over his head.*] My thanks to you, comrades, for your humble efforts on behalf of science! Our zoo has been enriched by a *chef-d'œuvre*. . . . We have captured a most rare specimen of an extinct insect which was extremely popular at the beginning of the century. Our city may be justly proud of itself. Scientists and tourists will flock to us. . . . Here in my hands I have the only living specimen of *bedbugus normalis*. . . . Move back there, citizens, the insect has fallen asleep, it has crossed its legs and wishes to rest! I invite all of you to the solemn opening of an exhibition in the Zoological Garden. The capture, so supremely important and so fraught with anxiety, has been successfully completed!

SCENE EIGHT

A room with smooth, opalescent, translucent walls. Hidden, bluish lighting from the ceiling. A large window on the left. A large table in front of the window. On the right, a bed let down from the wall. On the bed, lying under the cleanest of blankets, is PRISYPKIN. *He is filthy. Electric fans.* PRISYPKIN*'s corner is like a pigsty. The table is littered with cigarette butts and overturned bottles. A piece of pink paper has been stuck on the reading-lamp.* PRISYPKIN *is groaning. A* DOCTOR *paces the room nervously.*

PROFESSOR [*entering*]: How's the patient?

DOCTOR: I don't know, but I feel terrible. If you don't order a change of staff every half hour he'll infect everybody. Every time he breathes, my legs give way! I've put in seven fans to disperse his breath.

PRISYPKIN: A-a-a-a-a-a-h!

[PROFESSOR *runs over to him.*]

Professor! Oh, profes-s-s-or!!!

[PROFESSOR *takes one sniff and staggers back, clawing the air from dizziness.*]

Give me a drink. . . .

[PROFESSOR *pours a little beer into a glass and hands it to him.* PRISYPKIN *raises himself on his elbows.*]

PRISYPKIN [*reproachfully*]: You resurrect me and now you make fun of me! Like giving lemonade to an elephant!

PROFESSOR: Society hopes to raise you up to a human level....

PRISYPKIN: To hell with society and to hell with you. I didn't ask you to resurrect me. Freeze me back!

PROFESSOR: I don't know what you're talking about! Our lives belong to the collective and neither I nor anybody else...

PRISYPKIN: What kind of a life is it when you can't even pin a picture of your best girl on the wall? The tacks break on this bloody glass.... Comrade professor, give me a drink....

PROFESSOR [*filling glass*]: All right, only don't breathe in my direction.

[ZOYA BERYOZKINA *comes in with two piles of books. The* DOCTORS *talk with her in a whisper and leave.*]

ZOYA BERYOZKINA [*sits next to* PRISYPKIN *and unpacks books*]: I don't know whether this is what you want. Nobody knows anything about what you asked for. Only textbooks on horticulture have anything about roses, and daydreams are dealt with only in medical works – in the section on hypnosis. But here are two very interesting books more or less of your period – Hoover: *An Ex-President Speaks*... translated from the English.

PRISYPKIN [*takes the book and hurls it aside*]: No... I want something that... plucks at my heartstrings....

ZOYA BERYOZKINA: Well, here's a book by someone called Mussolini: *Letters from Exile.*

PRISYPKIN [*takes it and throws it aside*]: No, that's not for the soul.... I want something that gives me that melting feeling ... leave me alone with your crude propaganda.

ZOYA BERYOZKINA: I don't know what you mean . . . heart-strings, melting feeling . . .

PRISYPKIN: What is all this? What did we fight for? Why did we shed our blood, if I can't dance to my heart's content – and I'm supposed to be a leader of the new society!

ZOYA BERYOZKINA: I demonstrated your bodily movement to the director of the Central Institute of Callisthenics. He says he's seen things like that in an old collection of French post-cards, but now, he says, there isn't even anybody to ask about it. Except a couple of old women – they remember, but they can't demonstrate it because of their rheumatism.

PRISYPKIN: Why then did I bother to acquire such an elegant education? I could always *work* before the revolution.

ZOYA BERYOZKINA: Tomorrow I'll take you to see a dance performed by twenty thousand male and female workers on the city square. It's a gay rehearsal of a new work-system on the farms.

PRISYPKIN: Comrades! I protest! I didn't unfreeze for you to dry me up! [*Tears off the blanket, jumps out of bed, seizes a pile of books and shakes them out of the broadsheet in which they are wrapped. He is about to tear up the paper when he looks at it more closely. He runs from lamp to lamp, studying the text.*] Where . . . where did you get this?

ZOYA BERYOZKINA: It was being distributed to everybody in the streets . . . they must have put copies in all the library books. . . .

PRISYPKIN: Saved!! Hurrah!! [*He rushes to the door, waving the paper like a flag.*]

ZOYA BERYOZKINA [*alone*]: And to think that fifty years ago I might have died on account of this skunk. . . .

SCENE NINE

Zoo. In the centre a platform on which stands a cage draped with a cloth and decked with flags. Two trees behind the cage. Behind the trees two more cages with elephants and giraffes. On the left of the cage a rostrum and on the right a grandstand for guests of honour. MUSICIANS *standing around the cage.* SPECTATORS *approaching it in groups.* STEWARDS *with armbands assign them to their places according to profession and height.*

STEWARD: Over here, comrades of the foreign press! Closer to the platform! Move over there and leave room for the Brazilians! Their airship is now landing at Central Airport. [*Steps back and admires his arrangement of the guests.*] Comrade Negroes, mix in with the Britons and form nice multi-coloured groups with them. . . . Their Anglo-Saxon pallor will set off your complexions to even greater advantage! High-school students, over there to the left. Four old people from the Union of Centenarians have been assigned to you. They will supplement the professor's lecture with eyewitness accounts. . . .

[*Two* OLD MEN *and two* OLD WOMEN *are wheeled in in wheelchairs.*]

FIRST OLD MAN: *I* remember like it was now . . .

FIRST OLD WOMAN: No, it's me who remembers like it was now!

SECOND OLD WOMAN: You remember like it was now, but I remember like it was before.

SECOND OLD MAN: But I remember like it was before, like it was now.

FIRST OLD WOMAN: I remember how it was even before that, a long, long time before!

FIRST OLD MAN: I remember how it was before *and* like it was now!

STEWARD: Quiet there, eyewitnesses, no squabbling! Clear the way, comrades, make way for the children! Over here, comrades! Hurry, hurry!

CHILDREN [*marching in a column and singing*]:

We study
all day
But we know
how to play
We're through
with maths
And now we're off
to see the giraffes
We're going
to the zoo
Like the
grown-ups do!

STEWARD: Citizens who wish to please the exhibits and also to examine them for scientific purposes are requested to obtain various exotic products and scientific equipment from the official zoo attendants. Doses prepared without expert knowledge can be fatal. We ask you to use only the products and equipment supplied by the Central Medical Institute and the Municipal Laboratories of Precision Engineering.

[ATTENDANTS *walk around the zoo and the theatre.*]

FIRST ATTENDANT:

Comrade, when looking at germs
Don't be a dope!
Use a magnifying glass or a microscope!

SECOND ATTENDANT:

Take the advice of Doctor Segal
If accidentally spat upon
Be sure to use diluted phenol!

THIRD ATTENDANT:

Feeding time's a memorable scene!
Give the exhibits alcohol and nicotine!

FOURTH ATTENDANT:

Feed them with their favourite liquor!
They'll get gout and cirrhosis of the liver!

FIFTH ATTENDANT:

Give them nicotine in liberal doses!
A guarantee of arteriosclerosis!

SIXTH ATTENDANT:

Please give your ears the best protection.
These earphones filter every crude expression!

STEWARD [*clearing a way to the rostrum*]: The chairman of the City Soviet and his closest colleagues have left their highly important duties to attend our ceremony. Here they come to the strains of our ancient national anthem. Let's greet our dear comrades!

[*All applaud. A group of people with briefcases crosses the stage. They bow stiffly and sing.*]

PEOPLE:

The burdens of our office
Never tire or age us
There's a time for work
And a time for play
Greetings from the Soviet,
Workers of the Zoo!
We're the city fathers
And we're proud of you!

CHAIRMAN OF CITY SOVIET [*mounts rostrum and waves a flag; hushed silence*]: Comrades, I declare the ceremony open. The times in which we live are fraught with shocks and experiences of an internal nature. External occurrences are rare. Exhausted by the events of an earlier age, mankind is glad of this relative peace. All the same, we never deny ourselves a spectacle, which, however extravagant it may be in appearance, conceals a profound scientific meaning under its multicoloured plumage. The unfortunate incidents which have taken place in our city were the result of the incautious admittance in our midst of two parasites. Through my efforts, as well as through the efforts of world medicine, these incidents have been eradicated. However, these incidents, stirring a distant memory of the past, underline the horrors of a bygone age and the difficulties of the world proletariat in its mighty struggle for culture. May the hearts and souls of our young people be steeled by these sinister examples! Before calling on him to speak, it is incumbent upon me to move a vote of thanks to the director of our Zoo, who has deciphered the meaning of these strange occurrences and turned these ugly phenomena into a gay and edifying entertainment. Hip-hip . . . hurray! Hip-hip . . . hurray!

[*All cheer. The musicians play a fanfare as the* DIRECTOR *climbs to the rostrum. He bows on all sides.*]

DIRECTOR: Comrades! I am both delighted and embarrassed by your kind words. With all due consideration for my own part in the matter, it is incumbent upon me to express thanks to the dedicated workers of the Union of Hunters, who are the real heroes of the capture, and also to our respected professor of the Institute of Resurrection, who vanquished death by defrigeration. However, I must point out that it was a mistake on the part of our respected professor that led directly to the misfortunes of which you are aware. Owing to certain mimetic characteristics, such as its callouses and clothing, our respected professor mistakenly classified the resurrected mammal not only as a representative of *homo sapiens*, but even as a member of the highest group of the species – the working class. I do not attribute my success entirely to my long experience of dealing with animals and to my understanding of their psychology. I was aided by chance. Prompted by a vague, subconscious hope I wrote and distributed an advertisement. Here is the text:

'In accordance with the principles of the Zoological Garden, I seek a live human body to be constantly bitten by a newly acquired insect, for the maintenance and development of the said insect in the normal conditions to which it is accustomed.'

VOICE FROM THE CROWD: How horrible!

DIRECTOR: I know it's horrible . . . I was myself astonished by my own absurd idea . . . yet, suddenly, a creature presents itself! It looks almost human . . . well, just like you and me. . . .

CHAIRMAN OF CITY SOVIET [*ringing his bell*]: Comrade director! I must call you to order!

DIRECTOR: My apologies, my apologies! Of course, I immediately established from my knowledge of comparative bestiology and by means of an interrogation that I was dealing with an anthropoid simulator and that this was the most remarkable of parasites. I shall not go into details, particularly as you will see it all for yourselves in a moment, in this absolutely extraordinary cage. There are two of them: the famous *bedbugus normalis* and . . . er . . . *bourgeoisius vulgaris*. They are different in size, but identical in essence. Both of them have their habitat in the musty mattresses of time.

Bedbugus normalis, having gorged itself on the body of a single human, falls under the bed.

Bourgeoisius vulgaris, having gorged itself on the body of all mankind, falls on to the bed. That's the only difference!

While after the revolution the proletariat was writhing and scratching itself to rid itself of filth, these parasites built their nests and made their homes in this dirt, beat their wives, swore by Bebel,[1] and relaxed blissfully in the shade of their own jodhpurs. But of the two, *bourgeoisius vulgaris* is the more frightening. With his monstrous mimetic powers he lured his victims by posing as a twittering versifier or as a drooling bird. In those days even their clothing had a kind of protective coloration. They wore birdlike winged ties with tail coats and white starched breasts. These birds nested in theatre boxes, perched in flocks on oak trees at the opera to the tune of the *Internationale*, rubbed their legs together in the ballet, dressed up Tolstoy to look like Marx, hung upside down from the twigs of their verse, shrieked and howled to a disgusting degree, and – forgive the expression, but this is a scientific lecture – excreted on a scale far in excess of the normal small droppings of a bird.

Comrades! But see for yourselves!

[*He gives a signal and the attendants unveil the cage. The glass case containing the bedbug is on a pedestal. Behind it, on a platform, is a double bed. On the bed,* PRISYPKIN *with his guitar. A lamp with a yellow shade hangs above the cage. Above* PRISYPKIN'*s head is a glittering halo composed of post-cards arranged fanwise. Bottles are lying on the floor and spittoons placed around the sides of the cage, which is also equipped with filters and air-conditioners. Notices saying:* (1) *Caution – it spits!* (2) *No unauthorized entry!* (3) *Watch your ears – it curses! Musicians play a fanfare. Bengal lights. The crowd first surges back and then approaches the cage, mute with delight.*]

PRISYPKIN:

On Lunacharsky Street
There's an old house I know
With staircase broad and neat
And a curtain at the window!

DIRECTOR: Comrades, come closer, don't be frightened – it's quite tame. Come, come, don't be alarmed. On the inside of the cage there are four filters to trap all the dirty words. Only very few words come out and they're quite decent. The filters are cleaned every day by a special squad of attendants in gas-masks. Look, it's now going to have what they called 'a smoke'.

VOICE FROM CROWD: Oh, how horrible!

DIRECTOR: Don't be frightened. Now it's going to 'have a swig', as they said. Skripkin, drink!

[PRISYPKIN *reaches for a bottle of vodka.*]

VOICE FROM CROWD: Oh, don't, don't! Don't torment the poor animal!

DIRECTOR: Comrades, there's nothing to worry about. It's tame! Look, I'm now going to bring it out of the cage. [*Goes to the cage, puts on gloves, checks his revolver, opens the door, brings out* PRISYPKIN *on to the platform, and turns him around to face the guests of honour in the grandstand.*] Now then, say a few words, show how well you can imitate the human language, voice, and expression.

[PRISYPKIN *stands obediently, clears his throat, raises his guitar, and suddenly turns around and looks at the audience. His expression changes, a look of delight comes over his face. He pushes the* DIRECTOR *aside, throws down his guitar, and shouts to the audience.*]

PRISYPKIN: Citizens! Brothers! My own people! Darlings! How did you get here? So many of you! When were you unfrozen? Why am I alone in the cage? Darlings, friends, come and join me! Why am I suffering? Citizens! ...

VOICES OF GUESTS:

The children! Remove the children!
Muzzle it ... muzzle it!
Oh, how horrible!
Professor, put a stop to it!
Ah, but don't shoot it!

[*The* DIRECTOR, *holding an electric fan, runs on to the stage with the attendants. The attendants drag* PRISYPKIN *off. The* DIRECTOR *ventilates the platform. The musicians play a fanfare. The attendants cover the cage.*]

DIRECTOR: My apologies, comrades ... my apologies. ... The insect is tired. The noise and the bright lights gave it hallucinations. Please be calm. It's nothing at all. It will recover tomorrow. ... Disperse quietly, citizens, until tomorrow. Music. Let's have a march!

NOTES ON *THE BEDBUG*

SCENE ONE

1. *private pedlars*: Some forms of private enterprise were allowed between 1921 and 1928 under Lenin's New Economic Policy (N.E.P.).
2. *Nobile*: Umberto Nobile, Italian Arctic explorer whose dirigible crashed after a flight over the North Pole in 1928. The survivors were picked up by a Russian icebreaker.
3. *Mr Ryabushinsky*: The Ryabushinskys were a family of Moscow millionaires.
4. *Plekhanov*: Georgy Plekhanov (1875–1918), outstanding theorist of Marxism.
5. '*Kiss, kiss!*': Literally, 'bitter, bitter' (*gorko*). An ancient Russian custom at weddings. The guests demand that the bride and groom give each other a kiss to sweeten the bitter vodka the guests are drinking.

SCENE TWO

1. *Pierre Skripkin*: The hero has changed his name from the ridiculous-sounding Prisypkin to what he imagines to be the more elegant Skripkin, derived from *skripka* (violin). Ivan has become Pierre, in imitation of the practice, among the Russian upper classes, of assuming French first names.
2. *Apukhtin*: Alexei Apukhtin (1841–93), a worldly, sentimental poet despised by Mayakovsky.
3. *Nadson*: Semyon Nadson (1862–87), a melancholy, sentimental poet equally despised by Mayakovsky, and the frequent butt of his jokes.
4. *Liebknecht*: Karl Liebknecht (1871–1919), German Socialist leader.
5. *Nepmen*: Private businessmen during the N.E.P.
6. *Suvorov*: Alexander Suvorov (1729–1800), celebrated Russian field-marshal who was never defeated in battle.

SCENE THREE

1. See Scene 1, note 5.
2. *Perekop*: A Bolshevik force crossed the Straits of Perekop and drove the White armies out of the Crimea in November 1920.
3. *Botchkin*: In the original, Oleg has changed his name from the comical-sounding Botchkin, derived from *botchka* (barrel), to the poetic *Bayan*

(a Russian minstrel of ancient times). Mayakovsky was making fun of a minor poet he had known before the revolution, Vladimir Sidorov, who had actually adopted the pen-name Bayan.

4. *Kamarinsky*: A Russian folk dance.
5. '*Makarov's Lament for Vera Kholodnaya*': The lady was a famous Russian silent movie actress.
6. *Whites*: Men of the White Army, which opposed the Red Army during the Civil War.

SCENE FOUR

1. *Nadson and Zharov*: Semyon Nadson, see Scene 2, note 3. Alexander Zharov (b. 1904), a militant Conmmuist poet, and another frequent target of Mayakovsky's.

SCENE NINE

1. *Bebel*: August Bebel (1840–1913), a founder of the German Social-Democratic Party.

MARYA

Isaac Emanuilovich Babel

A play in eight scenes translated by Michael Glenny and Harold Shukman, with an introduction by Michael Glenny

INTRODUCTION TO *MARYA*

Isaac Babel was born in 1894 in Odessa, a town notable as a cradle of Russian-Jewish talent, especially of musical talent; both Yasha Heifetz and Benno Moïseivich came from there and were Babel's contemporaries. Babel himself was quite unmusical but excelled at languages. He loved Odessa and above all its Jewish quarter, the Moldavanka, where he had been born, and many of his best stories were written about that remarkable city and its underworld.

In 1916 Babel's first three stories were published by Gorky in his magazine *The Chronicle*. On Gorky's advice to give up writing for a while and gain experience, he joined the army, and when in 1920 war broke out between Poland and Soviet Russia he was sent as a war correspondent to cover the operations of Budyonny's First Cavalry Army.

The real beginning of his literary career was in 1924; in quick succession his 'Red Cavalry' and 'Odessa' stories were published. He wrote several film scripts, of which at least one is a highly original work of art: *Benya Krik*, about the king of the Odessa underworld.

In 1928 there was a warning rumble of trouble to come when 'Red Cavalry' was attacked for the second time by Budyonny as a 'slander on the First Cavalry Army'; fortunately for Babel he was vigorously defended by Gorky. With the end of the 'New Economic Policy' phase (N.E.P.), Party control of writers was tightened, but Babel stubbornly refused to subscribe to the fictions of 'Socialist Realism'.

In 1935 Gorky died and Babel at once felt the loss of his powerful protector. His only refuge throughout the years of Stalin's purges was an evasive silence. At ten a.m. on 15 May 1939 he was arrested at Peredelkino and tried on undisclosed charges by secret tribunal on 26 January 1940. The official date of his death was 17 March 1941.

Babel was not a prolific writer – he published only two cycles of short stories, a chapter of an unpublished novel, some separate short stories, a number of film scripts, and two plays. The extent of his unpublished work, which was almost certainly destroyed by the N.K.V.D., will probably never be known.

Babel's first play, *Sunset*, was published in 1928 and first performed in the same year by the Moscow Art Theatre.* In 1932–3 he spent several months in France and Italy, and it was during this happy interlude away from the pressures and frustrations of Stalin's Moscow that he started on his second play, *Marya*, finishing it while in the Caucasus later in 1933. The play was published in 1935, but its performance seems to have been banned when it was already in rehearsal.

Marya is an ambitious play in which Babel tried to do something very difficult to achieve on the stage. He set out to record, using the most sparing of dramatic means, the truth and the complexity of social change, to capture the instant when one era ended and another began.

Marya describes the dissolution of a whole order of society – the middle-class intelligentsia of pre-revolutionary Russia. The theme had, of course, been tackled by others, generally on an epic scale. Babel, by contrast, chose to bring it to life by showing a few hours in the lives of a small group of people, who act out in microcosm the historic upheaval in which most of them are but barely conscious participants.

The action occurs in the early months of 1920. Babel took great care in choosing this point in time. It was the moment before the Bolsheviks, after two and a half desperate and precarious years, turned the decisive corner which led them along the road to complete control of Russia. We should never for-

* A version of *Sunset*, adapted by Mordecai Richler, with the title *The Fall of Mendel Krik*, has been produced by B.B.C. Television.

get that until early 1921 the Bolsheviks were hardly more than one factor among many during seven bewildering years of war, revolutions, defeat, and civil war; years of hardship, hunger, and above all of confusion. Soon after the time when the action of *Marya* takes place there occurred on the same day (18 March 1921) two events which marked the final consolidation of the Bolshevik regime against its enemies within and without: Trotsky's ruthless suppression of the Kronstadt mutiny, proof that henceforth the Bolsheviks would crush by force the slightest internal opposition, even from fellow-Socialists; and the signature of the Treaty of Riga which ended the bitter year of war between Soviet Russia and Poland. There is therefore more than just artistic truth in Babel's placing of the real end of the old order in 1920 instead of in 1917, and the Russian public would have been keenly aware of the significance of the play's setting.

They would also have appreciated the skill with which Babel drew his characters. The Mukovnin family, on which the action centres, is a masterpiece of detached observation which sums up in three people the strength and the weakness of the class that had produced that unique social phenomenon, the Russian intelligentsia. The other characters, the Jewish businessman turned black marketeer (a type who was to become all too familiar in the subsequent seven years of the N.E.P.); the sheep-like demobilized peasant soldiers; the religious man who can only retreat into quietism; the disturbed, insecure ex-officer who cannot even be an efficient crook; the bewildered old nanny, her personality withered by servitude: all were once integrated into a society which with all its faults represented order and which in collapse leaves each one to resolve his crisis alone.

As a piece for the stage *Marya* is a considerable improvement on Babel's earlier play *Sunset*; it is much tighter and more consistent in structure. His boldest stroke was to keep his main character permanently off-stage. This successfully achieves two aims, one stylistic, the other symbolic: it throws the on-stage characters into sharper relief, and by Marya's physical absence from the despair and corruption of the old order it emphasizes her dedication to the new.

MICHAEL GLENNY

CHARACTERS

NIKOLAI VASILIEVICH MUKOVNIN, a former general
LUDMILA, his daughter
KATERINA VYACHESLAVOVNA FELSEN
ISAAC MARKOVICH BERNSTEIN
SERGEI ILLARIONOVICH GOLITSYN, a former prince
NEFEDOVNA, the Mukovnins' nanny
NIKITIN, BISHONKOV, PHILIP } disabled ex-soldiers
VISKOVSKY, an ex-captain of Horse Guards
KRAVCHENKO
MADAME DORA
POLICE INSPECTOR
KALMYKOVA, chambermaid at No. 86 Nevsky Prospekt
AGASHA, porter's wife
ANDREI, KUZMA } sweepers
SUSHKIN
SAFONOV, a workman
YELENA, his wife
NYUSHA
POLICEMAN
DRUNK
RED ARMY SOLDIER
TIKHON, a porter (voice off-stage)

The action occurs in Petrograd during the early years of the revolution.

SCENE ONE

An apartment on the Nevsky Prospekt; BERNSTEIN*'s room – dirty, littered with heaps of sacks, boxes and furniture. Two disabled ex-soldiers,* BISHONKOV *and* NIKITIN, *are unpacking bundles of foodstuffs.* NIKITIN *– a fat man with a big red face – has had both legs amputated above the knee.* BISHONKOV *has an empty sleeve pinned to his coat. Both are wearing medals, including the St George's Cross.* BERNSTEIN *is doing accounts with an abacus.*

NIKITIN: They've made it really tough now. It was all right when Sandberg was on at the Vyritsa check-point. He used to let us through. They've taken him off now.

BISHONKOV: They're getting vicious, Mr Bernstein.

BERNSTEIN: Is Korolyov still there?

NIKITIN: Still there? They knocked *him* off. They've made it really tough, I tell you. The guards at the check-points are all new.

BISHONKOV: The food lark's got too risky for our liking, Mr Bernstein. You get used to one guard, next thing you know he's not there. They don't just lift the stuff off you – you get a gunbarrel in your gut too.

NIKITIN: No use trying to play it clever, neither. They're up to a new dodge every day. ... Fr'instance, today we're heading for the railway station. They start shooting. Hullo, what's up, we said. Thought maybe they were kicking the Bolsheviks out. No such luck, it was *them*, blasting off at everybody – they shoot first and then ask questions.

BISHONKOV: They confiscated a bloody fortune in food today. Said they were going to give it to the kids. There's only kids now at Tsarskoye – a colony, they call it.

NIKITIN: Yer, kids all right. With beards.

BISHONKOV: Supposing I'm hungry – why shouldn't I get a bit of food for meself and take it home? 'Course I'm going to try and take some home if I'm hungry.

BERNSTEIN: Where's Philip? I'm worried about Philip. . . . What have you two done with him?

BISHONKOV: We didn't do nothing with him, Mr Bernstein. He lost his nerve.

NIKITIN: Someone drags him off. . . .

BISHONKOV: Vicious – that's what they are, Mr Bernstein.

NIKITIN: To look at Philip, now, you'd say there's a fine, grown man – but he's got no guts, he's weak. . . . We're driving along towards the station – all of a sudden there's shooting, people weeping, falling about all over the place. . . . I says to him, Philip, I says, let's slip round to Zagorodny through the gates, I know all the sentries there, they'll let us through. But he couldn't, lost his nerve. I can't go, he says, I'm scared. All right, I says, so you're scared – all you've got to do is to sit down and shut up. Look, you're safe if you're carrying vodka, all they give you is a poke in the snout – so what're you sweating about? All you've got is a belt full of vodka round you. . . . By that time he was flat on the ground. He's a strong man, strong as a horse, but he just hasn't got any guts.

BISHONKOV: We reckon he'll turn up, Mr Bernstein. Nobody much went after him, he should get away all right.

BERNSTEIN: How much did you pay for sausage?

BISHONKOV: The sausage cost us eighteen thousand roubles, Mr Bernstein, and the stuff's got a lot worse. Makes no difference nowadays whether it comes from Vitebsk or Petrograd – it's all churned out in the same state factory.

NIKITIN [*opens a concealed cupboard in the wall and starts piling food into it*]: They're ruining poor old Russia, everything's the same now – *state*.

BERNSTEIN: How much for barley?

BISHONKOV: Barley, Mr Bernstein, has gone up to nine

thousand and if you say a word, if you try and bargain – you don't get it. The dealers just aren't interested. Take it or leave it. Oh, they're getting cocky, these merchants, you'd never believe what they're like.

NIKITIN [*piling loaves into the cupboard*]: The missus baked this bread herself, Mr Bernstein, worked hard. ... Sent her respects, she did.

BERNSTEIN: How are the children – fit and well?

BISHONKOV: All the kids are fine, can't grumble. Well off they are, too – fur coats to wear and all. ... The wife wants to know if she can't come into town too.

BERNSTEIN: Well, I don't know. ... [*Does a sum on the abacus.*] Bishonkov!

BISHONKOV: Sir.

BERNSTEIN: We don't seem to have made any profit on this lot, Bishonkov.

BISHONKOV: I told you, Mr Bernstein – the job's got too difficult, too risky.

BERNSTEIN: We're not making any money, Bishonkov.

BISHONKOV: And you're not likely to, Mr Bernstein, the way things are going. ... Nikitin and me, we were sort of thinking we ought to switch to something else. Food, you see, well, it's bulky stuff: flour's bulky, barley's bulky, legs of veal – they're all bulky. We've got to switch to something else, Mr Bernstein – like saccharine now, or jewellery. ... Diamonds – lovely things ... just pop one inside your cheek and it's gone.

BERNSTEIN: Philip still hasn't come. ... I'm worried about him.

NIKITIN: They're beating him up, shouldn't wonder.

BISHONKOV: Way back in '18 you could make a living at being disabled – but now ...

NIKITIN: Can you wonder? Just look at people nowadays. In the old days they couldn't do enough for a wounded soldier – now it means nothing. 'How'd you get wounded?' they ask. 'Shrapnel shell took off both me legs,' says I. 'Well, what's special about that?' they say. 'Took 'em off, painlessly, both at once . . . can't have hurt you,' they say. 'What do you mean,' says I, 'can't have hurt me?' 'Well,' they say, 'it's a known fact: they even up your legs under chloroform, you don't feel a thing. The only trouble's your toes, they wriggle and itch even after they've been cut off, and that's all there is wrong with you.' 'And how,' says I, 'd'you reckon you know all that?' ''Course I know,' he says, 'what with all this education nowadays.' 'Fine sort of education – all you seem to have learned is how to kick wounded soldiers off a train. . . . What d'you want to kick me off the train for?' says I . . . 'I'm a cripple. . . .' 'We're kicking you off,' says he, ''cause we've got fed up with looking at cripples in Russia' – and he kicks me off like I was a pile of logs. . . . People, Mr Bernstein, they make me sick these days.

[*Enter* VISKOVSKY *in breeches and tunic, his shirt unbuttoned.*]

BERNSTEIN: Is that you?

VISKOVSKY: Yes. It's me.

BERNSTEIN: Where are your manners?

VISKOVSKY: Has Ludmila Mukovnin been to see you, Bernstein?

BERNSTEIN: I said – where are your manners? What if she has?

VISKOVSKY: I know you've got the Mukovnins' ring. And her sister Marya can't have brought it, so . . .

BERNSTEIN: . . . somebody else brought it. And it wasn't the fairies.

VISKOVSKY: How did you get that ring, Bernstein?

BERNSTEIN: Somebody gave it to me to sell it for them.

VISKOVSKY: Sell it to me.

BERNSTEIN: Why should I sell it to you?

VISKOVSKY: Have you ever tried being a gentleman, Bernstein?

BERNSTEIN: I'm always a gentleman.

VISKOVSKY: Gentlemen don't ask questions.

BERNSTEIN: These people want foreign currency for that ring.

VISKOVSKY: You owe me fifty pounds sterling.

BERNSTEIN: What for?

VISKOVSKY: For that deal with the cotton thread.

BERNSTEIN: Which you bungled. ...

VISKOVSKY: In the Horse Guards they didn't teach us to barter thread.

BERNSTEIN: You bungled it because you were impatient.

VISKOVSKY: All right, maestro. Give me time and I'll learn.

BERNSTEIN: What's the use of teaching you anything when you never do as you're told? Somebody tells you one thing, you go and do another. ... During the war you were a captain or a count or something – I don't know what you were in those days – maybe you have to be hot-headed in war, but in business you've got to be cool and keep your eyes open.

VISKOVSKY: Very good, sir.

BERNSTEIN: I'm annoyed with you, Viskovsky. I'm annoyed with you about another thing. What d'you mean by sending me that princess?

VISKOVSKY: I thought it was a good idea.

BERNSTEIN: You knew she was a virgin, I suppose?

VISKOVSKY: I know you only touch kosher ...

BERNSTEIN: That's just it, I can do without that sort of kosher. I'm a little man, Captain Viskovsky, and I don't want a princess coming to me like a madonna stepping down from a picture and looking at me with those eyes like silver spoons. ... What was it we said? Don't you remember? Make it a woman about thirty, we said, even about thirty-five, a housewife, who knows what the score is, who'd take my oatmeal and bread and a pound of cocoa for her kids –

and who wouldn't have said to me afterwards 'You filthy little money-grubber, you have soiled me, abused me.'

VISKOVSKY: There's always the younger Mukovnin girl in reserve.

BERNSTEIN: She talks too much. I can't stand women who never stop talking . . . why didn't you introduce me to her elder sister?

VISKOVSKY: Marya Mukovnin has gone off and joined the army.

BERNSTEIN: Now there was a woman for you – Marya Mukovnin. She looked good and you could talk to her. . . . You waited until she'd left before you told me she was going.

VISKOVSKY: It's not so simple with that girl, Bernstein. Not a simple matter at all.

NIKITIN: 'I don't give a monkey's about knocking off an old sod like you – you're past it anyway' – that's what he said to me and he meant it. . . .

[*A shot in the distance, then nearer; the shots grow more frequent.* BERNSTEIN *puts out the light and locks the door. Light through the windows, green glass; frost.*]

NIKITIN [*in a whisper*]: 'Ere we go again. . . .

BISHONKOV: What a life!

NIKITIN: Those ruddy sailors are still at it.

BISHONKOV: I ask you, Mr Bernstein, what sort of a life is this?

[*Knock at the door. Silence.* VISKOVSKY *pulls his revolver out of his pocket, releases the safety-catch. Another knock.*]

BISHONKOV: Who's there?

PHILIP [*from outside*]: It's me.

NIKITIN: Speak up . . . who's 'me'?

PHILIP: Open the door.

BERNSTEIN: It's Philip.

[BISHONKOV *opens the door. An enormous, shapeless creature sidles into the room, collapses against the wall, says nothing. A light flares. One side of* PHILIP'*s face is covered in weals. His head has fallen on his chest, his eyes are closed.*]

BERNSTEIN: Did you get shot at?

PHILIP: No.

NIKITIN: You must be all in.

[NIKITIN *and* BISHONKOV *remove* PHILIP'*s sheepskin coat and outer clothing, pull off a complete rubber suit and throw it on the floor.* PHILIP'*s fingers are torn and bleeding.*]

NIKITIN: They've fixed you all right. . . . And we call ourselves human. . . .

PHILIP [*his head sunk on his chest*]: Followed me . . . followed me, he did.

NIKITIN: Followed you?

PHILIP: Yeh.

NIKITIN: Man in leggings?

PHILIP: That's him.

NIKITIN: They're getting really hot on it now. . . .

BERNSTEIN: Did he follow you as far as the house?

PHILIP [*speaking with difficulty*]: No, he didn't get as far as here . . . the shooting started and he went to see.

[BISHONKOV *and* NIKITIN *lift up the wounded man and lay him on a bed.*]

NIKITIN: I *told* you to go through the gates. . . .

[PHILIP *groans. Shots in the distance, a burst of machine-gun fire, then silence.*]

NIKITIN: What a life!

BISHONKOV: 'Ere we go again. . . .

VISKOVSKY: Where's the ring, maestro?

BERNSTEIN: You are in a hurry for that ring, aren't you? You're itching for it. . . .

SCENE TWO

A room in the MUKOVNINS' *house. It is bedroom, dining-room, and study in one. Antique furniture, an old stove with flue running right through the room and out at a hole in the wall; a heap of chopped firewood under the stove. Behind a screen* LUDMILA MUKOVNIN *is getting dressed for the theatre. Curling-tongs are heating over a flame.* KATYA FELSEN *is ironing a dress.*

LUDMILA: You're out of date, my dear. . . . The audience at the ballet nowadays is fearfully smart. The Krymov sisters, Marya Meyendorf, they all look like fashion plates and they live well, believe me.

KATYA: Who can live well these days? Nobody.

LUDMILA: Some do. You're behind the times, Katya dear. Their lordships the proletariat are getting sophisticated and they like their women elegant. Do you think your Redko likes to see you looking like a slut? Not a bit of it. Their lordships the proletariat are getting sophisticated, Katya.

KATYA: I wouldn't use mascara if I were you, dear, and as for that sleeveless frock . . .

LUDMILA: My dear, you're forgetting that I'm going out with a boy-friend.

KATYA: He may be a boy-friend but he won't notice. . . .

LUDMILA: Don't say that. He has good taste and he has a way with women.

KATYA: Everyone knows that men with red hair are hot-blooded.

LUDMILA: My Bernstein's hair's not red, it's chocolate.

KATYA: Has he really got all that much money? I'm sure Viskovsky's making it all up.

LUDMILA: Bernstein has six thousand pounds sterling.

KATYA: I suppose he's made it all out of those cripples of his?

LUDMILA: Not a bit. Anybody else could have thought of it.

It's all share and share alike. Up to now they haven't been searching the disabled, so they could get the stuff through.

KATYA: Only a Jew would think of it.

LUDMILA: Well, Katya, far better to be a Jew than a drug addict like our men. . . . One's a drug addict, another goes and gets himself shot, another one becomes a cabby and waits for fares outside the Europa. *Par le temps qui court* the Jews are your best bet.

KATYA: I admit you won't find anyone more reliable than Bernstein.

LUDMILA: And then, we're women. Katya, we're ordinary women. You get tired of being 'on the loose', as the caretaker's wife says. We can't live without a man, we just can't.

KATYA: Will you have children?

LUDMILA: I shall have two little redheads.

KATYA: So you're going to be legally married?

LUDMILA: Jews won't have it any other way, Katya. They're mad about family life. A wife is somebody – they make a terrible fuss of children. And Jews are always grateful to their women. It's something noble, their respect for women.

KATYA: How do you know all this about the Jews?

LUDMILA: I can tell you that. Daddy once commanded a corps in Vilna and they're all Jews there. Daddy had a friend who was a rabbi. Their rabbis are all philosophers.

KATYA [*hands ironed dress over screen*]: Having supper after the theatre?

LUDMILA: We might.

KATYA: Oh yes, Ludmila, you'll have a few drinks, he'll get passionate and your legs will give way. . . .

LUDMILA: Nothing of the sort, my girl. I shall keep him on a string for a month or two – that's the way you have to treat Jews. I may not even let him kiss me yet.

[*Enter* MUKOVNIN *in felt boots; his dressing-gown has been made up from a red-lined greatcoat; he is wearing two pairs of spectacles.*]

MUKOVNIN [*reads*]: '... On October 16th, 1820, in the reign of the Emperor Alexander of blessed memory, a company of the Semyonov Regiment of Life Guards forgot their oath of allegiance and their military duty of obedience to their commanders and presumed to foregather on their own initiative late in the evening....' [*Raises his head.*] How did they show they had forgotten their oath of allegiance? By assembling after roll-call in the corridor and deciding to request the company commander to end regular platoon kit inspections. The regimental commander was in the habit of making such inspections. And what were the punishments meted out for this so-called mutiny? [*Reads*] 'N.C.O.s, confessed ringleaders, to be executed; men of No. 1 and No. 2 companies who had set a bad example, flogged; privates mentioned in paragraph 3, to run the gauntlet through the battalion six times as an example to others....'

LUDMILA: How frightful.

KATYA: We all know it was cruel in the old days, don't we?

LUDMILA: If you ask me, the Bolsheviks should jump at Daddy's book. It looks better for them if the old army's shown up.

KATYA: They only want topical stuff.

MUKOVNIN: I'm dividing the Semyonov tragedy into two chapters. The first will examine the causes of the outbreak, the second will describe the actual mutiny, the tortures, the deportations to the mines.... The book is to be a history of the barracks, not an inventory of famous names but the story of all those simple soldiers handed over to the tender mercies of Arakcheyev and deported for twenty years to military penal colonies.

LUDMILA: Daddy, do read Katya the chapter on Tsar Paul. I'm sure Tolstoy would admire it if he were still alive.

KATYA: But the newspapers keep asking for up-to-date stuff.

MUKOVNIN: Without an understanding of the past the way

into the future is closed to us. The Bolsheviks are completing the work of Ivan the First, gathering in the Russian lands. They need old regular officers like me if only to learn from the mistakes we made.

[*Doorbell rings. Bustling in lobby. Enter* BERNSTEIN *in fur coat carrying parcels.*]

BERNSTEIN: Good day to you, General Mukovnin. Good day to you, Miss Felsen. Is Ludmila at home?

KATYA: She's expecting you.

LUDMILA [*from behind screen*]: I'm dressing. . . .

BERNSTEIN: Good day to you, Ludmila. Well, you wouldn't send a dog out in this weather. Prince Hippolyte drove me here. Talked his head off, he did, and such rubbish. Not many like him around. We aren't late, are we, Ludmila?

MUKOVNIN: Broad daylight, and they're going to the theatre.

KATYA: The theatre starts at five o'clock these days.

MUKOVNIN: What, are they trying to save electricity?

KATYA: Partly it's the electricity, but also you can have everything stripped off your back if you come home late.

BERNSTEIN [*untying parcels*]: A nice leg of ham, general. I don't know about these things, but they did say it was corn-fed. Seems to have been fed on corn or something – I wasn't actually there at the time.

[KATYA *goes to a corner and smokes.*]

MUKOVNIN: Really, Mr Bernstein, you are much too kind to us.

BERNSTEIN: Some cracklings. . . .

MUKOVNIN [*not understanding*]: I beg your pardon?

BERNSTEIN: You wouldn't have eaten them in your father's house. But they think very highly of them where I come from. They're bits of goose skin. Taste them and tell me what you think. . . . How's the book going, general?

MUKOVNIN: It's getting on. I'm up to the reign of Alexander I.

LUDMILA: It reads like a novel, Isaac. To me it's just like *War and Peace* where Tolstoy talks about the soldiers. . . .

BERNSTEIN: Glad to hear it. Let them shoot each other on the streets, general, let them bash each other's heads against the wall, you've better things to do. Finish the book – we'll celebrate on me and I'll buy the first hundred copies. A little salami, general. Home-made salami from a German I know. . . .

MUKOVNIN: Mr Bernstein, I'll be angry with you . . .

BERNSTEIN: It would be an honour if General Mukovnin got angry with me. The salami is first-class. This German used to be quite a famous professor, and now he makes his living from sausages. . . . Ludmila, I strongly suspect we're going to be late.

LUDMILA [*behind screen*]: Ready!

MUKOVNIN: How much do I owe you, Mr Bernstein?

BERNSTEIN: You owe me one horseshoe from the horse that died on the Nevsky today.

MUKOVNIN: No, I'm serious.

BERNSTEIN: All right, so two shoes from two horses.

[LUDMILA *enters from behind the screen. She is dazzling, slender, rosy-cheeked. She wears diamond earrings and a black velvet sleeveless dress.*]

MUKOVNIN: Isn't she a beautiful daughter, Mr Bernstein?

BERNSTEIN: There's no denying it.

KATYA: There you are, Mr Bernstein, there's a real Russian beauty for you.

BERNSTEIN: I'm no expert but I approve.

MUKOVNIN: I must introduce you to my eldest daughter Marya.

LUDMILA: I ought to tell you, Marya's our favourite and would you believe it, the favourite daughter's gone and joined the army.

MUKOVNIN: Not quite the army, Ludmila. She's actually in the Political Section.

BERNSTEIN: Anything you want to know about the Political

Section just ask me, general. It's the same as the army.

KATYA [*taking* LUDMILA *to one side*]: I shouldn't wear those earrings if I were you.

LUDMILA: Wouldn't you?

KATYA: No. And then there's that supper. . . .

LUDMILA: You needn't worry about me, my sweet. . . . I wasn't born yesterday. . . . [*Kisses her.*] Katya, you really are a silly, sweet thing. . . . [*To* BERNSTEIN]: My boots . . . [*Turns away and takes off her earrings.*]

BERNSTEIN [*bustling about*]: Right away! [*He fusses around helping her to dress to go out – boots, fur cloak, headscarf.*]

LUDMILA: It amazes me that these things still haven't been sold. . . . Father, don't forget to take your medicine just because I'm out, and don't let him work, Katya.

MUKOVNIN: We're just going to have a quiet evening at home.

LUDMILA [*kissing her father on the forehead* : Isn't he a dear, Isaac? He's not like any other father.

BERNSTEIN: Such a father, he's a luxury.

LUDMILA: We're the only ones who understand him. Where did you leave Prince Hippolyte?

BERNSTEIN: At the gate. Wait, I told him. We must have discipline! We'll be there in a minute. All the best, general.

KATYA: Don't drink too much.

BERNSTEIN: Not much chance of that these days!

LUDMILA: 'Bye, daddy.

[MUKOVNIN *accompanies* LUDMILA *and* BERNSTEIN *to lobby. Voices and laughter off. Re-enter* MUKOVNIN.]

MUKOVNIN: A thoroughly charming and decent Jew.

KATYA [*curled up on the divan smoking*]: I think they're so tactless.

MUKOVNIN: But my dear Katya, how can you expect them to have any tact? Allowed to live only on one side of the street and chased off the other side by policemen. That's how it was in Kiev, on Bibikov Boulevard. Why should they be tactful? One can only marvel at their energy, their staying power, their toughness. . . .

KATYA: Well, that energy's spilling over into Russian life now and we're not like that, it just doesn't suit us.

MUKOVNIN: But I suppose fatalism does? Rasputin and that German Tsarina who ruined the dynasty – that suits us? Heine, Spinoza, Christ – nothing but good from that wonderful people . . .

KATYA: You used to praise the Japs once.

MUKOVNIN: And why not? They're a great nation and we can learn a lot from them.

KATYA: Now I can see who Marya takes after. You're a Bolshevik, Uncle Nikolai.

MUKOVNIN: I'm a Russian officer, Katya, and I would like to ask my brother-officers since when and why have they ceased to understand the rules of war. We have tormented and humiliated these people and until now they could put up no more than passive resistance – now they've gone over to the offensive and are fighting with skill, with forethought and desperation and I say they are fighting in the name of an ideal.

KATYA: An ideal? I don't know. We're unhappy and I don't see us ever being happy again. They have swept us away.

MUKOVNIN: Let them give old, sleepy, peasant Russia a shaking up and a good job too. There's so little time, Katya. Russia's only real emperor, Peter, said 'Delay means death.' Now that was a good watchword! And so, my brother-officers, you should have the guts to look at the map and see which of your flanks was turned, where and why you were beaten. . . . My motto is – keep your eyes open. And I won't change it.

KATYA: You must take your medicine, uncle.

MUKOVNIN: To my brothers-in-arms, those with whom I fought shoulder to shoulder, I say: *Messieurs, tirez vos conclusions.* Delay means death. [*Exit.*]

[*In the next room a Bach fugue is being played with cool precision on a 'cello.* KATYA *listens, then gets up and goes to the telephone.*]

KATYA: District Headquarters, please. ... Can I speak to Redko? Is that you, Redko? I just wanted to say ... I'm sure you're not the only man running the revolution, but you're the only one who can't find time to see the person ... the person you don't mind sleeping with when you feel like it. ... [*Pause.*] Take me out, Redko. Come and pick me up in the car. ... Well, of course, if you're busy. No, I'm not cross. What is there to be cross about? [*Hangs up.*]

[*The music stops. Enter* GOLITSYN, *a tall man in soldier's jacket and puttees, holding a 'cello.*]

KATYA: What was it they said to you in the café, Sergei – 'Don't play that sad stuff'?

GOLITSYN: 'Don't play that sad stuff, it tears our guts out.'

KATYA: They want something cheerful, Sergei. People want to forget themselves, they want to relax ...

GOLITSYN: Not all of them. Some ask for something with more feeling.

KATYA [*sits at piano*]: Who do you play to?

GOLITSYN: Dock workers.

KATYA: I suppose you go to the trade union. Do you get your supper there too?

GOLITSYN: Yes.

KATYA [*playing a popular tune*[1*]]: Try and follow me. This is what you ought to play in the café.

[GOLITSYN *plays, fluffs, gets it right.*]

* Notes are at the end of the play.

KATYA: Sergei, do you think I should learn shorthand?

GOLITSYN: Shorthand? I don't know.

KATYA [*hums tune*]: They need shorthand typists just now.

GOLITSYN: I really couldn't say. [*Plays the tune.*]

KATYA: Marya's the only real woman among us. She's strong and she's got nerve, she's completely genuine. Here we are moping away and she's happy in her Political Section. Have we invented some new law to replace happiness? There doesn't seem to be any other law.

GOLITSYN: Marya was never one for half-measures. That's the main thing about her. . . .

KATYA: She's right. [*Hums again.*] And she's got her affair with this Akim fellow. . . .

GOLITSYN [*stops playing*]: Who's this Akim?

KATYA: Their divisional commander, an ex-blacksmith. She mentions him in every letter.

GOLITSYN: What makes you think she's having an affair with him?

KATYA: I can read between the lines. . . . I wonder if I should go back to my family in Kazan? At any rate it's a home. . . . You at least go to see that monk of yours in the monastery – what do you call him?

GOLITSYN: Sionios.

KATYA: You go to Sionios. What does he teach you there?

GOLITSYN: You were talking about happiness, weren't you? . . . He teaches me to find happiness not in power over others, nor in endless greed – the greed which none of us can satisfy.

KATYA: Play, Sergei.

[*They play.*]

KATYA: Sionios – beautiful name.

SCENE THREE

LUDMILA *and* BERNSTEIN *are in his room. On the table are the remains of a meal, bottles. Part of the next room can be seen, where* BISHONKOV, PHILIP, *and* NIKITIN *are playing cards. The legless* NIKITIN *has been propped up on a chair.*

LUDMILA: Felix Yussupov was divinely handsome, played tennis brilliantly – he was champion of Russia. Still, even though he was so handsome, his looks somehow lacked virility, there was something doll-like about them. . . . I met Vladimir Larin at Felix's. To the very end the Tsar was incapable of seeing the nobility of that man's character. We used to call him 'the Teutonic knight'. . . . Friedrichs was a friend of Prince Sergei, the one who plays the 'cello . . . That evening there was a turn *hors programme*, Archbishop Ambrose. That old man took a fancy to me – can you imagine! – he kept on pouring me out more champagne cup and putting on such an expression – half pious and half lecherous. At first I made no impression on Vladimir, he admitted as much to me: 'You were snub-nosed, *si démesurément russe*, with such burning-red cheeks. . . .' At dawn we drove out to Tsarskoye Selo, left the car at the park gates and took a horse and carriage. He drove. 'Need I tell you, Ludmila, that I haven't taken my eyes off you all evening?' 'A fact which didn't escape Nina Buturlin, *mon prince*.' I knew that he and Nina had been having an affair – or rather, a flirtation. 'Buturlin, *c'est le passé*, Ludmila. . . .' '*On revient toujours à ses premiers amours, mon prince*.' Vladimir didn't have the title of grand duke, he was the son of a morganatic marriage, the Tsarina refused to meet their family. . . . Vladimir used to call that woman an evil genius. And then – he was a poet, a mere boy, he never understood a thing about politics. . . . We arrived at Tsarskoye.

Somewhere over the lake it was dawn and quite near us a nightingale started to sing. . . . Again he said: '*Mademoiselle Boutourline, c'est le passé.*' '*Mon prince*, the past sometimes comes back and when it does it can be terrible. . . .'

[BERNSTEIN *puts out the light, flings himself at* LUDMILA, *throws her down on the divan. There is a struggle. She extricates herself, straightens her hair and her dress.*]

BISHONKOV [*throwing down a card*]: Beat that. . . .

PHILIP: What a hope!

NIKITIN: . . . well, so they led him up to the fence with his hands tied. 'All right, friend,' they said, 'turn round.' And he said: 'I don't need to turn round, I'm a soldier, you can knock me off this way round. . . .' The fences in those parts are sort of hurdles about half as high as a man. . . . It was night-time, on the edge of the village; beyond the village nothing but open fields except for a bit of a gully. . . .

BISHONKOV [*taking the trick*]: That's done for you!

PHILIP: Bet you it hasn't.

NIKITIN: . . . so they led him out and took aim. One moment he was standing by the fence, the next it was just as if he'd been pulled off the ground with his hands tied and all, like God had snatched him off the face of the earth. He flew over that hurdle – sideways too – they fired . . . no good, too dark, he ducked, twisted and got away.

PHILIP [*putting down his cards*]: He's a hero.

NIKITIN: He was a hero. A real dare-devil. I knew him as well as I know you. . . . He was free for six months, then they caught him.

PHILIP: They didn't shoot him – not after he'd got away?

NIKITIN: They did. I reckon it wasn't fair. If a man's jumped out of the grave, seen the other world you might say and come back – that means his number's not up yet.

PHILIP: Nobody cares these days.

NIKITIN: I say they did him wrong. It's the law in every

country: if the firing squad miss you – good luck to you, you're a free man.

PHILIP: Except in Russia . . . in Russia they catch up with you and shoot you.

BISHONKOV: Except in Russia.

LUDMILA: Put the light on.

[BERNSTEIN *switches on the light.*]

LUDMILA: I'm going. [*Turns round, looks at* BERNSTEIN, *bursts into laughter.*] Don't pout, come over here . . . look, can't you see . . . first I've got to get used to you. . . .

BERNSTEIN: Get used to me! You make me sound like a new boot.

LUDMILA: I won't deny that I have some feeling for you, but it's a feeling that has to be encouraged to grow. . . . When Marya comes back from the army you'll get to know us all better: nothing is allowed to happen in our family without her. . . . Daddy gets on well with you, but he's helpless on his own – you've seen what he's like. . . . And then there's still plenty to straighten out: what about your wife?

BERNSTEIN: What's my wife got to do with it?

LUDMILA: I know that Jews are very attached to their children.

BERNSTEIN: God, d'you have to bring that up?

LUDMILA: That's why, for the time being, until everything's arranged, you're just to sit beside me and behave yourself, be patient. . . .

BERNSTEIN: The Jews have been waiting for the messiah for so long, they're patient by nature. Have another drink – just one.

LUDMILA: I've drunk an awful lot already.

BERNSTEIN: I was sent this wine from a battleship. The Grand Duke had a little case of it on board.

LUDMILA: How *do* you get all this stuff?

BERNSTEIN: I get it from places where nobody else can get it from. . . . Just one more glass.

LUDMILA: On condition that you sit still and behave yourself.

BERNSTEIN: The synagogue's the place for sitting still.

LUDMILA: When you came to see us you put on your frock-coat, just as if you were going to the synagogue. A frock-coat, my dear Isaac, is what high-school headmasters wear at graduations and businessmen wear at memorial dinners.

BERNSTEIN: Then I won't wear a frock-coat.

LUDMILA: And another thing – theatre tickets. Never, my dear, buy tickets for the front row of the stalls – it's the sign of a social climber, a *parvenu.*

BERNSTEIN: But I *am* a social climber.

LUDMILA: You also happen to be a thoroughly nice man, but no one will realize it until you show them. Even your name is wrong. . . . Nowadays you only need to put an announcement in the newspapers, in *Izvestiya,* and you can change it. . . . If I were you I should change it to Alexei . . . do you like Alexei as a name?

BERNSTEIN: Yes, I like it. [*Puts out the light again and flings himself at her.*]

NIKITIN: They're at it again.

PHILIP [*listening*]: Made herself at home, hasn't she?

BISHONKOV: I like Miss Ludmila better than all the others – she's decent to everybody. . . . All the others are real tarts . . . she calls me by my first name.

[VISKOVSKY *joins the card-players, stands behind* NIKITIN *and watches the game.*]

LUDMILA [*pulling herself away*]: Call me a cab. . . .

BERNSTEIN: All right. . . . I don't suppose I shall be getting much further tonight anyway. . . .

LUDMILA: Call me a cab this minute!

BERNSTEIN: There are thirty degrees of frost out on the street, I wouldn't like to send a mad dog out there.

LUDMILA: My clothes are all in a mess. . . . How am I going to show myself at home?

BERNSTEIN: You've only yourself to blame.

LUDMILA: How vulgar. . . . Don't talk to me like that.

BERNSTEIN: I see I've said the wrong thing again.

LUDMILA: I've got toothache, I tell you, it's unbearable.

BERNSTEIN: God . . . what have your teeth got to do with it?

LUDMILA: Get me something for it . . . I'm in pain.

[*Exit* BERNSTEIN; *he bumps into* VISKOVSKY *in the next room.*]

VISKOVSKY: Take it easy, maestro.

BERNSTEIN: She's got toothache.

VISKOVSKY: Too bad.

BERNSTEIN: So she *says*. . . .

VISKOVSKY: She's putting it on, bound to be.

PHILIP: She's making it up, Mr Bernstein, she hasn't got the toothache. . . .

LUDMILA [*pats her hair in front of the mirror. Stately, gay, flushed, she walks round the room and sings*]:

My love is the strongest of all,
He is fair, he is cruel, he is tall. . . .

BERNSTEIN: I'm not so green as that, Viskovsky – it's a long, long time now since I started shaving.

VISKOVSKY: Yessir.

LUDMILA [*picking up the telephone receiver*]: Three, seventy-five, two, please. Is that you, daddy . . . ? I'm fine. Nadya Johannson and her husband were at the theatre. Isaac and I are dining at his flat. . . . You simply must go and see Spessivtseva, she reminds one of Pavlova. . . . Have you taken your medicine? You must look after yourself and get well. . . . Your daughter's very clever, daddy, quite ingenious. . . . Is that you, Katya . . . ? Your orders have been carried out, ma'am. *Le manège continue, j'ai mal aux dents ce soir.*

[*Walks about the room, sings, pats her hair.*]

BERNSTEIN: If she goes on like this much longer, I won't be at home next time she comes. . . .

VISKOVSKY: You're the boss here.

BERNSTEIN: *Other* people can ask me questions about my wife and children, but not *her*.

VISKOVSKY: Yessir.

BERNSTEIN: These people are not worthy so much as to do up my wife's shoelace, if you want to know – her shoelace, I tell you.

SCENE FOUR

At VISKOVSKY'*s. He is in riding-breeches, boots, without a jacket, and shirt collar open. On a low sofa sprawls* KRAVCHENKO, *short, in uniform, and* MADAME DORA – *a skinny woman in black, with a Spanish comb in her hair and large dangling earrings.*

VISKOVSKY: At one go, Yasha. . . . [*Sings.*]

KRAVCHENKO: How much do you need, then?

VISKOVSKY: Ten thousand pounds. At one go. . . . Ever seen a pound sterling, Yasha?

KRAVCHENKO: What, from flogging thread?

VISKOVSKY: To hell with thread. Diamonds, three carat, like pale-blue water, pure without a flaw. They won't look at anything else in Paris.

KRAVCHENKO: But I bet there aren't any like that left.

VISKOVSKY: There are diamonds in every house, but you've got to know how to get hold of them. The Rimsky-Korsakovs have got them and the Shakhovskoys. There are plenty of diamonds around in old St Petersburg.

KRAVCHENKO: You'll never make a Communist business-man, Viskovsky.

VISKOVSKY: Oh yes I will. My father was in business, he traded his land for racehorses. The old guard may have surrendered, comrade Kravchenko, but it's far from dead yet.

KRAVCHENKO: You should call the Mukovnin girl in. She's pining in the corridor.

VISKOVSKY: I'll turn up in Paris like a lord.

KRAVCHENKO: Where's that Bernstein got to?

VISKOVSKY: He's sitting it out in the lavatory, or maybe he's playing '66' with the Lithuanian and Shapiro. [*Opens door.*] Hey, miss, come and sit by the fire. ... [*Goes out into corridor.*]

DORA [*kissing* KRAVCHENKO'*s hands*]: You are magnificent, I adore you!

[*Enter* LUDMILA *in fur wrap, and* VISKOVSKY.]

LUDMILA: I just can't understand it. We made an arrangement. ...

VISKOVSKY: More precious than gold.

LUDMILA: I was to come at eight. It's a quarter to nine now, and he didn't leave the key. Where's he got to?

VISKOVSKY: A little matter of business. He'll be back.

LUDMILA: One can hardly call them gentlemen, these people. ...

VISKOVSKY: Have a drop of vodka, my dear.

LUDMILA: I think I will. I'm frozen. Still, I can't understand it. ...

VISKOVSKY: Ludmila, allow me to introduce Madame Dora, a citizen of the Republic of France – *Liberté, Egalité, Fraternité.* Among her other attractions she possesses a foreign passport.

LUDMILA [*extending her hand*]: *Enchantée.*

VISKOVSKY: You know Yasha Kravchenko. Subaltern during the war, now a Red artilleryman. He's on the 10-inch guns at Kronstadt and can point them in any direction.

KRAVCHENKO: Viskovsky's in good form tonight.

VISKOVSKY: In any direction. You never know, Yasha. They'll tell you to demolish the street where you were born – and you'll do it. Shell the kindergarten! You'll do it, Yasha, just as long as they let you go on living and strumming your guitar and going to bed with your skinny women. You're fat, so you like them thin. You'll do anything. You'd even deny your own mother three times if they told you to. Still, that's not the point, the point is they'll go further. They won't let you choose your own drinking friends, they'll give you lousy books to read and teach you to sing lousy songs. Then the Red artilleryman'll get angry, you'll get wild, you'll start getting wrong ideas. . . . Two gentlemen will pay you a visit: 'Let's go, comrade Kravchenko. . . .' 'Shall I bring my things with me?' 'There's no need, comrade Kravchenko, it'll only take a minute, this interrogation, just a triviality. . . .' And then it's curtains for you, Red artilleryman – and all for four kopecks. The cost of one Colt bullet is four kopecks, and not a farthing more. They've worked it out.

DORA: Jacques, take me home. . . .

VISKOVSKY: Here's to you, Yasha! To victorious France, Madame Dora!

LUDMILA [*she has been drinking all the time*]: I'll just pop along and see if he's back. . . .

VISKOVSKY: Just a little matter of business and he'll be here. Did you think up the story about your teeth yourself, duchess?

LUDMILA: Yes. Not bad, eh? [*Laughs.*] What else can a girl do these days? Jews must be taught to respect the woman they're interested in.

VISKOVSKY: When I look at you, you remind me of a little sparrow. Let's drink, little sparrow!

LUDMILA: I'm beginning to feel it now. What did you put in this filthy stuff, Viskovsky?

VISKOVSKY: A little sparrow. The strength of the Mukovnins has all gone to Marya, and all they left you is a row of milk teeth.

LUDMILA: That was a cheap thing to say.

VISKOVSKY: And I don't much like your small breasts. A woman's breasts should be lovely and big and helpless, like a ewe's.

KRAVCHENKO: We're going, Viskovsky.

VISKOVSKY: You're not going anywhere. Marry me, little sparrow.

LUDMILA: No, thanks, I'd rather have Bernstein. ... I know what it would be like married to you. One day you're drunk, next day you've got a hangover, and the next day you go off God knows where and shoot yourself or something. No, I think I'll stick to Bernstein.

KRAVCHENKO: Viskovsky, be a sport and let us go.

VISKOVSKY: You're not going anywhere. ... A toast! To woman! [*To Dora*] That's Ludmila ... her sister's called Marya.

KRAVCHENKO: Isn't Marya in the army?

LUDMILA: She's at the frontier.

VISKOVSKY: She's at the front, Kravchenko, at the front. The division is commanded by an ex-waiter.

LUDMILA: That's not true, Viskovsky. He's a metalworker.

VISKOVSKY: They call Akim 'the waiter'. Let's drink to women, Madame Dora! Women love junior officers, waiters, customs officials, Chinamen ... that's their job – to make love. If that leads to trouble – what are the police for? [*Raises his glass.*] 'Here's to the girls, the beautiful girls, who loved us and left us after an hour.' Not even an hour, really. A thread of gossamer, then it broke ... her sister's called Marya. ... Just imagine that you've fallen in love with a queen, Yasha. 'You're disgusting,' she says, 'get out.'

LUDMILA [*laughs*]: Sounds just like Marya.

VISKOVSKY: 'You're disgusting, get out,' she says. No hope for the Horse Guards. Then she goes to No. 16 Furshtat Street, Apartment No. 4. ...

LUDMILA: Stop it, Viskovsky!

VISKOVSKY: Here's to the Kronstadt artillery, Yasha! So they decided to move to Furshtat Street. Marya walked out of the house in a grey tailored suit, and bought violets at the Troitsky Bridge, and pinned them on to the lapel of her jacket. . . . The prince – he plays the 'cello, you know – the prince tidied up his bachelor flat, stuffed his dirty linen under a cupboard, took his unwashed plates to the basement. . . . Coffee and *petit-fours* for two were served. They drank their coffee. She had brought spring with her, her violets, and she sat on the divan with her feet up. He covered her strong, tender legs with a shawl, she gave him a shining smile, an encouraging, obedient, sad, encouraging smile. . . . She embraced his greying head. 'Prince, what is it, prince?' But the prince's voice came out like a choir-boy's. *Passe, rien ne va plus.*

LUDMILA: God, what a nasty mind you've got.

VISKOVSKY: Yasha, try to imagine, before your very eyes the queen is taking off her brassière, her stockings, her knickers. . . . Enough to make even you blush, Yasha. . . .

[LUDMILA *falls back laughing.*]

VISKOVSKY: She's left 16 Furshtat Street. . . . Where is her footprint, that I might kiss it? Where is her footprint? . . . Anyway, let's hope Akim is up to it. . . . What do you think, Ludmila?

LUDMILA: You've put something in this vodka, Viskovsky. My head's spinning.

VISKOVSKY: Come here, angel-face. [*Draws her closer to him with his arm round her shoulders.*] How much did Bernstein pay you for the ring?

LUDMILA: What are you talking about?

VISKOVSKY: That ring wasn't yours, it was your sister's. You sold someone else's ring.

LUDMILA: Leave me alone!

VISKOVSKY [*pushing her through side door*]: Come with me, my little love.

[DORA *and* KRAVCHENKO *are left alone in the room. The*

slow beam of a searchlight crosses the window. Dishevelled and goggle-eyed, DORA *drags herself over to* KRAVCHENKO, *kisses his hands, moans, babbles. Enter on tiptoe, barefoot,* PHILIP; *slowly and silently takes from the table wine, sausage, bread.*]

PHILIP [*quietly, head on one side*]: You don't mind, Mr Kravchenko?

[KRAVCHENKO *nods. Exit the cripple, stepping carefully.*]

DORA: You're my sun! My God! My all!

[KRAVCHENKO *says nothing, listens for something. Enter* VISKOVSKY, *lights cigarette with trembling hand. Door into next room is left open.* LUDMILA *is sprawled on the divan, and sobbing.*]

VISKOVSKY: Calm down, Ludmila. You'll get over it.

DORA: Jacques, I want to go home. ... Take me home, Jacques.

KRAVCHENKO: Wait a bit, Dora.

VISKOVSKY: One for the road – comrades!

KRAVCHENKO: Wait a minute, Dora.

VISKOVSKY: One for the road. Let's drink to the ladies.

KRAVCHENKO: You don't do that, captain.

VISKOVSKY: Here's to the ladies, Kravchenko!

KRAVCHENKO: You don't do that, captain.

VISKOVSKY: What don't you do?

KRAVCHENKO: You don't go having women when you've got the clap.

VISKOVSKY [*in officer's voice*]: Would you mind repeating that!

[*Pause, sobs cease.*]

KRAVCHENKO: I said, people who've got the clap ...

VISKOVSKY: Take your spectacles off, Kravchenko. I'm going to smash your face in!

[KRAVCHENKO *draws his revolver.*]

VISKOVSKY: Very well.

[KRAVCHENKO *fires. Curtain falls. Behind curtain are heard shots, falling bodies, woman's scream.*]

SCENE FIVE

The MUKOVNINS' *flat. Their old* NANNY *is curled up asleep on a chest in the corner. A lamp casts a pool of light on the table.* KATYA *is reading aloud a letter to* MUKOVNIN.

KATYA: '... I am woken at dawn by the bugle from head-quarters squadron. By eight o'clock I have to be at the political commissar's office, I am responsible for nearly everything there.... I may edit an article for the divisional newspaper, run literacy classes for the troops. Our new draft are all Ukrainians; with their speech, their vivacity, they remind me of Italians. For centuries old Russia has suppressed and denigrated their culture.... In our street in Petersburg, in our house opposite the Hermitage and the Winter Palace we might have been living in Polynesia – knowing nothing about our people, never even suspecting what they were really like.... Yesterday evening in class I read out the chapter from papa's book about the murder of Tsar Paul. The emperor so obviously deserved his fate that no one questioned it: they asked – this is typical of the matter-of-fact cast of mind of these simple people – about the disposition of the regiment, the layout of the rooms in the palace, which company of the Guards was on sentry-duty that night, who the conspirators were and in what way Paul had wronged them.... I keep dreaming that papa may be able to come out here to us in the summer, if only the Poles don't start giving trouble again.[1] Dear old papa, you will see a new army, new barracks – in complete contrast to the kind you describe in your book. By then the grass will be out in our park, the horses will be in much better shape thanks to the fresh fodder, saddles and bridles will be mended and ready.... I was talking to Akim, he's in favour, provided that you are well enough. . . . It is night now. I came off duty early and climbed up the worn, 400-year-old stairs to my room. I live in the attic, in a vaulted chamber which once served as the armoury of the counts Krasnitsky. The castle is built on a cliff, a blue river at its foot and meadows stretching away as far as the eye can see, with a dark wall of forest in the distance. . . . On every floor of the castle there is a loophole for a sentry: from here they watched the approach of the Tartars and the Russians and they would pour boiling oil on the heads of the besiegers. Old Hedwig, the last Krasnitsky's housekeeper, has prepared my supper and lit a fire in the fireplace, which is as deep and black as a cave. . . . Down below in the park the horses are chafing at their lines. . . . The troops from the Kuban are eating round a camp-fire and have started up a song. The snow is weighing down the trees, the branches of oaks and chestnuts are interlaced under its weight and an uneven silver blanket has covered the overgrown paths, the statues. They still stand there – youths brandishing spears, frozen naked goddesses with beckoning arms, with flowing hair and unseeing eyes. . . . Hedwig is nodding and dozing, the logs on the fire flare and fall. The centuries have made the bricks of these walls as resonant as glass – as I write to you they are alight with gold from the fire. . . . Alyosha's photograph is beside me on the table. . . . I am among the very people who killed him, not knowing who he was. I have just left them – I have even been helping to set them free. . . . Have I done right, Alyosha, have I fulfilled your last wish for me, to live with courage . . . ? I feel I am doing what he would have wanted me to do. . . . It's late, I can't sleep; partly from a vague feeling of unease about you, partly from fear of dreaming. Whenever I dream I see violence, suffering, death. My life is a curious mixture of closeness to nature and anxiety about you. Why doesn't Ludmila write more often? A few days ago I sent her a certificate signed by Akim stating that as I am on active service my family's home is exempt from having rooms requisitioned. Besides that there should be papa's permit to keep his library. If it has expired you must take it to be renewed at the People's Commissariat of Education in the Chernyshev Embankment building, Room 40. I shall be happy if Ludmila succeeds in marrying and starting a family, but the man must come and see us at home, he should get to know papa – if papa likes him, all will be well. And Nanny should see him too. . . . Katya is always complaining about the old woman and saying she does no work. Katya, my dear, Nanny's old, she brought up two generations of Mukovnins, she thinks and has feelings of her own, she's not just a simple peasant. . . . I've always thought there wasn't much of the peasant about her – in any case, what did we, living in our Polynesia, ever know about the peasants . . . ? I hear the food situation has got worse in Petersburg and that people who don't work are having their rooms and linen confiscated. . . . I'm ashamed of how well we live. Akim has taken me out hunting with him, I have a horse of my own, a Don cossack horse. . . .' [KATYA *raises her head.*] There you see, Uncle Nikolai, how well and happy she is.

[MUKOVNIN *covers his eyes with his palm.*]

KATYA: Don't cry, please. . . .

MUKOVNIN: I ask God – we each have our private God – why He gave me, a sinful, selfish old man, such children – Marya, Ludmila. . . .

KATYA: There, there, uncle. There's no need to cry. . . .

SCENE SIX

Police station at night. A drunk is huddled under a bench. He moves his fingers in front of his face, telling himself something. On the bench dozes a heavy old man, well dressed in a racoon coat and tall hat. The coat is open, revealing a bare grey chest. The INSPECTOR *is interrogating* LUDMILA. *Her fur hat has been knocked over to the side of her head, her hair is disordered, her fur coat has been pulled off one shoulder.*

INSPECTOR: Name?
LUDMILA: Let me go.
INSPECTOR: Name?
LUDMILA: Barbara.
INSPECTOR: Patronymic?
LUDMILA: Ivanovna.
INSPECTOR: Where do you work?
LUDMILA: At Laferme's cigarette factory.
INSPECTOR: Union card?
LUDMILA: I haven't got it on me.
INSPECTOR: What's this yarn you're spinning me?
LUDMILA: I'm a married woman . . . let me go.
INSPECTOR: What do you want to spin this yarn for? How long have you known Brilyov?
LUDMILA: Who? I've never heard of him.
INSPECTOR: Brilyov signed the orders for the thread, it went via you to Gutman. Where did you store it?
LUDMILA: What are you talking about? Store what?
INSPECTOR: You'll soon find out. . . . [*To a* MILITIAMAN] Call Kalmykova.

[*The* MILITIAMAN *brings in* SHURA KALMYKOVA, *chambermaid at 86 Nevsky Prospekt.*]

INSPECTOR: Are you the maid at No. 86 Nevsky Prospekt?
KALMYKOVA: I do work there part-time.

INSPECTOR: Do you recognize this citizen?

KALMYKOVA: That I do.

INSPECTOR: What do you know about her?

KALMYKOVA: I'll answer any questions you like. Her father's a general.

INSPECTOR: Does she work?

KALMYKOVA: I suppose some people might call it work.

INSPECTOR: Is she married?

KALMYKOVA: Makes a habit of it. She keeps a string of 'husbands'. One of them hid himself in the WC for the whole evening because of her teeth.

INSPECTOR: What teeth? What's all this about?

KALMYKOVA: She knows what teeth I'm talking about.

INSPECTOR [*to* LUDMILA]: Been inside before? How many times?

LUDMILA: I've been infected. . . . I'm ill. . . .

INSPECTOR [*to* KALMYKOVA]: We have to know how many previous arrests she has.

KALMYKOVA: I don't know and I won't say. . . . I can't say what I don't know.

LUDMILA: I can't stand it any more. . . . Let me go. . . .

INSPECTOR: Calm down. Look at me.

LUDMILA: My head's spinning. . . . I'm going to faint. . . .

INSPECTOR: Look at me!

LUDMILA: For God's sake, why should I look at you?

INSPECTOR [*in fury*]: Because I haven't slept for five nights. . . . Do you know what that means?

LUDMILA: I know.

INSPECTOR [*goes close to her, takes her by the shoulders and looks into her eyes*]: How many times have you been inside . . . tell me!

SCENE SEVEN

The MUKOVNINS' *flat, lit by oil lamps. Shadows on the walls and ceilings.* GOLITSYN *is standing in prayer before an icon illuminated by a small hanging lamp.* NANNY *is asleep on a chest.*

GOLITSYN: '... Verily, verily I say unto you, Except a corn of wheat fall into the ground and die it abideth alone: but if it die, it bringeth forth much fruit. He that loveth his life shall lose it; and he that hateth his life in this world shall keep it unto life eternal. If any man serve me, let him follow me; and where I am there shall also my servant be: if any man serve me, him will my Father honour. Now is my soul troubled; and what shall I say? Father, save me from this hour: but for this cause came I unto this hour....'

KATYA [*approaches silently until she is standing beside* GOLITSYN, *leans her head on his shoulder*]: I meet Redko in the General Staff building, Sergei, in what used to be the ante-room, there's a check-covered divan there.... Redko locks the door; afterwards he unlocks it....

GOLITSYN: Yes.

KATYA: I'm going away, to Kazan.

GOLITSYN: Go.

KATYA: Redko is always teaching, lecturing me – who to love, who to hate.... He says that only the masses count today – the law of great numbers. But I'm a number – one. Doesn't that count?

GOLITSYN: It should.

KATYA: There you are – it surely counts.... Now I'm free, Nanny.... There now, wake up. You'll sleep through the day of judgement.

NEFEDOVNA [*raising her head*]: Where's Ludmila?

KATYA: Ludmila will be back soon, Nanny, and I'm going away. There'll be nobody here to scold you.

NEFEDOVNA: Why should anybody scold me, there's nothing for me to do. . . . I was born to be a nanny, brought in for the children to bring them up, but they've all gone away. . . . The house is full of silly women, but no more children. One's gone off to the wars, the place is empty without her; the other walks the streets. . . . What sort of house is it where there are no children?

KATYA: We'll arrange for you to have some . . . by the Holy Ghost.

NEFEDOVNA: You're just as bad as her. D'you think I don't know? And it does you no good.

GOLITSYN: Go to Kazan, you're needed there. . . . Kazan is a wilderness, Katya, a wilderness where wild beasts are devouring one another. . . .

NEFEDOVNA: Now there's the Molostovs – merchant family, common as anything, they managed to see *their* nanny got a pension – fifty roubles a month. . . . Why don't you do something for me, prince, why doesn't somebody give me a pension?

GOLITSYN [*putting more wood on the stove*]: Nobody listens to me any more, Nefedovna, I've no influence any more.

NEFEDOVNA: They were no more than shopkeepers. . . .

[*The door opens.* MUKOVNIN *steps back to admit* PHILIP, *wrapped in rags, hooded, huge and shapeless. Half of* PHILIP'*s face is covered in livid scar-tissue; he is wearing felt boots.*]

MUKOVNIN: Who are you?

PHILIP [*moving closer to him*]: I'm a friend of Miss Ludmila's.

MUKOVNIN: What do you want?

PHILIP: There's been a bit of trouble, sir.

KATYA: Have you come from Bernstein?

PHILIP: That's right, ma'am, from Mr Bernstein. . . . It all started from nothing, like. . . .

KATYA: Ludmila?

PHILIP: Yes, she was there with a whole lot of 'em. . . . They went a bit too far, sir. There was Captain Viskovsky, all of a sudden Mr Kravchenko lost his temper ... started to quarrel, they'd both had a few too many....

GOLITSYN: General, let me talk to this comrade.

PHILIP: It wasn't nothing much, just a quarrel really. ... They'd both had a bit too much ... had guns on 'em....

MUKOVNIN: Where is my daughter?

PHILIP: We don't know, sir.

MUKOVNIN: Will you please tell me where my daughter is? You can tell me everything.

PHILIP [*scarcely audible*]: They took her off.

MUKOVNIN: Come on, man, I can take it. Out with it.

PHILIP [*louder*]: They took her off, sir.

MUKOVNIN: Arrested her – what for?

PHILIP: It seems all the fuss was because of some sickness. Mr Kravchenko said, 'You've given her a disease.' So Captain Viskovsky took a shot at him. They had guns, you see ... and then she ...

MUKOVNIN: Was it the Cheka?[1]

PHILIP: Some men came and took her away, I don't know who they were ... these people don't wear uniform nowadays, so there's no knowing, sir.

MUKOVNIN: I must go to Smolny,[2] Katya.

KATYA: You're not going anywhere, Uncle Nikolai.

MUKOVNIN: I must go to Smolny – at once.

KATYA: Uncle, dear ...

MUKOVNIN: Katya – it's a question of getting my daughter back to me. [*Goes to telephone, picks up receiver.*] Give me the Headquarters of the Military District. ...

KATYA: Don't, uncle!

MUKOVNIN: Hello. Give me comrade Redko, please. ... Mukovnin here. ... As to who I am, comrade, I can't tell you more than that – I used to be Quartermaster-General of the Sixth Army. ... Is that you, comrade Redko ... ? Good evening, Redko. This is Mukovnin speaking. How are you? I'm very sorry if I've interrupted your work. . . . This evening at No. 86 Nevsky Prospect my daughter Ludmila was arrested by armed men. I don't intend to pull strings with you, Redko – I know that it carries no weight with your organization – but I just want to report that it is essential for me to see my eldest daughter, Marya. The fact is, I haven't been well lately and I feel I must see Marya. We have sent her telegrams and express letters and I know that Katya has been to see you about it – but there has been no reply. . . . I wish to submit my request to be connected with her on a direct line. . . . I may add that I've been called to Moscow by General Brusilov[3] to discuss my return to the active list. . . . You say it was delivered to her . . . delivered on the eighth . . . ? Thank you very much indeed, Redko. [*Replaces receiver.*] All's well, they've found Marya, the telegram was handed over to her on the eighth. She'll be in Petersburg tomorrow, or the day after at the very latest. You must get Marya's room ready, Nefedovna – you must get up at the crack of dawn tomorrow and tidy it. . . . Katya's right – the room's in a mess. We've let everything go to pieces lately, there's dust everywhere. We must put on some loose covers. Have we any loose covers, Katya?

KATYA: Not for all the furniture, but there are some.

MUKOVNIN [*pacing about the room*]: We must put on loose covers at once. . . . It would please Marya to find the house as it was when she left it. After all, why not make it comfortable for her if we can. . . . And Katya is bored here . . . you never have any fun, Katya, you never go to the theatre, you don't keep up with life.

KATYA: When Marya comes back, then I'll go out again.

MUKOVNIN [*to* PHILIP]: I'm so sorry, what is your name?

PHILIP: Philip Andreyich.

MUKOVNIN: Why don't you sit down, Philip Andreyich . . . ? We haven't even thanked you for all your trouble. . . . We must offer something to Philip Andreyich. Nanny, have we something to give him? We keep open house, Philip Andreyich, what we have is simple enough but you're very welcome. You must meet my daughter Marya as soon as she arrives. . . .

KATYA: You must rest, Uncle Nikolai, you must go and lie down.

MUKOVNIN: All right, if you like I shan't worry about Ludmila for a moment longer. It's a lesson to her – a lesson for being childish, for playing with fire . . . the matter's closed. . . . [*Shudders, stops, falls into a chair.* KATYA *runs to him.*] It's all right, Katya, don't worry. . . .

KATYA: What is it?

MUKOVNIN: Nothing – my heart. . . .

[KATYA *and* GOLITSYN *support him and lead him away.*]

PHILIP: He doesn't look too good to me.

NEFEDOVNA [*laying a place at the table*]: Were you there when they took our young lady away?

PHILIP: Yes, I was there.

NEFEDOVNA: Did she put up a fight?

PHILIP: She fought at first, then she went quietly.

NEFEDOVNA: I can give you a potato and there's some cranberry jelly.

PHILIP: Would you believe it, grandma, when that trouble started at our place they had made a whole tub full of meat balls – one moment there they were, next moment they were gone.

NEFEDOVNA [*putting a potato in front of* PHILIP]: Did you get your face burned in the war?

PHILIP: I got my face burned before I joined up. Happened a long time ago

NEFEDOVNA: Is there going to be war? What are your people saying?

PHILIP [*eating*]: There'll be war, grandma, in August.

NEFEDOVNA: What, with the Poles?

PHILIP: That's right, with the Poles.

NEFEDOVNA: Haven't we given them everything they want already?

PHILIP: The Poles want to have a state that stretches from one sea to the other, grandma. Like it was in the olden days, that's what they want now.

NEFEDOVNA: Ah, the fools.

[*Enter* KATYA.]

KATYA: The general is very ill. We must get a doctor.

PHILIP: You won't get a doctor to come at this hour, miss.

KATYA: He's dying, Nanny, his nose has turned blue.... You can see even now how he'll look when he's dead....

PHILIP: Right now, miss, every doctor's door is bolted and barred, they wouldn't come out at night even if you took a gun to 'em.

KATYA: Then we must go to the druggist for oxygen....

PHILIP: Does the general belong to a union?

KATYA: I don't know ... we don't seem to know about anything here.

PHILIP: If you're not in a union they won't give it to you.

[*A sharp ring at the door.* PHILIP *goes to open it and comes back.*]

PHILIP: It's ... it's ... Miss Marya....

KATYA: Marya?! [KATYA *runs forward stretching out her arms, bursts into tears, stops, covers her face with her hands, then removes them. Before her is a Red Army* SOLDIER *of about twenty, a long-legged boy dragging a sack behind him.* GOLITSYN *enters, stops in the doorway.*]

SOLDIER: Evening.

KATYA: Oh my God, Marya!

SOLDIER: Miss Mukovnin's sent you some things to eat.

KATYA: Where is she ... ? Is she with you?

SOLDIER: She's with the division, they're going into action. ... I've brought some of her things for you – some boots....

KATYA: Did she come with you?

SOLDIER: They're fighting out there, comrade – how could she come?

KATYA: We've sent her telegrams, letters....

SOLDIER: Send as many as you like – makes no difference. They're on the move day and night.

KATYA: Will you be seeing her?

SOLDIER: 'Course I shall. If you want me to tell her something ...

KATYA: Yes, please ... tell her this ... tell her that her father is dying and we don't expect to save him. Tell her that when he was dying he called for her.... Her sister Ludmila isn't living with us any longer and she's been arrested. Tell Marya that we wish her luck and happiness, that we want her never to think of all those days, those hours that she was away from us....

[*The* SOLDIER *looks round, steps back.* MUKOVNIN *staggers in from his room. His eyes are glazed, his hair tousled; he is smiling.*]

MUKOVNIN: There, Marya, you were away – and I haven't been ill, I've been in splendid shape all the time, darling.... [*Sees the* SOLDIER.] Who's that? [*Repeating it more loudly*] Who's that ... ? Who's that? [*Falls.*]

NEFEDOVNA [*falls on her knees beside* MUKOVNIN]: Nicky, my Nicky ... are you going? Couldn't you wait for your old nanny?

[*The old man groans; convulsion; dies.*]

SCENE EIGHT

The MUKOVNINS' *flat, empty. Midday, brilliant sunshine streams in. Through windows are seen sunlit columns of the Hermitage, a corner of the Winter Palace. Upstage* ANDREI *and his mate* KUZMA, *a fat-faced boy, are polishing the parquet floor.* AGASHA *shouts through the window.*

AGASHA: Nyushka! Don't let that kid get himself dirty on the wall, damn you! Where are your eyes, in your backside? You've grown up as tall as a house but it hasn't given you any more sense. Tikhon, hey, Tikhon, you've left the shed open! Shut the shed! . . . Good day, Yegorovna. Can you let me have a pinch of salt until the first of the month? I'll have me coupons after the first and I'll let you have it back. The girl'll come round, then, you can give it to her in a jar. Hey, Tikhon, have you been round to the Novoseltsevs? When are they getting out?

TIKHON'S VOICE: They say they've got nowhere to go to.

AGASHA: They knew how to lord it once, so it won't hurt them to learn how to clear out now. Tell them they've got till Sunday and after that we won't mess about waiting any more, you tell them that. Look out, Nyushka, damn you, the kid's stuffing earth up his nose. Take him upstairs, go on, and then you can clean them windows. [*To floor-polisher*] How are you getting on, then?

ANDREI: Not so bad.

AGASHA: Not so good either, are you? What about them corners?

ANDREI: What corners?

AGASHA: The four of 'em. And you've made the floor all red. It's not supposed to be red. You've done it the wrong colour.

ANDREI: You can't get the materials nowadays, lady.

AGASHA: My eye! You'd do it all right if the money was there, wouldn't you?

ANDREI: Well, if you really want to know, missus, you wouldn't ask your worst enemy to clean your floors after this here revolution. With the revolution going on the dirt on the floors got three inches thick. You can't get it off, not with a plane, you can't. I ought to get a medal for cleaning floors after the revolution, and you're carrying on....

[*Enter from upstage* KATYA *in mourning and* SUSHKIN.]

SUSHKIN: The only thing I'm really keen on buying is furniture, I just can't resist antiques, I'm mad about antiques. But I tell you, Miss Felsen, buying anything big these days is just like tying a millstone round your neck. You buy a thing one day and the next day, before you know where you are, you're stuck with it.

KATYA: You're forgetting, Mr Sushkin, that everything here is the best. The Stroganovs had it all brought from Paris a hundred years ago.

SUSHKIN: That's why I'm giving you a thousand million roubles for it.

KATYA: What's a thousand million worth today in terms of bread?

SUSHKIN: Yes, but you've got to think of it in terms of the risk I run in buying it. To be stuck with a load of heavy stuff today ... They'll be after me. ... [*Changes tone of voice*] I've got some fellows waiting downstairs. ... [*Shouts down*] You can come up now, lads, and bring the ropes with you!

AGASHA [*coming forward*]: What's going on here, then?

SUSHKIN: I don't think I've had the pleasure....

KATYA: This is our house-superintendent.

AGASHA: Caretaker to you.

SUSHKIN: Pleased to meet you. Well, now, this is what we'll do. You help us to shift the furniture out, and we'll see you're all right.

AGASHA: Sorry, mister.
SUSHKIN: What do you mean, sorry?
AGASHA: Some people from the basement are being moved in here....
SUSHKIN: Well, of course, that's very interesting, but...
AGASHA: What are they going to do for furniture?
SUSHKIN: I'm afraid I don't know, and to be frank I don't care.
KATYA: Agasha, Marya said I should sell it....
SUSHKIN [*to* AGASHA]: Excuse me for asking, ma'am, but is it your furniture?
AGASHA: No, but it's not yours either.
SUSHKIN: In the first place that's neither here nor there, and in the second place I can tell you you're doing yourself no good.
AGASHA: You bring your permit and I'll let you have the furniture.
KATYA: The furniture belongs to Marya, you know perfectly well, Agasha.
AGASHA: I've forgotten everything I knew, miss. I'm learning it different now.
SUSHKIN: You're going to come a cropper if you don't watch it!
AGASHA: You come it with me and I'll throw you out.
KATYA: Let us leave, Mr Sushkin.
SUSHKIN: You're too big for your boots, woman.
AGASHA: You bring your permit and I'll let you take the stuff.
SUSHKIN: We'll discuss this elsewhere.
AGASHA: At the police station, for all I care.
KATYA: Let's go.
SUSHKIN: I'll go now, but I'll be back, and with others.
AGASHA: It's not right what you're doing, miss.

[*Exeunt.* ANDREI *and* KUZMA *finish their work and gather their tools.*]

KUZMA: She gave him what for.

ANDREI: No mucking about with her all right.

KUZMA: Was she here in the general's time, then?

ANDREI: Yes, but she used to keep in her place. Never poked her nose out.

KUZMA: I suppose the general was a bit of a tartar.

ANDREI: Tartar? No, not a bit. You'd come up and see him and he'd shake your hand and say good day to you. We liked him.

KUZMA: How could ordinary working people like a general?

ANDREI: I suppose we were just soft. But he never did no more than his fair share of harm. Chopped his own firewood, he did.

KUZMA: Was he old?

ANDREI: Not that old.

KUZMA: Still he died. . . .

ANDREI: You don't have to be old to die. Just when your time's up. And his was.

[*Enter* AGASHA, *a worker* SAFONOV, *who is a bony, morose youth, and his pregnant wife,* YELENA, *tall with a small bright face, young, not more than twenty, in last days of pregnancy. All are loaded with household goods, stools, mattresses, a primus.*]

ANDREI: Hang on a minute, I'll spread something out. . . .

AGASHA: Come in, Safonov, it's all right. This is where you're going to live from now on.

YELENA: Perhaps we should go somewhere more ordinary. . . .

AGASHA: Try something better for a change.

ANDREI: You'll soon get used to it, easy as anything.

AGASHA: The kitchen's over there on the left, there's the bathroom – you can wash. Come on, my lad, let's get the rest of the things. Yelena, you just sit quietly and don't walk around. You never know, you might lose your baby.

[*Exeunt* AGASHA *and* SAFONOV. ANDREI *collects his things – brushes, buckets.* YELENA *sits on stool.*]

ANDREI: Well, good luck in your new home.

YELENA: I don't know, it seems so big. . . .

ANDREI: When are you due?

YELENA: I'm going in tomorrow.

ANDREI: Nothing to it. You're going to the palace on the Moika, I s'pose?

YELENA: Yes, on the Moika.

ANDREI: One of the tsarinas built it for a shepherd. Now they call it the 'Mother and Child' and the women go there to have their babies. It's all organized, nothing to it.

YELENA: Well, it's tomorrow for me. You know, one minute I'm scared, the next I don't care.

ANDREI: You've got nothing to be scared of. Mind you, it's not like having a cold. It'll shake your innards up a bit for you. But you'll be through it in no time and then you won't recognize yourself.

YELENA: Trouble is I'm a bit narrow down there.

ANDREI: Don't worry, you'll widen up when they ask you to. . . . You want to see some women – all delicate, little hands and little feet, a posh hair-do, and they go and push out a hulking great brat with fists like hams. . . . [*Puts bag on shoulder.*] What do you want, a boy or a girl?

YELENA: I don't mind.

ANDREI: Yes, it doesn't matter. I reckon the kids being born today are going to have a marvellous life when they grow up. Well, I mean, it stands to reason, don't it? [*Picks up tools.*] Come on, Kuzma. [*To* YELENA] Don't forget, there's nothing to it. You'll get the hang of it. Come on, soldier boy.

[*Exeunt floor-polishers.* YELENA *opens windows, sun and street noises stream in. She sticks out her belly and carefully moves along the walls, touches them, peeps into adjoining rooms, switches on chandelier and switches it off. Enter* NYUSHA, *an enormous ruddy girl, carrying pail and cloths to clean windows. She stands on sill, tucks skirt above her knees, sun's rays stream on to her. She stands out against the spring sky like a statue bearing an arch.*]

YELENA: Will you come to our moving-in party, Nyusha?
NYUSHA [*bass voice*]: I will if I'm asked. What will there be?
YELENA: There won't be much, just what there is. . . .
NYUSHA: I wouldn't mind a drop of sweet red wine. [*Piercingly and suddenly breaks out singing*]

A cossack galloped across the steppes,
Across the Manchurian plain,
He galloped through the green orchard
With a glittering ring on his finger.
His girl had given him the ring
When he went off to fight in the war,
She gave it and said:
'I'll be yours in a year.'
But a year has gone by. . . .

NOTES ON *MARYA*

NAMES: Russian names are a problem for the translator, especially in plays, in which so much has to be conveyed by the spoken word. The question has two aspects – form and usage.

As to form, the difficulty is either in names that are hard to pronounce and thus act as a continual stumbling-block or names that have unfortunate phonetic associations when transliterated. In this play an example of the first type is the character whom we have renamed 'Nikitin'. His name in the original is 'Yevstigneyich'; we felt this to be awkward enough to English eyes to warrant substitution by a simpler but quite normal Russian surname. Of the second type is one of the main characters, whom we have called 'Bernstein'. It is a recognizably Jewish name and is so in both English and Russian; this is in keeping with Babel's intention when he gave this personage a Jewish name common enough in Russia but which is unsuitable for use in an English-language context. Transliterated it is 'Dymshits'.

The question of usage is more complex. A common hindrance for most non-Russian readers or audiences is the Russian form of address known as 'name and patronymic', e.g. 'Ivan Ivanovich' (John, Son-of-John) for a man or 'Katerina Vyacheslavovna' (Katherine, Daughter-of-Vyacheslav) for a woman. In Russia this is widely used and is extremely convenient. It is neither servile nor over-familiar, is suited to near or close acquaintance and perfectly bridges the gap between persons of different age, class, status or sex. In translation, however, it often appears clumsy and confusing and we have avoided it for that reason, replacing it with forms of address more familiar to English-speaking readers. Similar considerations apply to the diminutive forms of Russian names, which are more numerous and expressive than their English equivalents, but which, if they proliferate in a translated work, can also confuse. While regretfully sacrificing some degrees of nuance and charm, we have (except in two cases: 'Katya Felsen', where the diminutive form is used exclusively instead of the full form 'Katerina', and 'Philip Andreyich', where the author supplies no surname) avoided the use of patronymics and diminutives of Christian names, using only first name and surname or the two together. For the same reasons we have not used the feminine inflexion of surnames.

NOTES ON *MARYA*

SCENE TWO

1. *playing a popular tune*: The tune referred to is a scurrilous popular tune of the period known as 'The Apple' and sung in various forms by both Reds and Whites. The translators have found it impossible to reproduce a snatch of this song satisfactorily.

SCENE FIVE

1. . . . *if only the Poles don't start giving trouble again*: This and subsequent references to warfare against Poland places the action of the play in the early months of 1920, when the fledgeling state of Poland was fighting the equally new Soviet government to establish the eastern frontiers of Poland; military success eventually gained the Poles a considerably larger slice of territory than that accorded to them under the Versailles settlement. Babel himself took part in this bitterly fought campaign as a war correspondent with Budyonny's First Cavalry Army.

SCENE SEVEN

1. *Was it the Cheka?*: 'Cheka' = the secret police. This abbreviation is made from the initial letters, *ЧК*, of the first of the many names given to the secret police under the Soviet regime. Phonetically transliterated it is: '*Ch*rezvychainaya *K*ommissiya', meaning 'Extraordinary Commission'; even this is an abbreviation of its full title, which was 'Extraordinary Commission for Combating Counter-Revolution and Speculation'. The Cheka was created by Felix Dzerzhinsky in December 1917 as the security arm of the Bolshevik party. In 1922, when from being a party organization it became an organ of the state, it was renamed with the notoriously sinister initials O.G.P.U., which stood for 'Central State Political Administration'.
2. *I must go to Smolny*: 'Smolny' refers to the Smolny Institute in Leningrad which was founded as a convent and orphanage by the Empress Elizabeth in 1748. Catherine the Great converted it into a school for daughters of the nobility. During the October revolution in 1917, Lenin took over the buildings as his emergency headquarters and Smolny continued as Bolshevik headquarters for some time after their seizure of power.
3. *General Brusilov*: General A. A. Brusilov, born 1853. One of the most able Russian commanders of the First World War, he was responsible for the 'Brusilov breakthrough' in Galicia of July 1916. He remained in service after the October revolution and was appointed chairman

of the supreme command council during the Polish campaign of 1920–21, when he persuaded the Bolshevik government of the need to recall to service former tsarist regular officers who would promise loyalty to the Soviets.

THE DRAGON

Yevgeny Schwartz

A fairy tale in three acts translated by
Max Hayward and Harold Shukman with an
introduction by Harold Shukman

INTRODUCTION TO *THE DRAGON*

YEVGENY LVOVICH SCHWARTZ was born in 1897. His background was cultivated and middle-class, his father being a doctor of apparently radical leanings, his mother an amateur actress. His first career was on the stage, in the provinces, and then, in the early 1920s, in Petrograd, home of innumerable actors' studios and experimental 'workshops'. He was the favourite impromptu entertainer at the House of Arts, which, thanks to the efforts of Maxim Gorky, provided a roof and a meeting-place for many writers. Among them were Zamyatin, Mandelshtam and Zoshchenko.

In 1925 Schwartz left the stage to become a professional writer of children's stories and plays, in which he combined some earlier journalistic experience with his talents as a wit and raconteur. He also collaborated with his friend, Samuel Marshak, in editing children's magazines published by the State Children's Publishing House. Throughout his life he continued to write plays and stories for children, of which a collection appeared in 1959. He also wrote a number of comedy film scripts, one in conjunction with Zoshchenko. His best-known film was also his last work, *Don Quixote*, which won acclaim in the West in 1959, a year after his death.

Two themes run throughout Schwartz's work. In one he elevates love to the most powerful and most magical expression of life. This theme dominates those plays which kept his name in the Soviet repertory throughout the period when his other theme – to say nothing of his close association with the other 'cosmopolitan' (i.e. Jewish) writers and producers of Leningrad – might have earned him more serious consequences than criticism in journals. This love-theme is characterized by a series of heroes, some invented, others drawn from the stock of Hans Andersen and tradition, who are chiefly realistic figures set in a fairy-tale situation. Schwartz's treatment of this theme, although original, does not mark him out particularly as a commentator on human affairs, and it was not for these works that he was ultimately recognized as a controversial and important playwright.

He first devoted himself to his second theme in 1933, when he wrote *The Naked King*. Based on three Hans Andersen tales, *The Swineherd*, *The Princess and the Pea*, and *The Emperor's New Clothes*, its ostensible purpose was to satirize German Nazism, and many direct references in it indicate that Schwartz's attention was in fact focused on this particular form of totalitarianism. Nikolai Akimov, who was to produce all of Schwartz's plays, planned an elaborate and ambitious production at the Leningrad Comedy Theatre, but it was never mounted, for the official reason that it treated a crucial question of 'world-historical importance' as a joke. Schwartz's 'joke' in this and later work – which suffered similar treatment – was to expose the charlatan under the skin of the despot; it is the theme of his most important later plays, *The Shadow* (1940) and *The Dragon* (1943). His tyrants, however great their physical or political power, are all shown to be essentially weak and vulnerable. There is an example even in the non-political setting of one of his children's stories, *Red Riding-Hood*, where, in the manner of Kenneth Grahame's *Reluctant Dragon*, the big bad wolf turns out to be a lonely and scared creature, acting the part created for him by human fantasy but longing for a quiet life.

In *The Shadow* Schwartz develops the idea that people are prone to worship these phony despots, these shadows of real men, and it is only the intervention of his power-of-love theme, characterized by a girl in love with the doomed hero, that saves the situation and leads to the triumph of the true over the false. (In Hans Andersen's original tale the Shadow triumphs and the hero is shot.)

The Dragon is Schwartz's most outspoken and most hilarious debunking of political tyranny. His earlier despots – kings, ministers, and imitations of men – are replaced by the traditional nightmare creature of legend, the dragon, who can also assume human and 'humane' form, and is succeeded by the all too humanly villainous Mayor. The play was written in 1943 and, like *The Naked King* and *The Shadow*, it was promoted as an anti-fascist, anti-war 'pamphlet'. It was, none the less, attacked for its allegedly pessimistic note, its critics detecting in it the message that it was not worth fighting tyranny because one tyrant was always replaced by another equally despicable one. It was also attacked as anti-democratic, since Schwartz depicts the townsfolk as cowed, spiritually crippled opportunists who rationalize their plight by claiming that as long as they have one Dragon no other will dare to touch them. This idea, hinted at frequently in Schwartz's other works, suggests that his message is that people *want* a Dragon, or at any rate make the best of the dragons they get. The Dragon's successor, the hare-brained, scheming, ruthless and corrupt Mayor, derives his fantastic power from the same source as the Dragon's – the people's *desire* to keep a tyrant – and, as the hero, Lancelot, says at the end of the play, it is necessary to kill the Dragon in each individual before the town will be safe from tyranny. However firm Schwartz's conviction may have been that good, embodied in Lancelot, must triumph over evil, the fact remains that the dominant key of the play, and all the good lines, belong to his evil characters, and what he mainly exposes is the fatal relationship between people and their leaders.

The play had only one performance each in Leningrad and Moscow in 1944, and was then withdrawn. It was revived in 1962, at the height of the new wave of Schwartz's posthumous popularity, but again, in spite of favourable notices, was taken off and has not appeared in the Soviet repertory since. This also applies to *The Naked King* and *The Shadow*.

On the whole, both during his life and since, Schwartz has been spared much direct attack, and instead his controversial appeal has been submerged by the convenient means of small printings of his works, and by removing his 'inadequate' plays from the repertory, leaving his fairy tales for adults and stories for children to preach their seemingly innocuous message of love and kindness.

The present translation is from his collected plays, published in 1960.

HAROLD SHUKMAN

CHARACTERS

THE DRAGON
LANCELOT, a knight errant
CHARLEMAGNE, Keeper of Public Records
ELSA, his daughter
THE MAYOR
HENRY, his son, private secretary to the Dragon
CAT
FIRST and SECOND WEAVERS
HAT MAKER
MUSICAL-INSTRUMENT MAKER
BLACKSMITH
FIRST, SECOND, and THIRD GIRL-FRIENDS of Elsa
SENTRY
GARDENER
FIRST MAN
SECOND MAN
FIRST WOMAN
SECOND WOMAN
BOY
PEDLAR
GAOLER
FOOTMEN, GUARDS, TOWNSPEOPLE

ACT ONE

Large comfortable kitchen, very clean, a large fireplace at the back. Stone floor. The CAT *sleeps on a chair in front of fire.*

LANCELOT [*enters, looks round and calls out*]: Anybody at home? Hey there! Not a soul. The house is empty. The gate's open and so are the doors and windows. Good thing I'm an honest man, or my fingers would be itching and I'd be looking round for something worth stealing and then clear off as fast as I could go. But all I want is a rest. [*Sits.*] I'll wait. Cat! Will the people of the house be back soon? Eh? Aren't you saying anything?

CAT: No, I'm not.

LANCELOT: And why, if I might ask?

CAT: When it's nice and cosy it's better to sleep quietly and keep your mouth shut, my dear friend.

LANCELOT: Yes, but where are the people of the house?

CAT: They're out, and a very good job too.

LANCELOT: Don't you like them?

CAT: I love them with every hair of my fur, and with my paws and with my whiskers, but they're in terrible trouble. I only get peace of mind when they go out.

LANCELOT: I see. So they're in trouble. What kind of trouble? You're not saying anything?

CAT: No, I'm not.

LANCELOT: Why?

CAT: When it's nice and cosy it's better to sleep quietly and keep your mouth shut and not get mixed up in tomorrow's troubles. Miao.

LANCELOT: You frighten me, Cat. It's so cosy here in this kitchen, the fire's burning so nicely. I just can't believe that this nice roomy house is in for trouble. Come on, Cat, now tell me what's happened.

CAT: Let me be, stranger.

LANCELOT: Now listen, Cat. You don't know me. I'm as light as a feather and I get blown all over the place. I'm very good at minding other people's business. And I've been hurt a lot in the process. Nineteen superficial injuries, five serious injuries, and three near fatal. But I'm still alive, because I'm as light as a feather and as stubborn as a mule. So come on, Cat, tell me what happened. Suppose I can save your people. It wouldn't be the first time I've done that sort of thing. Come on, let's have it now. What's your name?

CAT: Minnie.

LANCELOT: I thought you were a tom.

CAT: Yes, I am a tom, but sometimes people are so unobservant. My people still can't get over the fact that I haven't had kittens yet. They say: what are you waiting for, Minnie? The poor dears. I'm not saying any more.

LANCELOT: But tell me who they are at least.

CAT: He's Charlemagne the Keeper of Public Records and she is his only daughter Elsa; she's a sweet, kind, quiet girl and she has such gentle little paws.

LANCELOT: Which one of them is in trouble?

CAT: Actually, it's her, but that means we're all in it.

LANCELOT: But what sort of trouble is it?

CAT: Miao. [*Sighs.*] We've had a dragon in the town for four hundred years.

LANCELOT: A dragon? Splendid!

CAT: He takes tribute from the town. He picks himself a new girl every year. And we hand her over without so much as a miao. And then he takes her off to his cave and that's the end of her. People say they die of sheer disgust. [*Hisses*] Get away. Hsss.

LANCELOT: Who are you saying that to?

CAT: To the Dragon. He's picked our Elsa. The filthy reptile. [*Hisses.*]

LANCELOT: How many heads has he got?

CAT: Three.

LANCELOT: Quite a lot. And how many feet?

CAT: Four.

LANCELOT: Oh well, that's not so bad then. With claws?

CAT: Five on each. And they're all about the size of a stag's horn.

LANCELOT: Is that so? And are they sharp?

CAT: Sharp as knives.

LANCELOT: I see. And does he breathe fire?

CAT: Yes.

LANCELOT: The real thing?

CAT: He burns down whole forests.

LANCELOT: I see. Has he got scales?

CAT: Yes, he has.

LANCELOT: And they're pretty thick I suppose?

CAT: They're pretty good.

LANCELOT: How good?

CAT: You couldn't cut them with a diamond.

LANCELOT: I see. I get the idea. How big is he?

CAT: As big as a church.

LANCELOT: I think I've got the picture. Thank you, Cat.

CAT: Are you going to fight him?

LANCELOT: We'll see about that.

CAT: Oh, do challenge him, I beg you. He'll kill you, of course. But at least until then we'll be able to lie here in front of the fire and dream what it would be like if by some fluke or miracle, in one way or another, by hook or by crook, possibly, somehow, you might kill him instead.

LANCELOT: Thank you, Cat.

CAT: Stand up.

LANCELOT: What's the matter?

CAT: Here they come.

LANCELOT: I only hope she takes my fancy. Oh, I do hope I like her. That's always such a great help. [*Looks through window.*] She's nice! She's really wonderful, Cat. But what's all this, why is she smiling? She doesn't seem at all worried. And her father's smiling all over his face as well. Have you been trying to fool me, Cat?

CAT: No. The saddest thing about the whole business is that they go on smiling. Shh! Good evening! It's supper-time, dear master and mistress.

[*Enter* ELSA *and* CHARLEMAGNE.]

LANCELOT: Good evening to you, my good sir, and to you, beautiful young lady.

CHARLEMAGNE: Good evening, young man.

LANCELOT: Your house looked so inviting, the gate was open, and I could see the fire in the kitchen, so I came in without being asked. Please forgive me.

CHARLEMAGNE: Please don't apologize. We keep open house.

ELSA: Do sit down, please. Give me your hat, I'll hang it up. I'll just lay the table. . . . Is something wrong?

LANCELOT: No, no.

ELSA: It looked as though you . . . were frightened of me.

LANCELOT: No, not at all . . . it was just that . . .

CHARLEMAGNE: Do sit down, my friend. I like visitors. I suppose it's because I've spent my whole life in this town and never been anywhere. Where have you come from?

LANCELOT: From the south.

CHARLEMAGNE: Did you have an exciting journey?

LANCELOT: A bit too exciting for me.

ELSA: You must be tired. Do please sit down.

LANCELOT [*sitting*]: Thank you.

CHARLEMAGNE: You can have a real good rest here. It's a nice quiet town. Nothing ever happens here.

LANCELOT: Never?

CHARLEMAGNE: Never. Well, it's true last week we had a bit

of a high wind and it nearly blew the roof off a house. But you wouldn't call that a great event.

ELSA: Supper's ready. Do come and eat. What's wrong?

LANCELOT: Forgive me but ... Did you say that this is a *nice quiet* town?

ELSA: Well, so it is.

LANCELOT: But ... er ... what about this ... Dragon?

CHARLEMAGNE: Oh, that. ... But you know we're really quite used to him. He's been living here four hundred years now.

LANCELOT: But ... I've heard that your ... daughter ...

ELSA: But, sir ...

LANCELOT: Call me Lancelot.

ELSA: Sir Lancelot, excuse me, please don't take offence, but I beg you, not a word about that.

LANCELOT: Why?

ELSA: Because there's nothing to be done about it.

LANCELOT: Do you really think so?

CHARLEMAGNE: No, there's nothing to be done about it. We've just been walking in the woods and we've talked it all over. When the Dragon takes her away tomorrow I shall die as well.

ELSA: Don't let's talk about it, father.

CHARLEMAGNE: Very well, very well.

LANCELOT: Let me just ask one more question. Has nobody ever tried to fight him?

CHARLEMAGNE: Not in the last two hundred years. Before that people were always taking him on, but he always killed them. He's a brilliant strategist and a great tactician. He always attacks suddenly, he bombards his opponent with rocks from above, then he swoops down straight at the head of his opponent's horse and breathes fire on it, so that the poor beast is completely demoralized. Then he tears the rider to bits with his claws. So at last people just gave up trying. ...

LANCELOT: Hasn't the whole town ever tried it?

CHARLEMAGNE: Oh yes.

LANCELOT: Well, what happened?

CHARLEMAGNE: He burnt down the suburbs and drove half the population mad with poisonous fumes. He really knows his business.

ELSA: Won't you have a little more butter?

LANCELOT: Thank you very much. I have to get my strength up. Do forgive me, please, for all these questions, but you say that no one ever even tries to take him on now? So he's really got very nasty?

CHARLEMAGNE: Oh no, not a bit. He's very decent, really.

LANCELOT: Decent?

CHARLEMAGNE: Yes, really. There was once an outbreak of cholera here and the town medical officer asked him to breathe fire on the lake and boil the water. The whole town drank boiled water and we were saved from an epidemic.

LANCELOT: Was that a long time ago?

CHARLEMAGNE: Not at all. Only eighty-two years. But good deeds aren't forgotten.

LANCELOT: What are his other good deeds?

CHARLEMAGNE: He got rid of the gypsies for us.

LANCELOT: But gypsies are very nice people.

CHARLEMAGNE: What a dreadful thing to say! It's true I've never seen a gypsy in my life. But we had lessons on them in school and they're really frightful people.

LANCELOT: But why?

CHARLEMAGNE: They're vagrants by nature and by blood. They have no sense of law and order, otherwise they'd settle down somewhere and not wander about all over the place. Their songs are decadent and their ideas are disruptive. They steal children. They get in everywhere. We're completely rid of them now. But only a hundred years back anybody with dark hair had to prove he had no gypsy blood.

LANCELOT: Where did you get all this stuff about the gypsies?

CHARLEMAGNE: Our Dragon told us. The gypsies actually had the nerve to oppose him in the first years of his rule.

LANCELOT: What wonderful people. They never knuckle under.

CHARLEMAGNE: Please, you really mustn't talk like that.

LANCELOT: What does he eat, your Dragon?

CHARLEMAGNE: The town gives him a thousand cows, two thousand sheep, five thousand chickens and two hundred-weight of salt per month. In summer and autumn we supplement this with the total produce of ten vegetable gardens in lettuce, asparagus, and cauliflower.

LANCELOT: That doesn't leave much over for you.

CHARLEMAGNE: We're not complaining. Why on earth should we? So long as he's here no other dragon would dare to touch us.

LANCELOT: But as far as I know all the other dragons were killed off ages ago.

CHARLEMAGNE: But suppose you're wrong? I assure you that the only way to be free of dragons is to have one of your own. Let's drop the subject, please. Why don't you tell us something about your travels.

LANCELOT: Very well. Do you know what a complaints book is?

ELSA: No.

LANCELOT: Well, let me tell you. About five years' walk from here in the Black Mountains there's a huge cave. In this cave there is a writing book, and it's half full already. Nobody ever touches it and yet every day a new page is filled in. Who do you think does the writing? The world! The mountains, the grass, the rocks, the trees and rivers see what people are doing. They see the crimes of all criminals, the miseries of everybody who suffers for nothing. The complaints of mankind travel from branch to branch, from raindrop to raindrop, from cloud to cloud, and come to that cave in the Black Mountains, and this is how the book is written. If there were no such book in the world the trees would wither away from the burden of all this misery, and the water would turn brackish. Who do you think this book is meant for? It's for me.

ELSA: For you?

LANCELOT: For me and a few others. We keep our eyes open and we're everywhere. We heard about this book and we took the trouble to find it. Once you've seen that book you can never rest again. The complaints in that book! They cannot be left unanswered. And that's what we do.

ELSA: But how?

LANCELOT: We look into other people's affairs. We help people who need help and we destroy people who must be destroyed. Shall I help you?

ELSA: How?

CHARLEMAGNE: How can you help us?

CAT: Miao.

LANCELOT: I've been fatally wounded three times, and each time by people I was saving against their own will. So even if you don't ask me, I'm going to challenge the Dragon to fight. Do you hear that, Elsa?

ELSA: No, don't! He'll kill you, and that would poison the last hours of my life.

CAT: Miao.

LANCELOT: I am going to challenge the Dragon.

[*Noises off: increasing whistle, din, howl, roar. Windows rattle. Sudden glow of flame through window.*]

CAT: Talk of the devil!

[*Howling and whistling stop abruptly. Loud knock at the door.*]

CHARLEMAGNE: Come in.

[*Enter a richly dressed* FOOTMAN.]

FOOTMAN: My lord Dragon wishes to see you.

CHARLEMAGNE: Do show him in.

[FOOTMAN *flings open the door. Pause. Enter slowly a middle-aged, well-built, young-looking, fair-haired* MAN, *of military bearing. He has cropped hair. He smiles all over his face. Altogether his manner, though somewhat bluff, is not without a certain charm. He is rather deaf.*]

MAN: Well now, my friends! Hullo, Elsa, my sweet. You have a visitor I see. And who is it?

CHARLEMAGNE: He's a traveller, he's just passing through here.

MAN: What's that? Talk up, man. Report clearly, like a soldier.

CHARLEMAGNE: He's a traveller!

MAN: Not a gypsy?

CHARLEMAGNE: Goodness gracious, no! He's a very nice man.

MAN: What's that?

CHARLEMAGNE: A *nice* man.

MAN: I see. [*To* LANCELOT] I say, my man, why don't you look at me? What are you staring at the door for?

LANCELOT: I'm waiting for the Dragon to come in.

MAN [*laughs*]: I am the Dragon.

LANCELOT: You? But they told me you were huge and had three heads and claws!

DRAGON: Oh, but I'm off duty today. I'm in mufti.

CHARLEMAGNE: You see, Sir Dragon has been living among people so long that he sometimes turns into a man himself and drops by just like an old friend.

DRAGON: Yes, we're friends right enough, my good Charlemagne. I'm more than just a friend to you all. I'm your childhood friend. What's more, I'm the childhood friend of your fathers, your grandfathers, and your great-grandfathers. I remember your great-great-grandfather when he was running round in short pants. Brings a tear to me eyes, dammit. [*Laughs.*] Look at our visitor there with his eyes popping out of his head. Didn't think I was that sentimental, did you?

Well, did you? He's stuck for words, the bounder. There, there, don't worry. [*Laughs.*] Elsa!

ELSA: Yes, Sir Dragon.

DRAGON: Give me your mitt.

[ELSA *gives her hand to the* DRAGON.]

DRAGON: Ah, you little mischief, you little scamp. What a warm little paw you have. Stick your chin up now! Smile! That's it. [*To* LANCELOT] What do you say to that, stranger, eh?

LANCELOT: I'm just looking.

DRAGON: Good man! A smart reply. Go on looking. No fuss here, just like the army. We take things as they come. Eat something!

LANCELOT: I've eaten, thanks.

DRAGON: Well, have some more. What brings you here?

LANCELOT: Business.

DRAGON: What's that?

LANCELOT: Business.

DRAGON: What business? Come on, out with it! Eh? Maybe I can help you. What have you come here for?

LANCELOT: To kill you.

DRAGON: What's that again? I can't hear you.

ELSA: No, no, he's only joking. Shall I give you my hand again, Sir Dragon?

DRAGON: What is all this?

LANCELOT: I challenge you to battle. Do you hear, Dragon?

[DRAGON *says nothing and goes purple in the face.*]

LANCELOT: I challenge you to battle. That's the third time. Do you hear?

[*There is a terrible, deafening, triple roar. Despite the power of this roar which makes the walls shake, it is not unmusical. There is nothing human about it. It is the* DRAGON *roaring, with clenched fists and stamping his feet.*]

DRAGON [*suddenly stops roaring and says quietly*]: Idiot. Well, what have you got to say now? Scared?

LANCELOT: No.

DRAGON: No?

LANCELOT: No.

DRAGON: Very well then. [*Slight movement of his shoulders and is suddenly transformed in the most startling way. A new head appears. There is no sign of the old one. He now appears as an earnest-looking staid man with greying fair hair, high forehead, and narrow face.*]

CAT: There's nothing to it, Lancelot. He's got three of them, and he changes them when he feels like it.

DRAGON [*his voice is as changed as his face. It is soft and clipped*]: Your name Lancelot?

LANCELOT: Yes.

DRAGON: Any relative of the well-known knight errant of that name?

LANCELOT: A distant relative.

DRAGON: Challenge accepted. Knights errant and gypsies, it's the same thing. You have to be got rid of.

LANCELOT: You won't find it so easy.

DRAGON: I've already got rid of eight hundred and nine knights, nine hundred and five persons, rank unknown, one drunken old man, two lunatics, two women – the mother and aunt of two girls I'd selected as tribute – and one boy of twelve – a brother of one of the girls. On top of that, I've destroyed six armies and five unruly mobs. Wouldn't you like to sit down?

[LANCELOT *sits down.*]

LANCELOT: Thank you.

DRAGON: Do you smoke? Do carry on, please don't worry about me.

LANCELOT: Thank you. [*Takes out his pipe and fills it slowly.*]

DRAGON: Do you know what happened the day I was born?

LANCELOT: A disaster.

DRAGON: A terrible battle. Attila himself was defeated on that day. You can imagine what slaughter that means. The earth was drenched in blood, great black mushrooms had grown up under the trees. Graveyard mushrooms they called them. And I crawled out of the ground after them. I am the child of war. I *am* war. The blood of dead Huns flows in my veins, and it's cold blood. In battle I am cool, calm, and my aim is deadly. [*At the word 'deadly' the* DRAGON *makes a slight movement with his hand. A dry crackle is heard, and a flame shoots from his forefinger. It lights Lancelot's pipe.*]

LANCELOT: Thank you. [*He draws his pipe with pleasure.*]

DRAGON: You're against me, so you must be against war?

LANCELOT: Not at all. I've been fighting all my life.

DRAGON: You're a stranger. But we here came to understand each other a long time ago. The whole town will be horrified by this and they'll be glad at your death. There won't be much glory in it for you, you know.

LANCELOT: No.

DRAGON: So you're just as set on this as ever?

LANCELOT: Even more.

DRAGON: You're a worthy opponent.

LANCELOT: Thank you.

DRAGON: I shall take you seriously.

LANCELOT: Splendid.

DRAGON: Which means that I'm going to kill you straight away, here and now.

LANCELOT: But I'm unarmed.

DRAGON: Do you think I'm going to give you time to arm yourself? I told you I was going to take you seriously. I'm going to attack suddenly, right now.... Elsa, get a broom.

ELSA: What for?

DRAGON: I'm just about to incinerate this chap and you can sweep up the ash.

LANCELOT: Are you afraid of me?

DRAGON: I don't know what fear is.

LANCELOT: Then why are you in such a hurry? Give me till

tomorrow. I'll find some weapons and we'll meet on the battlefield.

DRAGON: But why?

LANCELOT: So the people won't think you're frightened.

DRAGON: They won't hear anything about it. These two will keep their mouths shut. You are about to die – bravely, quietly and without glory. [*He raises his hand.*]

CHARLEMAGNE: Stop!

DRAGON: What's the matter?

CHARLEMAGNE: You can't kill him.

DRAGON: What?

CHARLEMAGNE: Don't be angry with me, I beg you. I am utterly devoted to you, but I am also the Keeper of Records, you know.

DRAGON: What's that got to do with it?

CHARLEMAGNE: I have a document which you signed three hundred and eighty-two years ago. And it has never been annulled. It's not that I'm raising any objections, it's just that I'm reminding you. It's got your signature, 'Dragon'.

DRAGON: Well, so what?

CHARLEMAGNE: This is my daughter after all. And I want her to live a little longer. It's only natural.

DRAGON: Come to the point.

CHARLEMAGNE: I must protest, whatever happens. You are not allowed to kill him. Anyone who challenges you is safe till the day of battle – that's what you wrote under solemn oath. And it's the challenger, not you, who picks the day – that's what it says in the document. And it also says that the whole town must help the challenger and nobody will be punished. That's also on your solemn oath.

DRAGON: When did I sign that?

CHARLEMAGNE: Three hundred and eighty-two years ago.

DRAGON: Oh, but then I was only a silly, sentimental youth with no experience.

CHARLEMAGNE: But the document is still in force.

DRAGON: That's just one of those things. . . .

CHARLEMAGNE: But the document . . .

DRAGON: That's enough about documents. We're not children.

CHARLEMAGNE: But you signed it yourself. . . . I can go and fetch it.

DRAGON: Stay where you are!

CHARLEMAGNE: Here's a man who's going to try and save my daughter. What's wrong with loving your own child? And then, why shouldn't we show hospitality, what's wrong with that? So why are you looking at me in that awful way? [*Puts hand over his face.*]

ELSA: Father, father!

CHARLEMAGNE: I protest.

DRAGON: Very well, I'll wipe out the whole nest, this very moment.

LANCELOT: And the whole world will know you are a coward!

DRAGON: How will they know?

[*The* CAT *jumps through the window and hisses from outside.*]

CAT: I'll tell everything to everybody, you old lizard.

[*The* DRAGON *starts roaring again, and his roar is just as powerful, but this time one can clearly hear a hoarse groaning quality.*]

DRAGON [*suddenly stops roaring*]: Very well. We'll fight tomorrow as you ask. [*Exit quickly. Outside there is a howling raging din. Walls shake, lamps flicker, noise gradually dies.*]

CHARLEMAGNE: He's flown off. What have I done? What have I done? What a selfish old fool I am! But what else could I do? You're not angry with me, Elsa?

ELSA: No, of course not.

CHARLEMAGNE: I feel so weak all of a sudden. Excuse me, I must lie down. Don't bother to come with me. Stay with our guest. Entertain him, he's been so kind to us. Excuse me, I must go and lie down. [*Exit.*]

[*Pause.*]

ELSA: What did you want to go and start all this for? I don't hold it against you, but everything was all so clear and straightforward. It's not so bad to die young. You don't grow old like the rest.

LANCELOT: What a thing to say! Just think! Even the trees sigh when they're cut down.

ELSA: But I'm not complaining.

LANCELOT: But aren't you sorry for your father?

ELSA: But he'll die just when he wants to. That's real happiness.

LANCELOT: And you don't mind leaving all your friends?

ELSA: No. If it weren't for me, the Dragon would take one of them.

LANCELOT: What about the man you're supposed to marry?

ELSA: How do you know about that?

LANCELOT: I guessed. You won't be sorry about him?

ELSA: But, you know, the Dragon has made Henry his private secretary, just to make it easier for him.

LANCELOT: So that's how it is. Well, then of course it won't be so hard to leave him. But what about the town? Won't you be sorry to leave that?

ELSA: But I'm really doing all this for the town.

LANCELOT: And the town takes your sacrifice without turning a hair.

ELSA: Oh no! I shall die on Sunday, and right up to Tuesday the whole town will be in mourning. Nobody will eat meat for three whole days. And they'll have special buns with their tea called 'poor maids of honour' in memory of me.

LANCELOT: That's all?

ELSA: What more can they do?

LANCELOT: They could kill the Dragon.

ELSA: But that's impossible.

LANCELOT: The Dragon has warped your mind, so you don't see things as they really are any more. But we're going to put all that right.

ELSA: Don't. If what you've just said about me is true, I'd rather die.

[*Enter* CAT.]

CAT: Eight girl-friends of mine and our forty-eight kittens have been all over town and told everybody about the big fight. Miao. The Mayor'll be here any minute.

LANCELOT: The Mayor? Splendid!

[*Enter the* MAYOR, *running*.]

MAYOR: Hullo, Elsa. Where's the stranger?

LANCELOT: Here I am.

MAYOR: I must ask you first of all to keep your voice down, not to wave your arms about, don't make any sudden movements and don't look me in the eye.

LANCELOT: Why?

MAYOR: Because my nerves are in a shocking state. I have every nervous and mental disease known to medicine and three more still undiagnosed. How would you like to be mayor under the Dragon?

LANCELOT: Well, when I've killed the Dragon you'll be all right.

MAYOR: All right? Ha, ha! All right, ha, ha. All right, ha, ha. [*Mechanically. Has hysteria, drinks some water and calms down.*] Your impertinent challenge to the Dragon is a catastrophe. Everything was going just right. The Dragon was beginning to use his good influence to keep down my deputy, a thorough scoundrel if ever there was one, and his whole gang of crooked corn merchants. Now you come along and spoil everything. The Dragon will be so busy getting ready for the fight that he'll have to neglect official business just at the moment when he was getting interested in them.

LANCELOT: But don't you understand, you poor man, I'm going to save the town?

MAYOR: The town, ha, ha. The town, ha, ha. The town, ha, ha. [*Drinks some water and calms down again.*] My deputy's such a crook I'd sacrifice two towns to get rid of him. Better five dragons than a rotter like my deputy. Please go away!

LANCELOT: I won't.

MAYOR: Thank you very much, now I've got a cataleptic fit coming on. [*A wry smile is fixed on his face.*]

LANCELOT: But I'm going to save you all. Don't you understand?

[*Silence.*]

Don't you understand?

[MAYOR *is silent.* LANCELOT *sprinkles water on him.*]

MAYOR: No, I don't understand you. Who asked you to fight him?

LANCELOT: The whole town wants me to.

MAYOR: That's what you think. Just look out of the window. The town's leading citizens have come to beg you to clear out.

LANCELOT: Where are they?

MAYOR: There they are, crouching against the wall. Come closer, my friends!

LANCELOT: Why are they on tiptoe?

MAYOR: Because of my bad nerves. My friends, tell Lancelot what you want. Come on. One, two, three!

VOICES OFF [*in chorus*]: Go home, clear off!

[LANCELOT *turns from window.*]

MAYOR: You see! If you have a spark of common decency, hearken to the voice of public opinion.

LANCELOT: I will not.

MAYOR: Thank you very much. You've given me a slight fit of dementia. [*Puts one arm akimbo, other elegantly extended like teapot spout*] I'm a kettle, boil me!

LANCELOT: I see now why these wretched people came here on tiptoe.

MAYOR: Why?

LANCELOT: So as not to wake up the real people. I'll go and have a word with them. [*Runs out.*]

MAYOR: Boil me! What can he do anyway? Once the Dragon gives the word we'll put him in gaol. Don't worry, Elsa dear. Our dear Dragon will take you into his arms at the appointed hour, to the very second. Don't worry.

ELSA: Very well.

[*Knock on door. Enter* HENRY – *the footman who announced Dragon earlier.*]

MAYOR: Hullo, Henry my boy.

HENRY: Hullo, father.

MAYOR: Have you just come from him? There won't be any fight of course? Have you brought the warrant for Lancelot's arrest?

HENRY: The Dragon's orders are, first, to fix the battle for tomorrow, second, to supply Lancelot with arms, and third, try to use your brains a bit more.

MAYOR: Thank you very much, now my reason has gone altogether. Reason! Cooee! Answer me! Come back!

HENRY: I am to speak with Elsa alone.

MAYOR: I'm going, I'm going, I'm going. [*Exits hurriedly.*]

HENRY: Hullo, Elsa.

ELSA: Hullo, Henry.

HENRY: You hope Lancelot will save you?

ELSA: No. Do you?

HENRY: I don't either.

ELSA: What does the Dragon wish to tell me?

HENRY: He told me to say that *you* must kill Lancelot, if needs be.

ELSA [*horrified*]: What?

HENRY: Yes, with a knife. Here it is, it's poisoned.

ELSA: I will not.

HENRY: The Dragon told me to say that in that case he would kill all your friends.

ELSA: Very well. Tell him I'll do my best.

HENRY: And to that the Dragon said I was to say, any hesitation will be punished as disobedience.

ELSA: I hate you!

HENRY: And to that the Dragon said I was to say that he knows how to reward a good servant.

ELSA: Lancelot will kill your Dragon.

HENRY: And to that the Dragon told me to say, we shall see what we shall see.

ACT TWO

Town square. To right, town hall with tower with SENTRY *on it. Centre, huge, grim brown building without windows, with enormous iron door from floor to roof. Gothic inscription on door, 'Humans strictly forbidden'. Left, massive old fortress wall. Middle of square, well with ornamental railings and roof.* HENRY, *not in livery, in an apron is polishing the brass furnishings on the cast-iron door.*

HENRY [*humming*]: Hey diddle de, we shall see. We shall see. Said the Dragon to me.

[MAYOR *runs out of town hall, wearing a strait-jacket.*]

MAYOR: Hullo, Henry me boy. You sent for me?

HENRY: Hullo, father. I just wanted to know how things are going in there. Is the council meeting over?

MAYOR: What a hope! It's taken us all night to agree on the agenda.

HENRY: I bet you're really in a state.

MAYOR: You never said a truer word. In the last hour and a half they've had to change my strait-jacket three times. [*Yawns.*] I don't know whether it means we're going to have rain or what, but my blasted schizophrenia's really playing me up. It's me delirium, that's what it is. . . . Hallucinations and obsessions and all that sort of thing you know. [*Yawns.*] Got a cigarette?

HENRY: Yes.

MAYOR: Undo me and let's have a smoke.

[HENRY *undoes his father. They sit down on the steps of the palace and light up.*]

HENRY: Now when are you going to decide about the weapons?

MAYOR: What weapons?

HENRY: Weapons for Lancelot.

MAYOR: Who's Lancelot?

HENRY: Are you in your right mind?

MAYOR: Course I'm not. A nice son you are, forgetting how ill your poor old father is. [*Shouts*] Oh ye people, love ye one another. [*Calms.*] See, I'm quite dotty.

HENRY: There, there, father, you'll get over it.

MAYOR: I know I'll get over it, but it's a nuisance all the same.

HENRY: Now listen to me, I've got some important news. Old man Dragon's worried.

MAYOR: I don't believe it.

HENRY: No, really. The old boy's been out all night, working his wings off, flying around God knows where. He only got back at dawn. He had that awful fishy smell he always gets when he's worried. You know?

MAYOR: I see, I see.

HENRY: And this is what I've managed to find out: our dear Dragon has been flying around all night just to get all the low-down on the brave Sir Lancelot.

MAYOR: And?

HENRY: I don't know what sort of low-down places he's been to, in the Himalayas, on Ararat, in Scotland or in the Caucasus, but anyway he's found out that Lancelot is a professional hero. I just despise people of that sort. But old Drag, bless his little heart, as a professional villain, evidently attaches some importance to them. He's really been carrying on, what with swearing and cursing, and moaning and groaning. Then the old boy felt like a drink of beer. He guzzled a barrel full of his favourite brew, and without a word he spread his wings again and he's still cruising around up there like a blooming skylark. Doesn't it worry you?

MAYOR: Not a bit.

HENRY: Dad, tell me, you're older than me, and you've seen more of life . . . tell me honestly what do you think about this fight? Please tell me. Do you think Lancelot might . . . Only give me a straight answer, without any of the official stuff . . . Lancelot couldn't win, could he? eh, dad, tell me.

MAYOR: Listen here, Henry lad, I'll tell you then, and just what I really think, with no funny business. You know, my dear boy, I'm really devoted to our dear Dragon. I give you my word of honour. We might almost be relations. Now, how shall I put it, well, I would even sort of, er, well, you know, give my life for him. Honest to God, may I be struck down on this very spot. [*Moves away.*] Now you mark my words, he'll win all right. He'll win all right, our wonderful, darling, marvellous, heavenly, adorable Dragon. Oh, how I love him! I love him, and that's all there is to it. There's your answer.

HENRY: Dad! You just don't want to talk straight with your only son, do you?

MAYOR: No, I don't, my boy. . . . I'm not out of my mind yet. That is, I am, of course, but not that much. It was the Dragon who told you to sound me out, wasn't it?

HENRY: Dad, what an idea!

MAYOR: Good for you, my boy. You managed the conversation very well. I'm proud of you. Believe me, not just because I'm your father, but because you are so good at your job, a real old hand. Have you memorized my answer?

HENRY: Of course.

MAYOR: And the bit about our wonderful, darling, marvellous, heavenly, adorable Dragon?

HENRY: I've got it all.

MAYOR: Well, just you pass it on like that.

HENRY: All right, dad.

MAYOR: Ah, Henry, what should I do without you, my brave little nark! ... You'll go a long way, my boy. How are you off for money?

HENRY: I'm all right just now, but thanks all the same, dad.

MAYOR: Come on now, don't be afraid to ask. I've got plenty. I had a fit of kleptomania yesterday. Take some....

HENRY: Thank you, I don't need it. But come on, tell me the truth....

MAYOR: Now really, Henry, my boy – asking for the truth, just like a child. I'm not just anyone, you know. I'm the Mayor. I haven't told the truth even to myself for so many years I've forgotten what it is. It makes me sick, I can't stomach it. You know what comes of the blessed truth, don't you? Let's drop it, son. Three cheers for the Dragon, hip, hip!

[SENTRY *on tower strikes halberd on floor.*]

SENTRY [*shouts*]: Atten-shun! Eyes to the sky! His excellency is now proceeding over the Grey Mountains!

[HENRY *and the* MAYOR *jump up and stand to attention and look up to sky. A distant drone is heard, and dies away.*]

SENTRY: Stand easy! His excellency has now turned back and is hidden from view in smoke and flame!

HENRY: He's out on patrol.

MAYOR: I see, I see. Now listen, I want to ask you one little question. Did the Dragon really leave without a word, eh, Henry?

HENRY: Not a word, dad.

MAYOR: Aren't we to kill him?

HENRY: Who?

MAYOR: This saviour of ours.

HENRY: Tut, tut, father.

MAYOR: Out with it. Didn't he say anything about doing in Sir Lancelot on the quiet? Don't be shy, tell me. . . . We all know these things happen. Well, Henry?

HENRY: My lips are sealed.

MAYOR: Very well, then. I understand. Orders are orders.

HENRY: May I remind you, Mr Mayor, that at any moment now the weapons are to be handed to the hero at a solemn ceremony. The Dragon himself wishes to honour the ceremony with his presence, and here you are with still nothing ready.

MAYOR [*yawns and stretches*]: All right then, I'll go. We'll find him some sort of weapons in no time at all. He won't complain. Do up my sleeves for me. . . . Here he comes. It's Lancelot.

HENRY: Get him away from here. Elsa will be here any moment and I must have a word with her.

[*Enter* LANCELOT.]

MAYOR [*hysterically*]: Hail to thee, hail, George the Dragon-killer! Oh, excuse my mistake. I took you for him in my delirium. You are so like him.

LANCELOT: I'm not surprised. He's a distant relative of mine.

MAYOR: What sort of a night did you have?

LANCELOT: I wandered round.

MAYOR: Make friends with anyone?

LANCELOT: Of course I did.

MAYOR: Who?

LANCELOT: The frightened citizens of your town set their dogs on me. But your dogs have a lot of sense. So I made friends with them. They understand me because they love their masters and wish them well. We chatted till dawn.

MAYOR: Didn't you catch any fleas?

LANCELOT: No. They're nice clean dogs.

MAYOR: You don't remember their names, I suppose?

LANCELOT: They asked me not to tell.

MAYOR: I can't stand dogs.

LANCELOT: That's too bad.

MAYOR: They're much too simple for me.

LANCELOT: Do you think it's so simple to love people? You know dogs know only too well what their masters are like. It makes them weep but they love them all the same. That's real hard work. Did you send for me?

MAYOR: For me, the cow jumped over the moon, hey diddle diddle, the cat and the fiddle. For me, the mouse ran up the clock, hickory dickory dock. For me, little Miss Muffet sat on a tuffet. Or to cut a long story short, I did send for you.

LANCELOT: What can I do for you?

MAYOR: Millers have just got in a new delivery of cheese. Nothing goes better on a girl than modesty and a dress you can see through. At sunset wild ducks flew over the cradle. They're waiting for you at the council meeting, Sir Lancelot.

LANCELOT: Why?

MAYOR: Why do lime-trees grow on Dragon Street? Why dance when you want to kiss? Why kiss when hooves beat? The members of the council have to see you personally before they can decide which weapons will suit you best. Let's go and show ourselves.

[*Exeunt.*]

HENRY [*repeats earlier jingle*]: Hey diddle de, we shall see. We shall see. Said the Dragon to me.

[*Enter* ELSA.]

HENRY: Elsa!

ELSA: Yes, here I am. You sent for me?

HENRY: I did. What a pity there's a sentry up there. If it weren't for that highly unfortunate obstacle, I would take you in my arms and kiss you.

ELSA: And I would slap you!

HENRY: Oh, Elsa, Elsa. You always were a trifle too much on the virtuous side. But it suited you. There are depths behind that modesty of yours. Old Draggers certainly has a flair for girls. He always picked the most promising one, the naughty old thing. And hasn't Lancelot been after you yet?

ELSA: Shut up!

HENRY: But of course he hasn't. He'd go out and fight, even if it weren't you but some old hag. He doesn't mind who he saves. That's how he was brought up. He hasn't even had a proper look at you.

ELSA: We've only just met.

HENRY: That's no excuse.

ELSA: Did you call me just to tell me that?

HENRY: Oh, no. I called you to ask if you will marry me.

ELSA: Stop it!

HENRY: I mean it. I am authorized to tell you the following: if you do as you're told and kill Lancelot, should it become necessary, then as a reward the Dragon will let you off.

ELSA: I won't.

HENRY: Let me finish. Instead of you he will take another completely unknown girl from the lower classes. She was already lined up for next year anyway. Take your choice – a senseless death, or a life full of all the lovely things you've only dreamt of, and that so rarely it's a real shame.

ELSA: He's lost his nerve.

HENRY: Who? Old Draggers? I know all his faults. He's pig-headed, crude, parasitical, anything you like. But he's no coward.

ELSA: Yesterday he was threatening, today he's bargaining.

HENRY: That's my doing.

ELSA: You?

HENRY: I'm the one who can really get the better of the Dragon if you want to know. I can get anything I like out of him. I just waited for the right moment. I'm not such a fool as to give you up to anybody.

ELSA: I don't trust you.

HENRY: Yes, you do.

ELSA: Anyway, I cannot kill a man.

HENRY: But I see you've brought the knife all the same. There it is in your belt. I have to go, my dear. I must put on my ceremonial uniform. But I go with an easy mind. You will carry out your orders both for your own sake and for mine. Just think! We have a whole life ahead of us, if you want it. Think about it, Elsa my dear. [*Exit.*]

ELSA: Oh my God! My cheeks are burning as if I'd kissed him. What a disgrace! He nearly talked me into it.... So that's the sort of person I am. But what do I care? I've really had enough. I've always been the most meek and mild person. I've always been so trusting. And where has it got me? Yes, they respect me all right, but it's the others who have all the fun. They'll be sitting at home now, picking out their prettiest dresses, ironing pleats and curling their hair. They're getting ready to come and enjoy the sight of my unhappiness. I can just see them sitting there making up in front of their mirrors, saying: 'Poor Elsa, poor dear. And she was so sweet.' Here I am all alone on the square and worrying myself to death. And there's that idiot of a sentry gaping at me and thinking about what the Dragon's going to do to me today. And he'll be alive tomorrow having his rest after duty. He'll go for a walk to the waterfall, where the river's so gay that even the most miserable people smile when they see it splashing. Or maybe he'll go to the park where the gardener has grown those wonderful pansies with eyes, which blink and wink and can even read books, so long as the letters are big and there's a happy ending. Or he'll go for a sail on the lake, which the Dragon once made boil and where the mermaids have been so quiet ever since. They don't even drown anybody any longer, but just sit at the edge of the lake selling lifebelts. But they're just as beautiful as ever and the soldiers like to go and gossip with them. And this silly soldier will tell the mermaids about the jolly music, how everybody cried and how the Dragon carried me off. And they'll start sighing 'Oh, poor Elsa, poor dear. Such nice weather, and she can't be here to enjoy it.' But I do want to enjoy it! I want to see everything, hear it and feel it. So there! I want to be happy. So there! I brought the knife to kill myself. But I won't. So there!

[LANCELOT *comes out of town hall.*]

LANCELOT: What a joy to see you!

ELSA: Why?

LANCELOT: Oh, my dear young lady, I'm having such a trying day my soul cries out for a moment's peace. And now, as good luck has it, I meet you.

ELSA: Have you been at the meeting?

LANCELOT: Yes, I have.

ELSA: Why did they ask you to it?

LANCELOT: They offered me money to back out of the fight.

ELSA: And what did you say?

LANCELOT: I told them what poor fools they were. But don't let's talk about them. You're even more beautiful today than you were yesterday, Elsa. That's a sure sign that I really like you. Do you believe that I can save you?

ELSA: No, I don't.

LANCELOT: I'm not offended. That shows how much I like you.

[*Enter Elsa's* GIRL-FRIENDS.]

FIRST FRIEND: Here we are!

SECOND FRIEND: *We're* Elsa's best friends.

THIRD FRIEND: We've been like sisters for so many years. Ever since we were children.

FIRST FRIEND: She was the cleverest of all of us.

SECOND FRIEND: She was the nicest of all of us.

THIRD FRIEND: And nobody was ever so kind to us. She would do any sewing you wanted, and help you with your homework, and cheer you up when you felt really unhappy.

FIRST FRIEND: We're not late, are we?

SECOND FRIEND: Are you really going to fight him?

THIRD FRIEND: Sir Lancelot, do you think you could get us

places on the roof of the town hall? They won't refuse you, if you ask. We do so want to have a good view of the fight.

FIRST FRIEND: Oh, dear, now we've made you angry.

SECOND FRIEND: Now you won't talk to us.

THIRD FRIEND: But we're not such bad girls as all that, you know.

FIRST FRIEND: You think we came on purpose to stop you saying good-bye to Elsa.

SECOND FRIEND: But it wasn't on purpose.

THIRD FRIEND: Henry told us not to leave you alone with her until the Dragon gives permission. . . .

FIRST FRIEND: He told us to come and chat with you. . . .

SECOND FRIEND: And so here we are, like chatterboxes.

THIRD FRIEND: If we weren't chattering we'd be crying. But of course you can't imagine what a disgrace it is to cry in front of strangers.

[CHARLEMAGNE *comes out of town hall.*]

CHARLEMAGNE: The meeting is over, Sir Lancelot. A decision about your weapons has been taken. Forgive us. Have pity on us, poor murderers that we are.

[*Trumpets sound.* SERVANTS *enter laying carpets and placing chairs. They put one large luxurious chair in the middle, and simpler chairs to its right and left. Enter* MAYOR *surrounded by other* OFFICIALS. *He's in a good mood.* HENRY *is in full dress.*]

MAYOR: That was a good one. What was it she said, 'I thought all the boys knew how to do it'? Ha, ha, ha. Do you know this one, it's very funny: a gypsy had his head chopped off . . .

[*Trumpets sound.*]

MAYOR: Ah, everything's ready. Remind me to tell it to you after the ceremony. . . . Come along, gentlemen, come along. We'll soon get through this.

[*The* OFFICIALS *stand to right and left of the big chair.* HENRY *stands behind it.*]

MAYOR [*bowing to empty chair mechanically*]: Overwhelmed and overcome by the trust which you, your excellency, have shown in us by allowing us to take such important decisions, we beg you to take the place of honour. We beg you once, we beg you twice, we beg you thrice. We are distressed, but there it is. We shall have to carry on by ourselves. Take your seats, gentlemen. I declare the mooting ... [*Pause.*]

Water!

[SERVANT *brings water from well.* MAYOR *drinks.*]

I declare the mating ... Water! [*Drinks. Clears his throat. In high-pitched voice*] I declare [*bass voice*] the muting ... water! [*Drinks. High-pitched*] Thank you, darling. [*Bass*] Clear off, you scoundrel! [*Normal voice*] I hope you're happy now, gentlemen, it's my split personality again. [*Bass*] What are you up to now, you silly old girl? [*High voice*] Can't you see I'm chairing a meeting. [*Bass*] That's no job for a woman. [*High voice*] I don't like it myself, duckie. Don't make things harder. Let me read the minutes. [*Normal voice*] Proposed: to supply one Lancelot with arms.

Agreed: to do same, but reluctantly. Hey, you there. Bring those weapons!

[*Trumpets sound. Enter* SERVANTS. *The first brings* LANCELOT *a small brass bowl, to which narrow leather straps have been fixed.*]

LANCELOT: That's a barber's bowl.

MAYOR: Yes, but we have appointed it to stand in as a helmet. This brass tray will serve as your shield. Don't worry, in our town, even *things* know their place. They'll carry out their duties conscientiously. Unfortunately we have no armour in stock. But we have a lance. [*Hands* LANCELOT *a sheet of paper.*] This is to certify that the lance is actually under repair, as witnessed by this signature and seal. Just present this to Sir Dragon during the fight and everything will be all right. Well, that's the lot, then. [*Bass*] Close the meeting, you silly old woman. [*Falsetto*] That's what I'm doing, blast the thing. Everybody's so bad tempered and nobody knows why. [*Sings*] One, two, three, four, a knight went out to fight a war. . . . [*Bass*] Close the meeting, you old bitch. [*Falsetto*] What do you think I'm doing? [*Sings*] Here comes Draggles in full flight. And goes bang-bang at that poor knight. I declare the jolly old meeting closed.

SENTRY: Attention! Eyes to the sky! His excellency is over the Grey Mountains and is proceeding here with terrific speed.

[ALL *jump up and stand frozen with their eyes to the sky. A distant roar which grows with horrifying speed. Stage darkens. Complete darkness. The roar stops.*]

SENTRY: Attention! His excellency is hovering above us, covering the sun like a cloud. Hold your breath!

[*Two greenish lights flash.*]

CAT [*whispers*]: Lancelot, it's me, the Cat.

LANCELOT [*whispers*]: I know. I saw your eyes.

CAT: I shall be sleeping on the fortress wall. Find a moment to come to me and I shall miao something very nice to you. . . .

SENTRY: Attention! His excellency is diving head first down to the square.

[*Deafening whine and roar. Blinding light. In the big chair sits a tiny little* MAN *with his legs up. He is deathly pale and elderly.*]

CAT [*from fortress wall*]: Don't worry, dear Lancelot. That's his third head. He changes them when he feels like it.

MAYOR: Your excellency, in the municipality entrusted to me there have been no incidents. Number of persons in gaol: one. Present . . .

DRAGON [*cracked falsetto*]: Clear off! Everybody clear off, except the stranger.

[ALL *exit, leaving* LANCELOT, DRAGON, *and* CAT, *which sleeps on wall curled up.*]

How are we feeling?

LANCELOT: Very well, thank you.

DRAGON: What are these bowls on the ground?

LANCELOT: My weapons.

DRAGON: I suppose that was their idea.

LANCELOT: Yes.

DRAGON: The scoundrels. I suppose you're annoyed.

LANCELOT: No.

DRAGON: Come off it! My blood is cold, but even I would be annoyed. Are you frightened?

LANCELOT: No.

DRAGON: Come off it! These people of mine would frighten anybody. You won't find any more like them anywhere. That's *my* doing. I've made them what they are.

LANCELOT: But they're people all the same.

DRAGON: That's only on the outside.

LANCELOT: No.

DRAGON: If you could see their hearts, you would shudder.

LANCELOT: No.

DRAGON: You'd even run away. You wouldn't die for cripples like these. I made them cripples, my dear fellow. I crippled them properly. The human spirit is very hardy. Cut a man's body in half and he pegs out. But break his spirit and he'll eat out of your hand. No, you won't find any others like these anywhere. Only in my town. Spirits without arms, without legs, deaf and dumb spirits, spirits in chains, sneaking spirits, damned spirits. Why do you suppose the Mayor has to pretend to be mad? It's to hide the fact that he has no spirit at all. Threadbare spirits, venal spirits, gutted spirits, dead spirits. Ha! What a pity the spirits are invisible so you can't see them.

LANCELOT: It's as well for you that you can't.

DRAGON: How do you mean?

LANCELOT: People would take fright if they could see with their own eyes what has happened to their spirits. They would rather die than remain slaves. Who'd feed you then?

DRAGON: The devil knows, you may even be right. What do you say, shall we begin?

LANCELOT: Let's.

DRAGON: You'd better say your farewell to the girl you're going to die for. Hey, boy!

[*Enter* HENRY *running.*]

Bring Elsa, and look smart about it!

[*Exit* HENRY *ditto.*]

How do you like this girl I've chosen?

LANCELOT: I like her very, very much.

DRAGON: I'm glad to hear it. I like her very, very much as well. A splendid girl. Very well behaved.

[*Enter* ELSA *and* HENRY.]

Come over here, my dear. Now, let's have a proper look at you. That's it. Very good. What pretty bright eyes! You may kiss my hand. There's a good girl! What nice warm lips! That means you have an easy conscience. Want to say bye-bye to Sir Lancelot?

ELSA: Whatever you say, Sir Dragon.

DRAGON: That's what I'm telling you to do. Go and say a few nice words to him. [*Whispers*] Very, very nice words. Kiss him good-bye. It's all right as long as I'm here. And then kill him. Don't worry, don't worry. I shall be here all the time. I'll watch you do it. Go on, now. Talk to him over there, if you like. My eyesight's excellent. I shall see everything. Off you go.

[ELSA *joins* LANCELOT.]

ELSA: Sir Lancelot, I've been told to say good-bye to you.

LANCELOT: Very well, Elsa. Let's say good-bye, just in case. It'll be a hard fight and anything can happen. Before we part I want to tell you that I love you, Elsa.

ELSA: You love *me*?

LANCELOT: Yes, Elsa. I liked you so much yesterday when I saw you through the window walking home quietly with your father. And now you look lovelier to me every time

I see you. So now I see how it is. And when you kissed the Dragon's paw just now, I wasn't angry, I was just terribly upset. Now I'm really certain, Elsa. I love you. Please don't be angry. I did so want you to know this.

ELSA: And I'd been thinking that even if it had been some other girl in my place you'd still have challenged the Dragon.

LANCELOT: Of course I would! I can't stand them, these Dragons. But for your sake I'd strangle him with my bare hands, disgusting as that would be.

ELSA: So you love me?

LANCELOT: Very much! It frightens me to think that if I'd turned left instead of right at the cross-roads yesterday, we should never have met. Isn't that a terrible thought?

ELSA: Yes.

LANCELOT: It doesn't bear thinking about. I don't think there's anybody in the whole world who's closer to me now than you, and I look on this town as my own because you live here. If I . . . I mean if we don't manage to see each other again, don't forget me.

ELSA: I never will.

LANCELOT: Don't forget me. Now that's the first time today you've looked into my eyes. And I felt their warmth going all through me as though you'd caressed me. I'm always on the move, I'm a restless man, and all my life has been spent in hard fighting. What with dragons, ogres, giants and so forth. There's always something to be done. . . . It's difficult work and you get no thanks for it. But I've always enjoyed it. I've never got fed up, and I've often fallen in love.

ELSA: Often?

LANCELOT: Well, of course. If you wander round the world fighting all the time you can't help it. You're bound to meet girls. They're always getting captured by bandits, carted off by giants or ogres. And these monsters always pick the best girls, especially the ogres. So you can't help falling in love now and again. But now it's very different.

'It wasn't really serious with the others. It was just for fun. If we were alone now, Elsa, I would kiss you. Honestly, I would. And I'd take you away from here. We would speed away together over mountains and forests – it would be so easy. I would get you a horse with a saddle you could ride for ever and not get tired. I'd be there at your side and I'd never take my eyes off you. And nobody in the world would ever dare to hurt you.

[ELSA *takes him by the hand.*]

DRAGON: Good girl! She's got him where she wants him.

HENRY: Yes, she's no fool, your excellency.

LANCELOT: Elsa, you look as though you're going to cry.

ELSA: I am.

LANCELOT: Why?

ELSA: Because I'm sorry.

LANCELOT: Who for?

ELSA: For you and me. There'll be no happiness for either of us, Lancelot. Why did I have to be born under the Dragon?!

LANCELOT: Elsa, listen to me, I always speak the truth. We *will* be happy, believe me.

ELSA: Oh, please don't go on!

LANCELOT: And you and I will walk through the forest joyful and happy. Just you and me.

ELSA: No, please don't.

LANCELOT: And there'll be a clear sky above us. There'll be no one up there to swoop down on us.

ELSA: Is it true?

LANCELOT: It's true. How can people know in this poor town of yours what love really is? I will love you so much that all your fear, weariness and mistrust will disappear for ever. And you will go to sleep with a smile on your lips and wake up with a smile on your lips, and you will call to me. That's how much you'll love me. And you'll respect yourself as well. You'll be able to hold up your head and you won't have a worry in the world. And when I kiss you,

you'll see yourself what a wonderful person you are. And the trees in the forest will talk softly to us and the birds and the animals as well, because true lovers understand everything and are at one with the whole world. And everybody will like us, because true lovers bring good luck.

DRAGON: What's he on about over there?

HENRY: He's reading her the lesson. Honour thy father and thy mother, wash your hands before meals, and that sort of stuff. A real bore. . . .

DRAGON: Ah, look! She's put her hand on his shoulder! Good girl!

ELSA: Well, even if we never live to see such happiness, all the same I'm happy now. These monsters are watching us. But we're a whole world away from them. No one has ever spoken to me like this before, my dear. I didn't know there were such people as you in the world. Until yesterday I was as meek as a mouse. I didn't dare think about you. But in the night I crept downstairs and drank the wine you left in your glass. Only now I see that this was my way of kissing you secretly at dead of night to thank you for standing up for me. You can't imagine how confused in our feelings we are, we poor downtrodden girls. A little while ago I thought I hated you. But this was just my way of falling in love with you, almost without knowing it. Oh, my darling! I love you, and what a joy it is to say it. And what a joy . . . [*Kisses* LANCELOT.]

DRAGON [*stamping with impatience*]: Now she'll do it, now she'll do it!

ELSA: And now let go of me, my dear. [*Frees herself. Takes out dagger.*] Do you see this? The Dragon told me to kill you with it. Do you see?

DRAGON: Come on, come on, come on!

HENRY: Get on with it!

[ELSA *throws dagger down well.*]

The little bitch!

DRAGON [*roars*]: How dare you!

ELSA: Don't say another word! Do you think I'll let you swear at me now he has kissed me? I love him and he will kill you.

LANCELOT: That's the plain truth, Sir Dragon.

DRAGON: Oh, well. I suppose there's nothing for it but to fight. [*Yawns.*] As a matter of fact I'm not at all sorry. I recently worked out an interesting new stroke – you move paw X in direction Y. I shall now try it out in practice. Orderly, call the guard!

[HENRY *exits running.*]

And you go home, you silly girl, we'll have a little heart-to-heart about it after the fight.

[*Enter* HENRY *with* GUARD.]

Listen, guard, what was it I wanted to tell you? . . . Oh, yes, take this young lady home and keep an eye on her there.

[LANCELOT *steps forward.*]

ELSA: Don't. Keep your strength. When you've killed him, come to me. I shall wait for you and I shall go over in my mind every word you've said to me today. I believe in you.

LANCELOT: I shall come for you.

DRAGON: Now that's enough. Off you go.

[GUARD *leads* ELSA *away.*]

Boy, take the sentry off the tower and put him in the dungeon. We'll have to have his head chopped off tonight. He heard the girl shouting at me and he might let on about it in the barracks. Go and see to it. Then you can come back and smear my paws with poison.

[*Exit* HENRY *running.*]

DRAGON [*to* LANCELOT]: And you stay where you are, do you hear? And wait. I won't tell you when I'll begin. Real war always begins suddenly. Understand? [*He slides off the chair and goes into the palace.*]

[LANCELOT *goes up to the* CAT.]

LANCELOT: Well, Cat, what was that nice something you were going to miao to me?

CAT: Look along to the right, Lancelot my friend. That cloud of dust over there is a donkey kicking. And five men are trying to make it go. Now I'll sing him a little song. See how he's coming towards us? But he's going to dig his heels in again by that wall over there and you can go over and talk to his drivers. Here they come.

[Over the wall can be seen the DONKEY*'s head in a cloud of dust. Five* DRIVERS *shout at it.* HENRY *runs across the square.]*

HENRY *[to* DRIVERS*]*: What are you up to there?

TWO DRIVERS: We're taking our goods to market, your honour.

HENRY: What goods?

TWO DRIVERS: Carpets, your honour.

HENRY: Move on, then, move on. You're not allowed to stop in front of the palace.

TWO DRIVERS: The donkey won't budge, your honour.

DRAGON'S VOICE: Boy!

HENRY: Move on, move on! *[Runs into palace.]*

TWO DRIVERS *[in chorus]*: Good day, Sir Lancelot. We are your friends, Sir Lancelot. *[Clear their throats simultaneously.]* Don't mind us both talking at once. We've been working together since we were children and we're so used to it we think and talk as one. We even fell in love on the same day at the same instant and got married to twin sisters. We've woven a good many carpets in our time, but we never made a better one than the one we made last night for you. *[Take carpet off donkey's back and spread it on ground.]*

LANCELOT: What a beautiful carpet!

TWO DRIVERS: Ah, don't make 'em like this any more – double weave, wool and silk, and the dyes made to our own secret process. But it's not the wool, the silk or the dyes that makes it what it is. *[Whisper]* It's a flying carpet.

LANCELOT: Wonderful! Tell me quickly how to fly it.

TWO DRIVERS: It's very easy, Sir Lancelot. This corner here, with the picture of the sun on it, is for going up. This one here with the earth's for coming down, like. This one with swallows is for stunting. And this one here's for fighting dragons. You raises it and it goes into a steep dive straight at his head. And here we've woven in a jug of wine and some things for you to eat when you've killed him. No need to thank us. Our great-grandfathers was always watching out for you, our grandfathers waited for you, and now here you are at last.

[*Exeunt quickly and* THIRD DRIVER *comes to* LANCELOT *with cardboard box.*]

THIRD DRIVER: Good day, sir. Excuse me, would you just turn your head this way, and now this way, if you please? Perfect. I'm a master hatter. I make the best hats and caps in the world. I'm quite a celebrity here, every dog knows me.

CAT: And every cat, too.

THIRD DRIVER: See that? I don't even have to take a measurement. A look is enough, and you've got a hat that makes you look really wonderful. And that's my great joy in life. There's one lady here, for instance, whose husband only loves her when she's wearing one of my hats. She even sleeps in it, and tells everyone that she owes her happiness to me. All night I've been working for you, sir, crying like a baby from misery.

LANCELOT: Why?

THIRD DRIVER: It was a special job, and such a sad one. It's a hat to make you invisible.

LANCELOT: Wonderful!

THIRD DRIVER: As soon as you put it on you vanish and then the poor hatter never knows if it suits you. Here you are, but please don't try it on while I'm here. I couldn't stand it, no, I couldn't stand it! [*Hurries out.*]

[FOURTH DRIVER *comes up to* LANCELOT. *He is a*

bearded gloomy man with a bundle on his shoulder. Undoes it. It contains a sword and lance.]

FOURTH DRIVER: Here's your sword and lance! It took us all night. And good luck to you! [*Exits.*]

[FIFTH DRIVER *comes to* LANCELOT. *He is a small grey-haired man carrying a musical instrument.*]

FIFTH DRIVER: I am a maker of musical instruments, sir. My great-great-great-grandfather started making this little instrument here. We've been working on it for generations now and it's been in human hands so long it's almost human itself. It'll keep you good company in battle. Your hands will be busy with your sword and lance, but it will take care of itself. It tunes itself, changes broken strings and starts playing all by itself. It does an encore if you want it to, and if you don't it shuts up. That's right, isn't it? [*Instrument answers with tune.*] Do you see? We knew, we all knew you were wandering around alone, so we got busy making weapons for you. We've been waiting hundreds of years. We were so much under the Dragon's thumb that all we could do was sit and wait. And now the time has come. Kill him and set us free. Is that right? [*Instrument gives tune,* FIFTH DRIVER *exits bowing.*]

CAT: When the fight starts, me and the donkey will hide in the barn at the back of the palace, so I don't get my fur singed by the odd flame. Shout if you need anything. Here in his pack the donkey has strong drinks, cherry pie, a whetstone for your sword, spare points for the lance and needle and thread for the carpet.

LANCELOT: Thank you. [*Steps on to carpet, picks up weapons, places musical instrument at his feet. Puts on hat and disappears.*]

CAT: Good craftsmanship. They've done a good job. Are you still there, Lancelot?

LANCELOT'S VOICE: No. I'm climbing steadily. Good-bye, friends.

CAT: Good-bye, dear friend. Oh, what a lot of excitement and trouble. No, it's much nicer when you've lost all hope. You just doze and don't expect anything. Isn't that right, Donkey?

[DONKEY *twitches his ears.*]

I'm afraid I can't talk with my ears. Let's talk in words, Donkey. We don't know each other very well, but as we're working together we may as well have a friendly miao. It's torture to wait in silence. Let's have a miao.

DONKEY: I won't miao.

CAT: Well, let's talk then. The Dragon thinks Lancelot's still here, but he's taken off. Funny, isn't it?

DONKEY [*gloomily*]: *Very* funny.

CAT: Why don't you laugh then?

DONKEY: They'll beat me. As soon as I laugh out loud people say there's that damned donkey braying again, and they beat me.

CAT: Oh, I see. So when you make that horrible shrill noise you're really laughing, then?

DONKEY: Yep.

CAT: And what do you laugh about?

DONKEY: It depends. . . . I start thinking and then something funny comes into my head. Take horses, they make me laugh.

CAT: Why?

DONKEY: Well, they're so daft.

CAT: Forgive me for being nosy, but there's something I've been meaning to ask you for a long time. . . .

DONKEY: What is it?

CAT: How can you eat thistles?

DONKEY: What's wrong with them?

CAT: I know in grass you get tasty stalks, but thistles are so dry!

DONKEY: Well, I like things with a sharp taste.

CAT: What about meat?

DONKEY: What about meat?

CAT: Ever tried any?

DONKEY: You don't eat meat, you carry it. That's what they put in my cart, you ass.

CAT: Well, what about milk, then?

DONKEY: I used to drink it when I was a baby.

CAT: Well, thank heavens that gives us something nice and pleasant to chat about.

DONKEY: Yes, it is nice. Me Ma was so nice and kind and the milk was so warm. You could have a real good guzzle. It was heaven. It didn't half taste good.

CAT: Some people prefer to lap their milk.

DONKEY: Well, I'm not one of them.

CAT [*jumping up*]: Hear that?

DONKEY: It's that bloody Dragon stamping his hooves.

[*Sound of triple roar from* DRAGON.]

DRAGON: Lancelot! [*Pause.*] Lancelot!

DONKEY: Cuckoo! [*Starts braying*] Heehaw, heehaw.

[*Palace doors fly open. Dimly seen through fire and smoke are three huge heads, enormous paws, glittering eyes.*]

DRAGON: Lancelot. Come and admire me before battle commences. Where are you?

[HENRY *runs out on to square. Rushes round looking for* LANCELOT, *looks down well.*]

DRAGON: Where the hell is he?

HENRY: He's hiding, excellency.

DRAGON: Hey, Lancelot, where are you?

[*Sound of sword striking.*]

Who dares to strike me?!

LANCELOT'S VOICE: It's me, Lancelot.

[*Blackness. Threatening roar. Flash of light.* HENRY *flees into town hall. Sound of battle.*]

CAT: Let's take cover.

DONKEY: About time, too.

[CAT *and* DONKEY *run off. The square fills up with* POPULACE. *They are unusually quiet. They whisper together and gaze at the sky.*]

FIRST MAN: It's agony the way this fight drags on and on.

SECOND MAN: I know. Two minutes already and still no result.

FIRST MAN: I hope they get it all over in one go.

SECOND MAN: Dear, dear. Life was so nice and quiet. It's lunch-time already, but who can eat at a time like this? It's dreadful. Good day, gardener. What are you looking so miserable for?

GARDENER: My tea roses have come out today. And then I've got bread roses and wine roses, too, you know. One look at them is as good as a meal. The Dragon promised to have a look at them and give me money for more experiments. But he's fighting instead. This terrible thing could ruin the fruits of many years' labour.

PEDLAR [*in a whispered patter*]: Who wants a lovely smoked glass? See the old Dragon go up in smoke.

[ALL *laugh quietly.*]

FIRST MAN: How utterly scandalous! Ha, ha, ha!

SECOND MAN: See him go up in smoke! The idea!

[*They buy glass.*]

BOY: Mummy, who's the Dragon running away from up there?

ALL: Sssshhh!

FIRST MAN: He's not running away, little boy, he's simply manoeuvring.

BOY: But he's got his tail between his legs.

ALL: Sssshhh!

FIRST MAN: His tail is where it is according to plan, little boy.

FIRST WOMAN: Imagine! Six minutes the war's been on, and there seems no end to it. It's got everyone worried. The shopkeepers have put up the price of milk three times.

SECOND WOMAN: That's nothing. On the way here we saw something that gave us a really nasty turn. Sugar and butter were being rushed from the shops to the warehouses, being as they're the first things to be evacuated if there's a war.

[*Cries of outrage. The crowd shies to one side. Enter* CHARLEMAGNE.]

CHARLEMAGNE: Good day to you. [*Silence.*] Aren't you talking to me?

FIRST MAN: No, we're not! Not since last night.

CHARLEMAGNE: Why?

GARDENER: Terrible people. They let strangers into their house. Upset the Dragon. That's even worse than walking on the grass. And then they ask why.

SECOND MAN: Speaking for myself, I stopped talking to you from the moment they put a guard round your house.

CHARLEMAGNE: And a dreadful thing that is, too. Don't you agree? D'you know, the stupid guards won't let me get through to see my own daughter. They say the Dragon has forbidden anyone to see Elsa.

FIRST MAN: Well, I don't doubt that in their own eyes they're perfectly justified.

CHARLEMAGNE: Elsa's all alone there. It's true she looked quite happy when she nodded to me from the window, but that must have been just to put my mind at rest. Dear me, I have no place to go to.

SECOND MAN: What do you mean, no place to go to? Have they sacked you as archivist?

CHARLEMAGNE: No.

SECOND MAN: Well, what place are you talking about, then?

CHARLEMAGNE: Surely you know what I'm talking about?

FIRST MAN: No. Since you made friends with this outsider we talk different languages.

[*Battle noises. Clang of swords.*]

BOY [*pointing to sky*]: Mummy, mummy! He's upside down. Someone's hitting him and making sparks fly.

ALL: Ssshhh! ! !

[*Trumpets sound. Enter* HENRY *and* MAYOR.]

MAYOR: Oyez, oyez! To prevent an epidemic of eye disease, and for no other reason, sky-gazing is forbidden. You will hear about the aerial situation from communiqués which will be issued by the Dragon's personal secretary as and when required.

FIRST MAN: That's more like it!

SECOND MAN: And about time too.

BOY: Mummy, why is it bad for us to watch him being beaten?

ALL: Ssshhh.

[*Enter Elsa's* GIRL-FRIENDS.]

FIRST FRIEND: The war's been on ten minutes now. Why can't that Lancelot just surrender?

SECOND FRIEND: He must know it's impossible to beat the Dragon.

THIRD FRIEND: He's only doing it to upset us.

FIRST FRIEND: I left my gloves at Elsa's. But nothing matters any more. I'm so tired of this war that I can't worry about anything.

SECOND FRIEND: I've become quite numb, too. Elsa wanted to give me her new slippers as a memento but I'm not giving them a thought.

THIRD FRIEND: Think of it! If it weren't for this stranger the Dragon would have taken Elsa off ages ago. And we would be sitting quietly at home having a good cry.

PEDLAR [*in shifty whisper*]: Here y'are then, a marvellous scientific instrument, a mirror they call it. You look downwards and see the sky. Going cheap. See the Dragon at your feet.

[ALL *laugh quietly*.]

FIRST MAN: How utterly scandalous! Ha, ha, ha.

SECOND MAN: See him at your feet! Some hope!

[*They buy mirrors. Little groups form and look in the mirrors. Noise of battle fiercer.*]

FIRST MAN: My God, how awful!

SECOND MAN: The poor Dragon!

FIRST MAN: He's stopped breathing flame.

SECOND MAN: He's only smoking now.

FIRST MAN: Such tricky manoeuvres.

SECOND MAN: If you ask me . . . No, I'd better not say.

FIRST MAN: I can't make head or tail of it.

HENRY: Here is a communiqué issued by the city council: The battle is nearing its end. The enemy has lost his sword. He's broken his lance. The flying carpet has been found to contain moth, which is rapidly undermining the enemy's aerial supremacy. Cut off from his base, the enemy cannot get moth-balls and is trying to beat the moths out of it with his hands, thus losing his freedom of movement. The Dragon refrains from annihilating the enemy only because of his love of war. He wants to perform more feats of bravery and make the most of his own unbelievable prowess.

FIRST MAN: Ah, now I understand.

BOY: But Mummy look, somebody is giving it to him in the neck, honest.

FIRST MAN: He has three necks, little boy.

BOY: Well, look now, he's getting it in all three.

FIRST MAN: An optical illusion, little boy.

BOY: You're telling me it's an illusion! I'm always in fights myself and I know when someone's getting beaten. Ouch! What are you doing?

FIRST MAN: Get the kid out of here.

SECOND MAN: I don't believe it. I can't believe my eyes! Get me an eye specialist.

FIRST MAN: It's falling down here. I can't bear it. Get out of the way! Mind out!

[DRAGON*'s head falls into the square with a crash.*]

MAYOR: A communiqué, a communiqué. My kingdom for a communiqué!

HENRY: Here is a communiqué from the council: Rendered

powerless and having lost everything, Lancelot has been partly taken prisoner.

BOY: Why partly?

HENRY: Why not? It's a military secret. His remaining parts are still resisting sporadically. Just one thing, the Dragon has released one of his heads on sick leave, and put it into the first line of reserves.

BOY: I still can't understand . . .

FIRST MAN: What is there to understand? Haven't you ever lost a tooth?

BOY: Yes.

FIRST MAN: Well, you're still alive, aren't you?

BOY: But I've never lost my head.

FIRST MAN: So what!

HENRY: Listen now to a commentary on the background to the day's news. You might ask, why in actual fact is two a greater number than three? The answer is simple. You have two heads on two necks: two plus two makes four. Q.E.D. And what is more, they are firmly in place.

[*The* DRAGON'*s second head falls with a crash into the market-place.*]

We interrupt our commentary to bring you a news item. Military operations are proceeding in accordance with the Dragon's plans.

BOY: Is that all?

HENRY: For the moment.

FIRST MAN: I've lost two thirds of my respect for the Dragon. Charlemagne, my dear friend! Why are you standing over there on your own?

SECOND MAN: Come over here and be with us.

FIRST MAN: It's utterly scandalous that the guards won't let you in to see your only daughter.

SECOND MAN: Why don't you speak?

FIRST MAN: Surely you're not angry with us?

CHARLEMAGNE: No. I'm a bit confused. A little while ago

you wouldn't have anything to do with me, and you weren't play-acting. Now you're only too pleased to see me, and you're still not pretending.

GARDENER: Ah, Master Charlemagne, it doesn't bear thinking about. It's too terrible for words. Terrible to think of the time wasted running to lick the paw of this one-headed monster. The flowers I could have grown in that time!

HENRY: We continue our commentary on the news.

GARDENER: Clear off! We've heard enough!

HENRY: That's what you think! It's war-time. You have to be patient. So, as I was saying. There is one God, one sun, one moon, and there is one head on the shoulders of our sovereign. To have only one head is – human, it is humane in the highest sense of the word. Furthermore, it is highly advantageous from the purely military point of view. It greatly reduces the front. It's three times easier to defend one head than three.

[DRAGON'*s third head falls with crash into market-place. Burst of shouts. Now all talk loudly.*]

FIRST MAN: Down with the Dragon!

SECOND MAN: We've been swindled from start to finish.

FIRST WOMAN: This is wonderful. Nobody to boss us around any more.

SECOND WOMAN: I feel quite drunk with happiness! I swear it.

BOY: Mummy, that means there won't be any school. Hurray!

PEDLAR: Roll up, ladies and gentlemen. Here's a lovely new toy. You pull the string and off comes his head.

[ALL *laugh out loud.*]

GARDENER: Very clever.

ALL: Hurray! Down with him! Down with old spud-face. Let's get the lot of them.

HENRY: Here is a communiqué.

ALL: We won't listen. We'll shout as much as we like and we like shouting a lot. Hurray! Come on. Let's get the lot of them!

MAYOR: Guard! Hey!

[GUARD *runs on to square.*]

MAYOR [*to* HENRY]: Talk to them. Start gently and then give them what for. Atten-tion!

[ALL *fall silent.*]

HENRY [*very mildly*]: Now do please listen to this communiqué. As a matter of fact the situation at the front is quite frankly not in the least bit interesting. Everything is pretty much all right. We're declaring a sort of minor state of siege. The penalty for spreading rumours [*threateningly*] is decapitation, and no fines accepted. Right? Everybody home! Guard, clear the square! [*The square empties.*] Well? How did you like that?

MAYOR: Be quiet, son.

[*Dull, heavy thud, causing earth tremor.*]

MAYOR: That's the Dragon's body crashing by the mill house.

DRAGON'S FIRST HEAD: Boy!

HENRY: What are you rubbing your hands for, father?

MAYOR: Ah, my boy. Because power has just fallen into them, all by itself.

DRAGON'S SECOND HEAD: Mr Mayor, come here. Give me water. Mr Mayor!

MAYOR: Everything is just fine, Henry. He trained them to take orders from anybody who holds the whip.

HENRY: Yes, but you saw what happened on the square just now...

MAYOR: Oh, that was nothing. Let a dog off its lead and it'll dash about like mad, but it'll always go back to its kennel by itself.

DRAGON'S THIRD HEAD: Boy! Come over here. I'm dying!

HENRY: Aren't you afraid of Lancelot, dad?

MAYOR: No. You don't think it was all that easy to kill off the Dragon, do you? I bet you Sir Lancelot is lying senseless on his flying carpet, and that the wind is carrying him well away from us.

HENRY: But suppose he comes down again, all of a sudden?

MAYOR: We'll finish him off in a jiffy. He's knocked out, I can assure you. The late lamented was quite a fighter, if nothing else. Let's go. We've got to get out our first decrees. The main thing is to carry on as if nothing had happened.

DRAGON'S FIRST HEAD: Boy! Mayor!

MAYOR: Come on. We haven't got time. [*Exeunt.*]

DRAGON'S FIRST HEAD: Why did I hit him with my second left paw? I should have used the second right.

DRAGON'S SECOND HEAD: Hey, is there anybody there? Miller! You used to kiss my tail whenever you met me. Hey, Brown! You once gave me a pipe with three mouthpieces and inscribed 'Yours for ever'. Anna-Louise, where are you now? You said you loved me. You carried parings of my claw in a velvet bag on your breast. We learnt to understand each other many years ago. Where are you all now? Give me water. Look, look, the well is just here. Just a mouthful, half a mouthful. Just wet my lips, then.

DRAGON'S FIRST HEAD: If only I could have another go. I'd crush the lot of you.

DRAGON'S SECOND HEAD: Just one drop of water, somebody.

DRAGON'S THIRD HEAD: If only I'd trained one of them to be loyal to me. But there just wasn't the material.

DRAGON'S SECOND HEAD: Ssshhh. There's someone near, I can tell. Come here. Give us water.

LANCELOT'S VOICE: I can't.

[LANCELOT *appears on market-place. He is on his magic carpet, leaning on his bent sword. He is holding his magic hat. The musical instrument is at his feet.*]

DRAGON'S FIRST HEAD: You won by a fluke. If I'd hit you with my second right . . .

DRAGON'S SECOND HEAD: Ah, well. Good-bye.

DRAGON'S THIRD HEAD: My only consolation is that what I've left you are burnt-out, threadbare, dead spirits. . . . Ah, well, good-bye.

DRAGON'S SECOND HEAD: Only one man around, and he's the one who killed me! What a way to die!

ALL THREE HEADS [*in unison*]: This is the end. Good-bye. [*They die.*]

LANCELOT: They're dead, but I can't say I feel all that well. My hands don't obey me. I can't see properly. And I seem to hear someone calling me all the time: 'Lancelot, Lancelot.' It's a familiar voice. A sad voice. I don't want to go, but this time I think I have to. What do you think, am I dying?

[*Musical instrument plays.*]

Yes, you make it all sound so fine and noble. But I feel very ill. I'm badly wounded. Not yet, not yet. . . . The Dragon's dead and that's a great relief. Elsa! I killed him! True, I shall never see you again, Elsa. You'll never smile at me again, never kiss me, never murmur, 'Lancelot, what's the matter? Why so sad? Why is your head spinning so? Why do your shoulders ache? Who is calling you so persistently, Lancelot, Lancelot?' It's death calling me, Elsa. I'm dying. It's very sad, isn't it?

[*Musical instrument answers.*]

It's too bad. They've all hidden away. Anyone would think my victory was a major disaster or something. You can just wait a bit, Death. You know me. It won't be the first time I've looked you in the eye and not run off to hide. I won't run away. I can hear you. Just give me a minute or two to think. They've all hidden themselves away. All right. But now they'll be sitting at home gradually coming to their senses, and are beginning to think straight for the first time. They're beginning to whisper and ask themselves why did we feed and look after that monster. It's through us that there's a man out there on the square dying all on his own. Well, now we shall be wiser. What a terrible battle it was up there in the sky all because of us. Poor Lancelot can hardly breathe. No, we must never let it happen again. Because of our weakness the strongest, the best, the most daring men have given their lives. Even the stones would have learnt the lesson. And we are people. That's what they're whispering in every house, in every little room. Do you hear?

[*Musical instrument replies.*]

Yes, just as I say. It means I'm not dying for nothing. Good-bye, Elsa. I knew I'd love you for the rest of my life.... But I didn't think my life would end so soon. Good-bye, town, good-bye, morning, noon, and evening. And now it's night already. Hey, you! Death is calling me ... he's in a hurry ... I can't think straight any more. There's ... there's something else I must say.... Hey, you! Don't be afraid. You can live without hurting widows and orphans. You can also have pity on one another. Have pity and you will be happy. It's true, I swear it, it's the pure truth, the purest truth on earth. That's all. I'm leaving. Good-bye.

[*Musical instrument answers.*]

ACT THREE

Luxuriously appointed hall in the Mayor's palace. Upstage, on either side of central door, two semi-circular tables, laid for supper. In centre, a small table, on which lies a heavy book in a gold binding. As the curtain rises an orchestra strikes up. A group of PEOPLE *shout, while looking towards the door.*

TOWNSPEOPLE [*quietly*]: One, two, three. [*Loudly*] Long live the Dragon-killer! [*Quietly*] One, two, three. [*Loudly*] Long live our leader! [*Quietly*] One, two, three. [*Loudly*] Our happiness is too great to comprehend. [*Quietly*] One, two, three. [*Loudly*] We can hear his footsteps!

[*Enter* HENRY.]

[*Loudly, but orderly*] Hurrah, hurrah, hurrah!

FIRST MAN: Oh, glorious liberator! Exactly one year ago you destroyed that accursed, repulsive, insensitive, hideous swine of a Dragon.

TOWNSPEOPLE: Hurrah, hurrah, hurrah!

FIRST MAN: Since then we have lived so well. We . . .

HENRY: Wait, wait, dear friends. Put more emphasis on the 'so'.

FIRST MAN: Very good. Since then we have lived ssso well.

HENRY: No, no, my friend. Not like that. Don't drag out the 's'. It sounds like an ambiguous hiss. Stress the 'o'.

FIRST MAN: Since then we have lived sooo well.

HENRY: You've got it. That's what I want. Why, you all know the Dragon-killer. He is a man simple to the point of innocence. He likes frankness and sincerity. Carry on.

FIRST MAN: We're beside ourselves with joy.

HENRY: Excellent. Wait a bit. Let's put in a bit of, what shall I say, uplift. . . . The Dragon-killer likes that sort of thing. [*Snapping his fingers*] Wait, wait, let me see. It's coming, it's coming. Yes, I've got it. Even the birdies are twittering it from the treetops. Evil is laid low, virtue has triumphed. Tweet-tweet, tweet-hurrah! Let's give it a run through.

FIRST MAN: Even the birdies are twittering it from the treetops. Evil is laid low, virtue has triumphed. Tweet-tweet, tweet-hurrah!

HENRY: You're not putting your back into it, my friend. If you don't watch out, you'll really have something to twitter about.

FIRST MAN [*merrily*]: Tweet-tweet. Tweet-hurrah.

HENRY: All right, that's better. Okay. We've already rehearsed the other bits, haven't we?

ALL: Yes, indeed, Mr Mayor.

HENRY: Right then. The Dragon-killer, the President of our Free City, will appear here in a moment. Just remember, speak in an orderly fashion, but at the same time in a free and easy democratic way. It was the Dragon who went in for all that ceremonial, but we . . .

SENTRY [*from centre door*]: Atten-tion! Eyes to the door! His Excellency the Lord President of the Free City is proceeding along the corridor. [*In a wooden bass voice*] Oh, you sweet thing! Oh, you are goodness itself! You killed the Dragon. Fancy that, now!

[*Music rings out. Enter* MAYOR.]

HENRY: Your Excellency Lord President of the Free City! I have no incidents to report and all's well. Ten men present. All of them are insanely happy. In the lock-up.

MAYOR: At ease, at ease, gentlemen. Good day, Mr Mayor. [*Shakes* HENRY*'s hand.*] Oh, but who are these people? Eh, Mr Mayor?

HENRY: Our fellow citizens have remembered that it was just a year ago today that you killed the Dragon. They've come to congratulate you.

MAYOR: Well, whatever next! What a pleasant surprise! Go ahead, then.

CITIZENS [*quietly*]: One, two, three. [*Loudly*] Long live the Dragon-killer! [*Quietly*] One, two, three. [*Loudly*] Long live our leader. . . .

[*Enter* GAOLER.]

MAYOR: Wait a minute. Good day, Gaoler.

GAOLER: Good day, your Excellency.

MAYOR [*to citizens*]: Thank you, gentlemen. I know only too well what you want to say. Brings a tear to my eyes, dammit. [*Brushes away tear.*] But you see, we're having a wedding here today, and I still have one or two little things to attend to. You may leave now, but come back later to the wedding. We'll have a real good time. The nightmare is over, and now we are really living. Isn't that so?

TOWNSPEOPLE: Hurrah, hurrah, hurrah.

MAYOR: Quite so, quite so. Slavery is a thing of the past and we are reborn. Do you remember what I was like under that wretched Dragon? I was sick, I was out of my mind. And now? Right as rain. To say nothing of you. You're always so joyful and happy, like my little birdies. Well, fly home now. Look sharp! Henry, see them off.

[*Exeunt* TOWNSPEOPLE.]

Well, how is everyone in prison?

GAOLER: Still there.

MAYOR: And my ex-assistant, how is he?

GAOLER: He's in a bad way.

MAYOR: Ha, ha! You're not pulling my leg, are you?

GAOLER: I swear he is.

MAYOR: But how, though?

GAOLER: He's up the wall.

MAYOR: Ha, ha! And a good job too. A disgusting character. You tell a joke, everyone else laughs except him – he says he's heard it before. Right, it'll do him good to sit in gaol a bit. Have you shown him my portrait?

GAOLER: Not half!

MAYOR: Which one? The one where I'm smiling radiantly?

GAOLER: That's the one.

MAYOR: How did he take it?

GAOLER: He wept.

MAYOR: Go on!

GAOLER: I swear it, he wept.

MAYOR: Ha, ha. That's nice to know. And what about those weavers who made the flying carpet for you-know-who?

GAOLER: They're a damned nuisance. They're on different floors, but it's as though they were in the same cell. Whatever one says the other says the same.

MAYOR: Yes, but at least they've got thin, haven't they?

GAOLER: You don't put on weight in my gaol!

MAYOR: What about the blacksmith?

GAOLER: He cut through the bars again. We've had to put a diamond window in his cell.

MAYOR: That's good, money's no object. But how did he take it?

GAOLER: He can't make it out.

MAYOR: Ha, ha. That's nice.

GAOLER: The hatter made little hats for the mice and the cats won't touch them.

MAYOR: Really? Why?

GAOLER: They think they're too nice. And the musician's singing makes you want to cry. I always plug my ears with wax when I go in there.

MAYOR: What's happening in the town?

GAOLER: It's quiet. They're writing, though.

MAYOR: Writing?

GAOLER: Yes, the letter 'L' on the walls. 'L' stands for Lancelot.

MAYOR: Rubbish. 'L' means we Love our President.

GAOLER: Ah, I see. So there's no need to lock up people who write it?

MAYOR: What do you mean, no need? Lock them up! What else do they write?

GAOLER: I hardly dare say. The President's a swine. His son's a crook.... The President [*deep giggle*]... I daren't tell you what they say. But mostly they write the letter 'L'.

MAYOR: They're crackers. They can't get that Lancelot fellow out of their minds. Still no news of him, I suppose?

GAOLER: He's vanished.

MAYOR: Have you had the birds in for questioning?

GAOLER: Yes.

MAYOR: All of them?

GAOLER: Yes. See this mark here? I got that from one of the eagles pecking me on the ear.

MAYOR: Well, what do they say?

GAOLER: They say they haven't seen him. Except for one parrot who came clean. I say 'Any news?' And he says

'News'. I say 'Lancelot?' and he says 'Lancelot'. But you know what parrots are like.

MAYOR: What about the snakes?

GAOLER: If they knew anything they'd have come crawling already. They're on our side. And then they're relatives of the late lamented. But there's no sign of them.

MAYOR: And the fish?

GAOLER: They're not saying anything.

MAYOR: Perhaps they know something, then?

GAOLER: No. Our fish experts have examined their eyes and they say that they don't know anything. To cut a long story short, Lancelot, alias St George, alias Perseus, the scoundrel – he has a different name in every country – well, his whereabouts have not yet been established.

MAYOR: Oh, well, blow him.

[*Enter* HENRY.]

HENRY: Charlemagne, the father of the happy bride, is here.

MAYOR: Ah? Just the man I wanted to see. Tell him to come in.

[*Enter* CHARLEMAGNE.]

All right, you can go now, Gaoler. Carry on the good work, I'm very pleased with you.

GAOLER: We do our little best.

MAYOR: Good for you. Charlemagne, you know the Gaoler, don't you?

CHARLEMAGNE: Not very well, your Excellency.

MAYOR: Well, not to worry, maybe you'll get to know him better some day.

GAOLER: Shall I take him now?

MAYOR: There he goes again, always in such a hurry. Now be off with you for the time being.

[*Exit* GAOLER.]

Well, now, Charlemagne, you've no doubt guessed why we've summoned you. What with this, that and the other, cares of state, you know, I haven't had a chance to come and see you myself. But you and Elsa know, from the notices posted round the town, that it's her wedding today.

CHARLEMAGNE: Yes, we know, sir.

MAYOR: We statesmen haven't got time to go making proposals. Going down on our knees and presenting flowers and what not. We don't make proposals, we give orders just like that. Ha, ha. One saves so much time, that way. Elsa's happy I trust?

CHARLEMAGNE: No.

MAYOR: Come, come . . . Of course she is. What about yourself?

CHARLEMAGNE: I'm in despair, sir.

MAYOR: How ungrateful of you! I kill the Dragon for you . . .

CHARLEMAGNE: I'm sorry, sir, but I just cannot believe that.

MAYOR: Yes you can.

CHARLEMAGNE: No I can't, I swear it.

MAYOR: Yes you can, yes you can. If even I can believe it, then I'm sure you can.

CHARLEMAGNE: I can't.

HENRY: He just doesn't want to.

MAYOR: But why?

HENRY: He's holding out for a better price.

MAYOR: All right. I offer you the post of my principal private secretary.

CHARLEMAGNE: I don't want it.

MAYOR: Nonsense, of course you do.

CHARLEMAGNE: I don't.

MAYOR: Don't haggle, there isn't time. You'll get government quarters near the park, not far from the market, a hundred and fifty-three rooms – all facing south incidentally. Fabulous salary. And every time you go to the office you get expenses, and you get a special allowance for going home again. Every time you go visiting you get a travel allowance, and if you just sit around at home you get an accommodation allowance. You'll be almost as rich as me. That's all. I trust I have your agreement.

CHARLEMAGNE: No.

MAYOR: Well, what do you want, then?

CHARLEMAGNE: Only one thing, just leave us in peace.

MAYOR: Leave you in peace – that's a good one! Why should I? Anyway, it's the proper thing to do from the official point of view. Dragon-killer weds damsel he saved. Sounds so plausible. Don't you see the point?

CHARLEMAGNE: Why do you torment us? I've now got a mind of my own, and that is painful enough. And now there's this wedding on top of it all. It's enough to drive anybody mad.

MAYOR: No it isn't, not at all. All this about mental illness is just so much poppycock, all imagination.

CHARLEMAGNE: Oh, my God, we're so helpless! The town is just as meek and mild as it ever was – it's terrible.

MAYOR: What sort of raving nonsense is this? What's so terrible? Are you and Elsa plotting revolt, or something?

CHARLEMAGNE: No. We went for a walk in the woods today and talked over the whole thing. Tomorrow, when her end comes, I shall die too.

MAYOR: What do you mean, when her end comes? What sort of nonsense is this?

CHARLEMAGNE: You don't really imagine that she'll survive the wedding, do you?

MAYOR: Why not? It'll be a wonderful, gay occasion. Anybody else would be only too glad to marry his daughter to a wealthy man.

HENRY: He is glad, too.

CHARLEMAGNE: No. I'm not. I'm getting on in years and I don't like to be rude, I don't like to say this to your face, but I must: this wedding is a great tragedy for us.

HENRY: What a tedious way he has of driving a bargain.

MAYOR: Look here, my dear man. I've made my final offer.

I suppose you want to come in on the whole business. Well, there's nothing doing. Everything that bare-faced Dragon used to grab is now in the hands of your leading citizens. I mean in mine and Henry's. Which is just as it should be. You won't get a penny of that money.

CHARLEMAGNE: Will you excuse me now, sir?

MAYOR: Yes, you may go. Only remember these three things: first: I expect you to be the life and soul of the party at the wedding. Second: don't either of you dare go and die on me. I'll thank you to stay alive for as long as I need you. You can tell your daughter that, too. Third: in future address me as 'your Excellency'. See this list? There are fifty names here. All your best friends. So you'd better behave or else the whole lot will disappear into thin air. You may go now. No, wait a minute. There'll be a carriage coming for you right away. You bring your daughter here, and no funny business. All right? Right.

[*Exit* CHARLEMAGNE.]

Well, everything's going fine.

HENRY: What did the Gaoler have to say?

MAYOR: Everything's as right as rain.

HENRY: And what about this 'L' they're writing?

MAYOR: Oh, they were always writing on the walls in the Dragon's day, weren't they? Who cares? They get a bit of fun out of it and what harm does it do us? Go and make sure there's nobody sitting in that chair.

HENRY: Oh, really! [*Feels the chair.*] There's nobody here, you can sit in it.

MAYOR: It's no laughing matter. He can sneak in anywhere in that invisible hat of his.

HENRY: Father, you simply don't understand the man. He's such a stickler for form, he would never dream of entering a house without first taking his hat off, and then the guard would nab him.

MAYOR: How do we know he hasn't lowered his standards

in the last year? [*Sits down.*] Now then, sonny boy, I have a little bone to pick with you. There's the matter of a small sum you owe me.

HENRY: What small sum, father dear?

MAYOR: You've bribed three of my flunkeys to watch my movements, read my papers and so on, haven't you?

HENRY: Heavens above, father!

MAYOR: Not so fast, sonny boy, don't interrupt. I gave them an extra five hundred out of my own pocket so they'd pass on only what I want them to. And so you see you owe me five hundred, my darling boy.

HENRY: I'm afraid not, father. This having come to my attention, I coughed up another six hundred.

MAYOR: And I, not to be outdone, threw in another thousand, you little monkey. So the balance is in my favour. And please don't give them any more, dear boy. With all this money they've got fat and lazy, they've got spoilt, and they've gone to seed. If we don't watch out they'll be turning on us both before long. And another thing. You really must lay off my private secretary. I've had to send the poor devil to a mental home.

HENRY: Oh, really, why?

MAYOR: Because he changed hands so many times a day, he didn't know who he was working for any more. He's even been giving *me* reports on myself. He's even been plotting against himself to get his own job. He's a decent, hard-working lad, it's a shame to see him suffer like this. Let's go and see him tomorrow at the home, and straighten out once and for all who he's working for. Oh Henry, my boy! Ah, my little pride and joy! After daddy's job was he, diddums?

HENRY: What will you say next, father!

MAYOR: Forget it, my dear boy, forget it. We're both men of the world. You know what I suggest? Let's be more straightforward about the whole business, let's keep it in the family, as between father and son, without bringing in any outsiders. Think of the money we'll save!

HENRY: Who cares about money, father!

MAYOR: True, true. . . . You can't take it with you . . .

[*Clatter of hooves and jingling bells.*]

MAYOR [*rushes to window*]: She's here! She's come, our beauty! What a carriage! It's a marvel. All inlaid with the Dragon's scales. And just look at Elsa! Enough to take your breath away. All got up in velvet. Say what you like, it's a nice thing to be in power. [*In a whisper*] Ask her a few questions.

HENRY: Who?

MAYOR: Elsa. She's been a bit quiet lately. Maybe she knows where whatsisname . . . [*looks round*] – Lancelot is. Only better be careful. I'll be listening here behind this curtain. [*Hides.*]

[*Enter* ELSA *and* CHARLEMAGNE.]

HENRY: Welcome to you, Elsa. You get prettier every day, it's one of the nicest things about you. The President is dressing. He asked me to give you his apologies. Sit down here, Elsa. [*Puts her into chair with back to curtain where Mayor is hiding.*] And perhaps you will wait in the ante-room, Charlemagne.

[CHARLEMAGNE *bows and leaves.*]

Elsa, I'm glad the President is busy putting on his regalia. I've been wanting to have a heart-to-heart with you for a long time now. Why don't you ever say anything? Eh? You don't want to talk? You know I'm very fond of you, in my own way. Talk to me.

ELSA: What about?

HENRY: Anything you like.

ELSA: I really don't know . . . I don't want anything.

HENRY: Come, now. Today's your wedding day. Oh, Elsa. . . . This is the second time I've had to make way for another man. Still, a Dragon-killer's a Dragon-killer. I'm not very easily impressed, but even I have to hand it to him. You're not listening to me.

ELSA: No.

HENRY: Oh, Elsa. . . . Have I really become such a stranger to you? Think what good friends we were as children. Remember when you had measles, I used to come and stand under your window so I could catch it, too? And you used to come and see me and tell me I was sweet and kind. Remember?

ELSA: Yes.

HENRY: Is it possible that those two children who were so close to each other suddenly ceased to exist? Is there nothing left of them in either of us? Let's talk to each other as we did in the old days, like brother and sister.

ELSA: Well, all right, let's talk, then.

[MAYOR *peeps from behind curtain and silently applauds* HENRY.]

You want to know why I've been so silent all this time?

[MAYOR *nods his head.*]

Because I have been afraid.

HENRY: Who are you afraid of?

ELSA: People.

HENRY: Really? Tell me their names. We'll just lock them up and you won't have any more trouble.

[MAYOR *takes out notebook.*]

Just tell me their names.

ELSA: That wouldn't help at all, Henry.

HENRY: It will, I promise you. I've tried it out myself. You sleep better, eat better, and feel better.

ELSA: Don't you see . . . I don't know how to explain it . . . I'm afraid of everyone.

HENRY: Ah, yes, I see . . . I understand only too well. You think everyone is cruel, including me. Right? You probably don't trust me, but, but . . . I'm also afraid of everyone. I'm afraid of my own father.

[*The* MAYOR *shrugs his shoulders and looks quizzical.*]

I'm afraid of our faithful servants, and I pretend to be cruel to make them afraid of me. Oh, what a tangled web we weave. . . . Go on talking and I'll listen.

[MAYOR *nods understanding.*]

ELSA: I don't know what else to say. . . . At first I was angry, then I was sad, and finally nothing mattered. I'm as meek now as I ever was. Anyone can do what they like with me.

[MAYOR *giggles loudly. Ducks back behind curtain.* ELSA *looks round.*]

Who is it?

HENRY: Take no notice. They're getting ready for the wedding feast. My poor, dear little sister. Such a shame that Lancelot has vanished into thin air. It's only now that I understand him. He was a marvellous man. We have all done him wrong. Is there no hope at all for his return?

[*Again* MAYOR *comes out from curtain. He is all ears.*]

ELSA: He . . . he won't come back.

HENRY: You mustn't think that. I have a sort of feeling that we'll be seeing him again.

ELSA: No we won't.

HENRY: Believe me!

ELSA: I like hearing you say it, but . . . we're not being overheard are we?

[MAYOR *sits down behind her arm-chair.*]

HENRY: Of course not, my dear. Today's a holiday. The spies have been given a day off.

ELSA: The thing is . . . I know what happened to Lancelot.

HENRY: Don't talk about it if it's painful for you.

[MAYOR *shakes his fist at* HENRY.]

ELSA: It's all right. I've kept quiet for so long that I feel I want to tell you everything now. I thought that I was the only one in this town who felt how sad this is. But you're being so kind to me today. . . . Anyway . . . Just a year ago, when the battle ended, the Cat ran on to the palace square. There he saw Lancelot, as white as a sheet, standing by the dead heads of the Dragon. He was leaning on his sword and smiling, so as not to upset the Cat. The Cat came rushing for me to help. But I was so closely guarded that not even a fly could have got in to the house. They chased the Cat away.

HENRY: Soldiers are so rude!

ELSA: Then the Cat got his friend the Donkey. He put Lancelot on the Donkey's back and smuggled him out of town by all the back streets.

HENRY: But why?

ELSA: Lancelot was so weak, the people could easily have killed him. And so they followed the path to the mountains. The Cat sat next to Lancelot so as to hear if his heart was still beating.

HENRY: It was, I trust?

ELSA: Yes, but it was getting more and more faint. Then the Cat called 'Halt!' and the Donkey stopped. Night had fallen. They were high up in the mountains, and it was as quiet and as cold as could be. 'Let's go home,' said the Cat. 'They can't hurt him any more. Let Elsa say her good-bye to him and then we'll bury him.'

HENRY: He was dead, poor Lancelot!

ELSA: Yes, Henry, dead. The stubborn Donkey said 'I won't turn round', and went on further. But the Cat came back – cats always do. He came back and told me the whole story, so now I'm not waiting for anybody any more. It's all over.

MAYOR: Three cheers! It's all over! [*Dances all round the room.*] It's all over! I'm the king of the castle! Nothing to be afraid of any more. Thanks, Elsa. This is a real holiday. Who'll have the nerve to say I didn't kill the Dragon now, eh? Eh?

ELSA: Was he listening?

HENRY: Of course.

ELSA: And you knew?

HENRY: Oh, Elsa, you'll have to stop this innocent maiden act. Thank God you're getting married today.

ELSA: Father! Father!

[*Enter* CHARLEMAGNE, *running*.]

CHARLEMAGNE: What is it, my darling? [*Makes to embrace her.*]

MAYOR: Keep your hands to yourself! And stand to attention when you address my bride-to-be!

CHARLEMAGNE [*at attention*]: There, there, don't get upset. Don't cry. What can we do? There's nothing to be done. What can we do?

[*Music starts.*]

MAYOR [*running to window*]: It warms the cockles of me heart! The guests are arriving for the wedding. The horses are all decked out with ribbons. And fairy-lights on the carriages. It's a joy to be alive and to know that no fool can get in your way. Smile then, Elsa. At the appointed hour, to the very second, the President of the Free City himself will take you to his bosom.

[*Doors are flung open wide.*]

Welcome, welcome, dear guests.

[*Enter* GUESTS. *They walk past* ELSA *and* MAYOR *in pairs. They talk primly, almost in a whisper.*]

FIRST MAN: Congratulations to the bride and groom. Everyone's so happy!

SECOND MAN: The houses are all lit up with coloured lights.

FIRST MAN: It's as light as day in the streets.

SECOND MAN: All the pubs are packed out.

BOY: They ain't arf fighting and swearing too.

GUESTS: Ssshhh.

GARDENER: Allow me to present you with these bluebells. I'm afraid they're ringing a little sadly just now, but don't worry. They'll have wilted by the morning and you won't hear them any more.

FIRST GIRL-FRIEND: Oh, Elsa dear, do cheer up a little. Or I'll start crying and spoil my mascara, and I made such a good job of it today.

SECOND GIRL-FRIEND: After all, he's not as bad as the Dragon, dear. He's got proper hands and feet, hasn't he, and none of those awful scales. And even if he is the President he's still human. You can tell us all about it tomorrow. It'll be so interesting.

THIRD GIRL-FRIEND: And then think of the good you'll be able to do for people. You could ask him to sack my dad's boss, for a start. Then my dad'll get his job, his wages'll be double, and we'll be so happy.

MAYOR [*counting guests in undertone*]: One, two, three, four. [*Counting places at table*] One, two, three. . . . It seems there's one guest too many. . . . Oh, yes, it's the little boy. Now, now, don't cry. You can eat out of the same plate as your mum. Well, we're all here now. Please take your places, ladies and gentlemen. We'll soon be over with the ceremony – we don't hold with pomp and circumstance – and then we'll get down to the banquet. I've got you a fish specially made to be eaten. It laughs when it's being cooked, and tells the cook when it's ready. And here's a turkey stuffed with its own chicks. Such a touching family scene, don't you think? And here are some sucking pigs which were not only fed but specially bred for us to eat. They can still sit up and beg with their trotters even though they've already been roasted. Don't howl, boy, there's nothing to be frightened of, it's great fun. And this wine here is so old it's in its second childhood, and that's why it's bubbling away like a baby. And here's vodka that's so pure that it looks as if there's nothing in the bottle. My God, it really is empty. Those damned flunkeys have been at it again. Doesn't matter, there's plenty more in the sideboard. You know, it's so nice to be rich. Are we all seated? Splendid. Hang on a minute. Before you start eating there's the little matter of the ceremony. It'll only take a moment. Elsa, give me your mitt.

[ELSA *gives her hand.*]

Ah, you little mischief, you little scamp. What a warm little paw you have. Stick your chin up now. Smile. All set, Henry?

HENRY: Aye, aye, sir.

MAYOR: Do your stuff, then.

HENRY: Ladies and gentlemen, unaccustomed as I am to public speaking, I fear that my remarks may lack polish. A year ago a conceited upstart challenged that bane of our lives, the Dragon, to a duel. A special committee, set up by the city council, established the following: all the wretch, who is now dead, had succeeded in doing was to inflict a slight wound on the monster, which merely enraged him. Then, our mayor, now President of our Free City, heroically flung himself at the Dragon and killed him once and for all, performing in the process various extraordinary feats of bravery.

[*Applause.*]

And thereby the canker of servility was for ever cut out of our body politic.

[*Applause.*]

As a token of its gratitude the city decided that in view of the fact that we used to give our prettiest maidens to the accursed monster, we can hardly deny the same simple and natural right to our beloved liberator.

[*Applause.*]

And therefore, in order, on the one hand, to give expression to the greatness of our President, and on the other, to the loyalty and devotion of our city, I shall now in my capacity as mayor perform the marriage ceremony. Organist, the wedding march!

[*Organ plays.*]

Notaries! Open the register of happy events.

[*Enter* NOTARIES *holding enormous fountain-pens.*]

For four hundred years the names of those poor girls given in tribute to the Dragon have been inscribed in this book.

We have now reached page 401, and the first name to be entered on this page will be that of the lucky girl whom our brave Dragon-killer is taking as his bride.

[*Applause.*]

Bridegroom, wilt thou take this woman to be thy lawful wedded wife?

MAYOR: For the good of my home town I am ready for anything.

[*Applause.*]

HENRY: Write that down, notaries. Watch out! Any blots and I'll make you lick 'em up. Good. That's the lot then. Oh, yes, I'm sorry. There's just one more little formality. It's the bride. Thou wilt, of course, take his Excellency to be thy lawful wedded husband? [*Pause.*] Well, come on, girl, out with it . . .

ELSA: No.

HENRY: Well, that's settled then. Write down 'I will'.

ELSA: Don't dare write anything of the sort.

[NOTARIES *stagger back.*]

HENRY: Elsa, don't hold up the proceedings.

MAYOR: She's not holding us up, my dear boy. When a girl says no, she means yes. Just write it down.

ELSA: I said no! I'll tear the page out of the book and trample on it.

MAYOR: Charming girlish tantrums, tears and all that sort of romantic stuff. Every girl has to have her little cry before the wedding, and then everything comes out all right in the wash. We'll just hold her by her little hand and do the necessary. Notaries . . .

ELSA: At least let me have my say! Please!

HENRY: Elsa!

MAYOR: No need to shout, dear boy. Everything is as it should be. The bride wants her say. She shall have it, and that will be an end of the formalities. It's all right, don't worry, let her, we're all friends here.

ELSA: My friends, my friends! Why are you tormenting the life out of me like this? It's just like a nightmare. But when the bandit is holding his knife over you, you can still escape. Somebody can come and kill him, or you can slip away from him ... but then suppose the bandit's knife suddenly flies at you by itself? Or his rope crawls towards you like a snake, to tie you up, hand and foot? Suppose even the curtain of his room, the harmless little curtain, suddenly flies at you to muzzle you? What would you say then? I used to think you were all obedient to the Dragon only in the way the bandit's knife obeys the bandit. But it turns out that you, my friends, are bandits too. I'm not blaming you, you're not even aware of it, but I implore you to come to your senses! Can it be that the Dragon didn't die, but only turned himself into a man, the way he used to? Only this time he turned himself into many people, and here they are killing me. Don't kill me. Wake up! Oh, my God, what misery! Cut through the web that binds you all. Is there no one who will come to my help?

BOY: I would, only my mum's got hold of my hand.

MAYOR: Well, that's over with. The bride has said her say. Life goes on as though nothing had happened.

BOY: Mum!

MAYOR: You keep quiet, my little lad. Now we're going to have the time of our lives. I've had enough of all this red tape. You just write down 'The marriage is hereby solemnized' – and now for the food. I just feel like a good meal.

HENRY: Notaries, write down 'The marriage is hereby solemnized'. Come on, then! Stop day-dreaming!

[NOTARIES *pick up their pens. Loud knock at the door.* NOTARIES *stagger back.*]

MAYOR: Who is it?

[*Silence.*]

You there, whoever you are, come back tomorrow, d'you

hear, tomorrow, in office hours, and see my secretary. I haven't got time now. I'm just getting married!

[*Again a knock.*]

Don't open the doors! Notaries, write!

[*The doors fly open by themselves. Nobody is to be seen through them.*]

Henry, come here. What's going on here?

HENRY: Oh, father, it's the usual thing. The innocent complaints of our dear Elsa have alarmed all those well-meaning inhabitants of the rivers, and woods, and lakes. Don't worry about them. . . . They can't touch us. They're just as invisible and just as powerless as so-called conscience and all that rubbish. We'll have two or three bad dreams – and that'll be the end of it.

MAYOR: No, I know it's him!

HENRY: Who?

MAYOR: Lancelot. He's wearing that invisible hat of his. He's standing right here. He can hear what we're saying. His sword is hanging over my head.

HENRY: My dear father, if you don't pull yourself together, I shall have to take over from you.

MAYOR: Strike up the band! My dear guests, please forgive that unintended hitch, but I can't stand draughts. It was a draught that opened the door, nothing more. Don't get excited, Elsa my sweet. I declare the marriage solemnized and duly signed and sealed. What was that? What's all the running for?

[*Frightened* FLUNKEY *enters, running.*]

FLUNKEY: Take it back! Take it back!

MAYOR: Take what back?

FLUNKEY: Take back your filthy money. I'm not working for you any more.

MAYOR: Why?

FLUNKEY: He'll kill me for all the vile things I've done.

MAYOR: Who's going to kill him? Eh? Henry?

[*Enter* SECOND FLUNKEY, *running.*]

SECOND FLUNKEY: He's coming along the corridor! I gave him a low bow, but he didn't say a word. He doesn't even look at people any more. My God, we're not half going to catch it for what we've done. We're in for it now. [*Rushes out.*]

MAYOR: Henry!

HENRY: Carry on as though nothing was wrong. Whatever happens. We'll be all right. It's our only hope.

[THIRD FLUNKEY *enters backwards. He shouts into empty corridor.*]

THIRD FLUNKEY: I can prove it! My wife will back me up! I always said they were a bad lot. I only took their money because my nerves were so bad. I've got documents to prove it. [*Disappears.*]

MAYOR: Look!

HENRY: Don't bat an eyelid, for God's sake!

[*Enter* LANCELOT.]

MAYOR: Well, hullo, fancy you turning up! Still, we're glad to see you. We're a bit short of crockery, but never mind. You can eat off a big plate and I'll use a little one. I'd send for more only those idiots of flunkeys have cleared off. . . . Ah, well, er, now here's me just on the point of entering holy wedlock as it were. Ha, ha. H'm, yes, we were just having a quiet little do on our own without any fuss. Nice and cosy like. . . . Come and meet my guests. But where are they? Oh, they're all looking for something they've dropped under the table. This is my son, Henry. You've met already, I think. Only a youngster, but he's Mayor already. He got on very fast after I . . . after we . . . I mean after the Dragon was killed. What's the matter? Please come in.

HENRY: Why don't you say something?

MAYOR: Yes, what is the matter? Did you have a good journey? What's happening in the world? Perhaps you'd like a rest after your journey? The Guard will show you the way.

LANCELOT: Hullo, Elsa.

ELSA: Lancelot! [*Runs to him*] Come in and sit down, come on. Is it really you?

LANCELOT: Yes, Elsa.

ELSA: And your hands are warm, and your hair's grown since I last saw you. Or is it just my imagination? But you still have the same cloak. Lancelot! [*Makes him sit on small chair in centre.*] Drink some wine. No, better not take anything of theirs. Just rest a bit and then we'll go home. Father! He's come, father! It's just like the first time he came. It was just when we were both thinking there was nothing else for it but to lie down and die without a word. Lancelot!

LANCELOT: Does that mean you still love me?

ELSA: Did you hear that, father? How many times did we dream of him coming back and asking 'Elsa, do you still love me?' And then I answer, yes, Lancelot. And then I ask, where have you been all this time?

LANCELOT: Far away. In the Black Mountains.

ELSA: Were you very ill?

LANCELOT: Yes, I was. You know, being mortally wounded is a pretty dangerous thing.

ELSA: Who nursed you?

LANCELOT: A woodcutter's wife. She was a good, kind woman. But she got a bit hurt when I kept calling her Elsa in my delirium.

ELSA: So you missed me?

LANCELOT: I did.

ELSA: And I was dying without you. They tormented me here.

MAYOR: Who did? I don't believe it! Why didn't you let us know about it? We soon would have put a stop to it!

LANCELOT: I know all about it, Elsa.

ELSA: You know?

LANCELOT: Yes.

ELSA: How do you know?

LANCELOT: Not far from the woodcutter's cottage in the Black Mountains there's a huge cave. In this cave there is a writing book, and it's nearly filled right up to the last page now. Nobody ever touches it and yet a new page is filled in every day. Who do you think does the writing? The world! The crimes of all criminals, the miseries of everybody who suffers for nothing – it's all in there.

[HENRY *and* MAYOR *tiptoe towards door.*]

ELSA: And was it in there about us, too?

LANCELOT: Yes, Elsa. Hey, you there! Murderers! Stay where you are!

MAYOR: Why do you say nasty things like that?

LANCELOT: Because I'm different from what I was a year ago. I set you free and look what you've done!

MAYOR: Oh, well, if you're going to complain about my work, I'll just pack it in and go into retirement.

LANCELOT: You're not going anywhere!

HENRY: Quite right, too. You simply can't imagine how he's behaved since you left. I'll let you have a list of all the crimes he's planned which haven't got into that book of yours yet, because he didn't have time to carry them out.

LANCELOT: Shut up!

HENRY: Well, I never! If you really go into it you'll find I'm not guilty of anything at all. I was taught to be what I am.

LANCELOT: So was everyone else. But why did you learn the lesson better than anybody else? You scoundrel.

HENRY: It's time we went, father. He's beginning to use bad language.

LANCELOT: You're not going anywhere. I came back a month ago, Elsa.

ELSA: And you didn't come to see me!

LANCELOT: Yes, I did, in my invisible hat, early in the morning. I kissed you very softly, so as not to wake you up. And then I went for a walk round the town. What I saw was frightful. It had been bad enough to read about it, but to see it with my own eyes was much worse. Hey, Miller!

[FIRST MAN *gets up from underneath table.*]

I saw you sobbing with ecstasy when you were shouting out to the Mayor 'Long live the Dragon-killer!'

FIRST MAN: It's true, I did cry. But, Sir Lancelot, I wasn't pretending.

LANCELOT: But you knew it wasn't him who killed the Dragon.

FIRST MAN: In private, I knew it ... But in public? ... [*Shrugs shoulders.*]

LANCELOT: Gardener!

[GARDENER *gets up from under table.*]

You taught your snapdragons to shout 'Hurrah for the President!'?

GARDENER: Yes, I did.

LANCELOT: And did they learn to do it?

GARDENER: Yes. But every time they shouted it they stuck their tongues out at me. I thought I'd try to get money for new experiments. ... But ...

LANCELOT: Brown!

[SECOND MAN *crawls out.*]

Is it true that when the Mayor got angry with you he put your only son into a dungeon?

SECOND MAN: It's true. And now the lad's got a hacking cough. It's very damp down there, you know.

LANCELOT: Yet after he'd done that you gave the Mayor a pipe inscribed 'Yours ever'?

SECOND MAN: What else could I do to soften his heart?

LANCELOT: What *am* I to do with you?

MAYOR: Don't you bother with them. You don't want to trouble yourself with this sort of thing. Henry and I know just how to deal with them. That'll be the best possible punishment for this lot. You just take Elsa by the hand and let us carry on as before. It'll be more humane and democratic that way.

LANCELOT: It's impossible. Come in, my friends!

[*Enter* WEAVERS, BLACKSMITH, HATTER, MUSICAL-INSTRUMENT MAKER.]

Even you let me down, too. I thought you'd manage without me. Why did you knuckle under and go to prison? After all, there were enough of you!

WEAVERS: They didn't give us a chance to get our bearings.

LANCELOT [*indicating* MAYOR *and* HENRY]: Take them away.

WEAVERS [*seizing* MAYOR *and* HENRY]: Come on!

BLACKSMITH: I checked the bars myself. They'll do. Come on!

HATTER: Here are some dunces' caps for you. I used to make such beautiful hats, but you turned me nasty in prison. Let's go!

MUSICAL-INSTRUMENT MAKER: In my cell I made a fiddle from black bread and spun the strings from a spider's web. It plays rather sadly and softly, but you only have yourselves to blame. And now you can march to our music to the place you'll never come back from.

HENRY: But this is all nonsense, we can't have this, it just isn't right. All of a sudden, this tramp, this beggar, who's never done a day's work . . .

WEAVERS: Get going!

MAYOR: Got going!

WEAVERS: Get going!

[*Simple, sad, hardly audible music.* HENRY *and* MAYOR *are led off.*]

LANCELOT: Elsa, I'm not the man you used to know. Have you noticed?

ELSA: Yes, but I love you even more.

LANCELOT: We can't go away . . .

ELSA: It doesn't matter. It can be just as much fun at home.

LANCELOT: We have some very tricky and boring work to do, even worse than embroidery. The Dragon has to be killed in each and every one of them.

BOY: Will it hurt?

LANCELOT: Not you, it won't.

FIRST MAN: What about us?

LANCELOT: I can see I've got my work cut out with you.

GARDENER: Be patient with us, Sir Lancelot. I do beg you to be patient. Tend us gently. The fires you light will help us grow. Take out the weeds carefully, or you might damage the new roots. You know, when you really come to think about it, when all is said and done, people need very careful treatment.

FIRST GIRL-FRIEND: And now let us have the wedding after all.

SECOND GIRL-FRIEND: Because happiness makes people beautiful.

LANCELOT: Well said! Let's have some music there!

[*Music starts up.*]

Give me your hand, Elsa! My friends, I love you all. Why should I take so much trouble over you, otherwise? And if I love you everything will be wonderful. And after all our trials and tribulations we're going to be happy, very happy at last!

PENGUIN CLASSICS

William James	Varieties of Religious Experience
Jack London	The Call of the Wild and Other Stories
	Martin Eden
Henry Wadsworth Longfellow	Selected Poems
Herman Melville	Billy Budd, Sailor and Other Stories
	Moby-Dick
	Redburn
	Typee
Thomas Paine	Common Sense
Edgar Allan Poe	The Narrative of Arthur Gordon Pym of Nantucket
	The Other Poe
	The Science Fiction of Edgar Allan Poe
	Selected Writings
Harriet Beecher Stowe	Uncle Tom's Cabin
Henry David Thoreau	Walden and Civil Disobedience
Mark Twain	The Adventures of Huckleberry Finn
	A Connecticut Yankee at King Arthur's Court
	Life on the Mississippi
	Pudd'nhead Wilson
	Roughing It
Owen Wister	The Virginian

FOR THE BEST IN PAPERBACKS, LOOK FOR THE

CLASSICS OF THE TWENTIETH CENTURY

Petersburg Andrei Bely

'The most important, most influential and most perfectly realized Russian novel written in the twentieth century' (*The New York Times Book Review*), *Petersburg* is an exhilarating search for the identity of the city, presaging Joyce's search for Dublin in *Ulysses*.

The Miracle of the Rose Jean Genet

Within a squalid prison lies a world of total freedom, in which chains become garlands of flowers – and a condemned prisoner is discovered to have in his heart a rose of monstrous size and beauty. Of this profoundly shocking novel Sartre wrote: 'Genet holds the mirror up to us: we must look at it and see ourselves.'

Labyrinths Jorge Luis Borges

Seven parables, ten essays and twenty-three stories, including Borges's classic 'Tlön, Uqbar; Orbis Tertius', a new world where external objects are whatever each person wants, and 'Pierre Menard', the man who rewrote *Don Quixote* word for word without ever reading the original.

The Vatican Cellars André Gide

Admired by the Dadaists, denounced as nihilist, defended by its author as a satirical farce: five interlocking books explore a fantastic conspiracy to kidnap the Pope and place a Freemason on his throne. *The Vatican Cellars* teases and subverts as only the finest satire can.

The Rescue Joseph Conrad

'The air is thick with romance like a thunderous sky...' 'It matters not how often Mr Conrad tells the story of the man and the brig. Out of the million stories that life offers the novelist, this one is founded upon truth. And it is only Mr Conrad who is able to tell it us' – Virginia Woolf

Southern Mail/Night Flight Antoine de Saint-Exupéry

Both novels in this volume are concerned with the pilot's solitary struggle with the elements, his sensation of insignificance amid the stars' timelessness and the sky's immensity. Flying and writing were inextricably linked in the author's life and he brought a unique sense of dedication to both.